A GIRL NEXT DOOR

Celebrations for the Adams family...

It is 1956 and Boots Adams is celebrating his sixtieth birthday with a good old-fashioned cockney knees-up. A good time is had by all, even though Gemma, James and the rest of the younger people insist that the music has to be rock and roll. The new generation is growing up fast, and changes are on the way in Adams Fashions too, where Boots and Sammy have difficult decisions to make regarding a take-over. Meanwhile, Polly cannot place a familiar face, and Anneliese encounters someone she never wishes to see again, and turns to Boots for help...

A GIRL
NEXT DOOR

by

Mary Jane Staples

Magna Large Print Books
Long Preston, North Yorkshire,
BD23 4ND, England.

British Library Cataloguing in Publication Data.

Staples, Mary Jane
    A girl next door.

A catalogue record of this book is
available from the British Library

ISBN 0-7505-2384-0

First published in Great Britain in 2004 by Corgi

Copyright © Mary Jane Staples 2004

Cover illustration © Larry Rostant by arrangement with
Transworld Publishers

The right of Mary Jane Staples to be identified as the author of
this work has been asserted in accordance with sections 77 and
78 of the Copyright, Designs and Patents Act, 1988

Published in Large Print 2005 by arrangement with
Transworld Publishers

Magna Large Print is an imprint of Library Magna Books Ltd.

Printed and bound in Great Britain by
T.J. (International) Ltd., Cornwall, PL28 8RW

THE ADAMS FAMILY

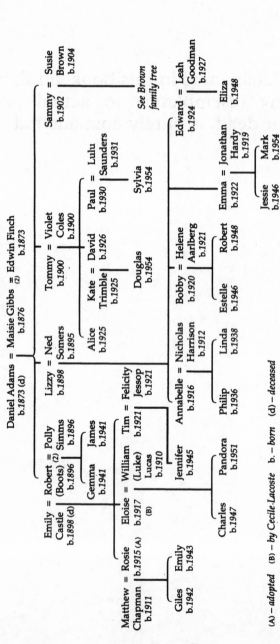

Daniel Adams = Maisie Gibbs = Edwin Finch
b.1873 (d)   b.1876   (2)   b.1873

Emily = Robert (Boots)   Lizzy   Tommy = Violet   Sammy = Susie
Castle   (2) Simms   b.1898   Ned   b.1900   Coles   b.1902   Brown
b.1898 (d)   b.1896   Somers   b.1900   b.1904
             b.1896   b.1895

Gemma   James
b.1941   b.1941

Eloise = William   Tim = Felicity
b.1917   (Luke)   b.1921   Jessop
(B)   Lucas   b.1921
         b.1910

Matthew = Rosie
Chapman   b.1915 (A)
b.1911

Giles   Emily
b.1942   b.1943

Jennifer
b.1945

Annabelle = Nicholas
b.1916   Harrison
            b.1912

Charles   Pandora
b.1947   b.1951

Philip   Linda
b.1936   b.1938

Alice   Kate = David   Paul = Lulu
b.1925   Trimble b.1926   b.1930 Saunders
         b.1925   b.1931

Douglas   Sylvia
b.1954   b.1954

Bobby = Helene   Edward = Leah
b.1920   Aarlberg   b.1924   Goodman
         b.1921   b.1927

Estelle   Robert   Emma = Jonathan   Eliza
b.1946   b.1948   b.1922   Hardy   b.1948
                             b.1919

Jessie   Mark
b.1946   b.1954

See Brown
family tree

(A) – adopted   (B) – by Cecile Lacoste   b. – born   (d) – deceased

THE BROWN FAMILY

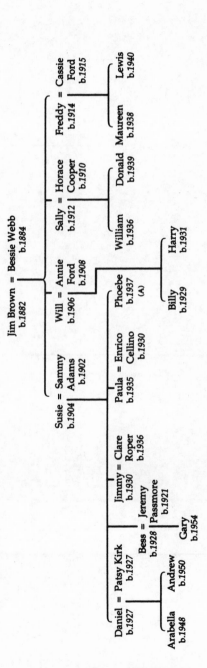

Chapter One

July, 1956.
The rock and roll movement, born, the public were informed, of the young people's enthusiasm for free expression in music, was reaching a peak of popularity in America and Britain. It has to be said, however, that the singer Liberace, with his jewel-encrusted get-ups, his photogenic piano and his equally photogenic minty-fresh choppers, still commanded a faithful following among older people.

America had something else going on in addition to rock and roll, something that was capturing the interest of all its citizens, young and old, as well as the rest of the world. A programme for exploring space. Heading their scientific team was a rocket genius, Wernher von Braun, the German who had built Hitler's flying bombs. Of course, some people, despite their interest, laughed at the idea of a spacecraft that could reach the moon, thousands and thousands of miles from Earth. And even if it could be managed, who was going to do what with it?

'Don't look at me, I'm up to my ears working on our property company's overheads,' said Sammy Adams, well-known business-man of Camberwell, south-east London.

'Try me,' said his son Daniel, an adventurous type.

'Try you not, honey,' said his American wife Patsy. 'I want you at home. Your granny and grandpa are coming to Sunday tea.'

'How about Edith Hammerglow down the road?' suggested Daniel's cousin, Bobby Somers, to his French wife Helene. 'She's always talking about an urge for faraway places.'

'That woman?' said Helene. 'She'd fall off her broomstick before she reached the rain clouds.'

'Who's going to give her first aid if she lands in our back garden?' asked Bobby.

'Ah, what an idiot,' said Helene, 'but you are still a nice man.'

That kind of dialogue was representative of the fact that in the UK nobody very much gave serious consideration to the possibility of placing a man on the moon.

Far more prominence was given to an event in the Middle East. General Nasser, dictator of Egypt, had summarily nationalized the Suez Canal, much to the anger and dismay of Sir Anthony Eden, Britain's Prime Minister. He was having to consider whether or not he could allow free passage of the Canal to be controlled by Egypt. Since its inception, the Canal had been Britain's lifeline to the

Middle East and the Far East, and what was presently left of its Empire in those regions. There were rumblings in 10 Downing Street.

Of interest to the Adams family was the news that in America the police and the FBI were conducting a nationwide manhunt for a young German Jew, Wilhelm Kleibert, who was wanted for the murder of an immigrant Ukrainian doctor, one Paul Rokovsky.

The murder had touched the life of Mrs Felicity Adams who, blinded during a German air raid on London, had been due to consult Dr Rokovsky in New York. An outstanding ophthalmic surgeon, he had restored the sight of several blinded American soldiers of the Second World War. Only a short time before Felicity and her husband were due to take the flight to New York, Kleibert had shot Dr Rokovsky dead.

During interrogation, Kleibert claimed that Rokovsky was actually a German medical practitioner responsible for hideous experiments on inmates of the notorious Auschwitz concentration camp. Kleibert himself had been an inmate, along with his brother and sister, twins. He had survived, his brother and sister had died as a consequence of experimental operations. His escape from police custody had been engineered by two FBI men who held written orders to take him to FBI headquarters. They turned out to be impostors, the orders a forgery.

11

That had been two months ago. The murder had taken place in December 1954, the trial constantly put back due to the delaying tactics of the defence and the complications of investigations that were mainly concerned with discovering whether or not the murdered man, Dr Paul Rokovsky, really did have a murky history. The defence claimed they had witnesses, concentration camp survivors, to prove he did, that he was actually Dr Gerhard Fischer, a German known to have worked at Auschwitz under Dr Mengele, for whom a hunt was also going on. Both were classified as major war criminals.

The FBI believed the impostors to be agents of Mossad, the Israeli security force, and that they intended to return to Israel in company with Kleibert. Airports and seaports were all being watched.

That murder crushed Felicity's hope of a successful operation.

Chapter Two

On a more homely note, in a house close to the heart of tranquil Dulwich Village, southeast London, Mrs Polly Adams woke up. It was well past nine, but it was Saturday morning and, further, everyone had gone to bed very late. Yesterday her husband, Robert Alfred Adams, known as Boots, had reached the age of sixty, and the celebrations, which had been attended by almost everyone in the extensive Adams families, had lasted until well past one in the morning.

Polly might have had a hangover, but had always escaped that morning-after affliction. During her years as a flapper, friends had known her to be squiffy, but never headless.

Sleepily, she turned her head to find out if Boots was awake, but saw only his pillow. She smiled. Did he have a hangover, and was he suffering it in the bathroom? Downstairs, the sounds of someone at work reached her ears. Her daily maid, Flossie Cuthbert, was busy doing a massive job of clearing up.

Boots, dressing gown over his pyjamas, came in then, carrying a tea tray.

'D'you fancy a cup of hot strong tea, Polly old girl?' he asked, placing the tray on a bedside table and sitting down on the edge of the bed.

'Hot strong tea?' said Polly. 'You old darling, don't you have a hangover?'

'Fortunately, no,' said Boots, and poured the steaming brew. 'There we are,' he said, handing her a full cup.

Polly sat up and took it. She smiled and looked him over. Sixty now, but he showed not a single trace of grey in his dark brown hair, nor any loss of firmness in his features.

That, she supposed, made it easy for him to accept his advancing years. But then, he had never quarrelled with old Father Time any more than he had quarrelled with the quirks and perversities of life and people. Advancing years were different for a woman who was as sensitive about her age as she was. She would be sixty herself in September, only two months away. God, how she hated the thought. Boots would have told her she looked nowhere near sixty, and it was true that the piquancy of her looks brought to mind her younger years. Certainly, her hair, as dark as burnt sienna, showed no more grey tints than his did. The whole family thought she and Boots remarkably well preserved. Polly, however, was sure her crow's feet would soon make her look a definite old lady.

'How do you do it?' she asked, sipping her tea.

'How do I do what?' countered Boots.

'Keep your wrinkles from showing?'

'Oh, in the same way that you keep yours at bay,' said Boots, 'by the grace of God.'

'Thanks for that sweet notion,' said Polly, who used creams in the reasonable belief that her Maker was far too omnipotent to attend to the wants of foolish individuals and their vanities. What was it about the Adams family that defied time? Boots's sister Lizzy, and his brothers, Tommy and Sammy, were all in their fifties, but looked younger than their years. And his mother, only two months short of eighty, was hardly grey-haired, wrinkled and bent. 'Well, whatever, we both survived a famous party. Congratulations on your stamina, old warhorse.'

'I could say the same about yours,' said Boots. 'What a woman.'

'Is that a compliment?' asked Polly.

'Spoken from the heart,' said Boots.

'Darling, it's been fifteen years,' said Polly. They had celebrated that particular wedding anniversary in March.

'Who's complaining?' said Boots. 'I'm not.' He thought of his long-lost Emily then, his first wife. Fifteen years, yes, that was also the amount of time he had been married to her before she was killed during a daylight air raid. Her image, that of a bright and energetic cockney woman, often took shape in his mind. But he had never regretted marrying Polly. What man could regret marrying a woman who, at the age of forty-five, had presented him with twins as endearing as Gemma and James? He lightly touched her shoulder. 'I'm a fortunate man, Polly.'

'Is that another compliment?' smiled Polly.

'It's well deserved,' said Boots.

Polly asked him what he had thought of the antics of the young people at his party, on the grounds that they had turned it into a rock 'n' roll merry-go-round. Boots said any modern merry-go-round at any man's sixtieth birthday was as entertaining as an old-fashioned knees-up, as long as he wasn't dragged into it himself.

'Wild,' said Polly.

'A knees-up?' said Boots.

'Rock 'n' roll,' said Polly, 'and I must speak to Gemma. It was her record player that started it all.'

'Give her my compliments,' said Boots, 'her record player was a hit.'

'A loud hit,' said Polly. 'The ceiling trembled and the floor shook. If the old people could survive all that, they could survive an earthquake. I must ring Stepmama this morning and find out if she's still alive. And you had better check on the health of your mother and stepfather.'

'I don't think that will be necessary,' said Boots.

In their house on Red Post Hill, his mother, Lady Finch, still known as Chinese Lady to her closest kin, was at breakfast with her husband, Sir Edwin Finch. Neither had a hangover, both had imbibed with respect for their ages. Mind, Chinese Lady did follow two glasses of port with a glass of champagne, but that was out of respect for her age combined with respect for her eldest son's sixtieth.

'Edwin,' she said, spooning marmalade over her buttered toast while thinking about

16

Boots, 'I just don't know how my oldest son can be sixty.'

'Maisie my dear,' said Sir Edwin, 'Boots achieved that in the natural way.'

'Yes, but it seems like only yesterday that he was just a talkative boy,' said Chinese Lady.

'It was his talkative talents and his many questions about life that made him the man he is.'

'If you mean airy-fairy, I couldn't agree more,' said Chinese Lady.

'I mean communicative and worldly,' said Sir Edwin.

'That still sounds like airy-fairy to me,' said Chinese Lady, 'but my goodness, I should think everyone in the family turned up to help him celebrate, as well as lots of friends. All that noise, I never heard the like at no-one else's birthday party. I was trying to talk to Lizzy about when she and Boots were growing up and Sammy was saving all his pennies and ha'pennies in his old socks, but I just couldn't hear what I was saying, and nor could Lizzy.'

'There'll be an even noisier celebration in September,' said Sir Edwin.

'Well, I don't know which celebration you mean, but I do know I couldn't live through a noisier one,' said Chinese Lady, refilling teacups and ignorant, of course, about Polly's reference to earthquake survival.

17

'I think you'll do very well, Maisie, it'll be on the occasion of your eightieth,' smiled Sir Edwin.

'Edwin,' said Chinese Lady. 'I don't want anyone to fuss about me being eighty.'

'We shall all fuss,' declared Sir Edwin, 'as we will a little later when Polly celebrates her own sixtieth.'

'Well, I can't stop Polly having her kind of celebration,' said Chinese Lady, 'but all I want is just a little private tea party with Boots and Polly and the others, and toasted muffins and a cake.'

'I doubt if the family will let you get away with that,' said Sir Edwin.

'Well, I just don't want no loud noise, nor any dancing like we had last night,' said Chinese Lady. 'What was everyone doing?'

'I think it's called jiving, or rocking and rolling,' said Sir Edwin. 'All to Gemma's record player.'

'Whatever it's called, it's not what I know as dancing,' said Chinese Lady, 'not like a nice waltz or a foxtrot. I could hardly believe my eyes at what some of my granddaughters were doing.'

'Modern young ladies aren't quite as shy or as modest as those of our day, Maisie,' said Sir Edwin.

'Well,' said Chinese Lady firmly, 'I don't mind girls not being shy, but I don't like them doing French dancing. That's what it was, French, showing a lot more than any respectable girls ought to.'

Sir Edwin coughed. True, there had been a profusion of high swirling skirts and an array of pretty, nyloned legs, all to the accompaniment of noisy encouragement from the young men and growing boys jigging in concert with the girls. 'Swing it, baby!' 'Keep rocking, Linda!' 'Go get 'em, Phoebe!' Linda was the eighteen-year-old granddaughter of Lizzy and Ned, Phoebe the nineteen-year-old adopted daughter of Sammy and Susie. And 'baby', no doubt, had been young Gemma herself, she who had introduced her record player and turned the party into the equivalent of a rousing knees-up. Sir Edwin could not fault any of them for their looks or – um – for their pretty legs. However...

'I don't think you and I would want to discourage the lively spirit of the young, Maisie,' he said.

'Well, Edwin,' declared Chinese Lady, 'all I can say is that if I do have a large family party on my eightieth, just make sure Gemma doesn't bring no kind of gramophone.'

'Very well, Maisie,' said Sir Edwin, 'I'll take good note of that.'

'Thank you, Edwin,' said Chinese Lady, and reached across the table to pat his hand. Her husband would be eighty-three in September, just before her eightieth; and she was devoting herself to his well-being. If she was still upright in her carriage and firm of body, Edwin was silver-haired, and leaner by the year. It would grieve her to lose him. 'Still, everyone was very complimentary about Boots, which made me feel he's turned out a lot better than I thought he would.'

'Maisie,' said Sir Edwin, 'you can believe me when I tell you you can be very proud of your—' He smiled. 'Of your only oldest son.'

'Well, it's nice of you to say so, Edwin,' said Chinese Lady, and gave him another affectionate pat.

Her youngest son, Sammy, and his wife Susie, were, like Polly, not yet up. Sammy was awake, but blearily so and wondering what had happened to his head.

'Susie, what went on last night?' he asked.

'You got drunk,' said Susie, sheets and blanket cosily cuddling her.

'Eh?'

'Tight as a lord,' said Susie, coming up to fifty-two and matching Polly in her fight to stay well preserved.

'Eh?' said Sammy, fifty-four and still mentally and physically energetic, except right now, when his whole being felt as if Satan's black angels had been hammering him all night. That included his head.

'Didn't I keep telling you after all that wine and champagne to stop having one

20

more whisky for the road?' said Susie, who had been wise enough to limit her liquid intake, although she did have two glasses of bubbly. 'You must've had six.'

'Suffering cats, I don't remember drinking anything,' said Sammy. 'I only know my head feels like a seasick hot-air balloon, and me mouth feels like it's been down a drain all night.'

'Oh, dear, what a shame, Sammy love, but lucky for you it's Saturday and you can stay in bed and nurse your fat head,' said Susie.

'Susie,' groaned Sammy, 'is someone boiling it? It feels like it.'

'Someone like a cannibal?' said Susie.

'Don't make jokes, Susie,' said Sammy, 'it ain't Christian at the moment.' He closed his bleary eyes. 'Did Boots make a speech last night?'

'Well, of course,' said Susie. 'He talked about what sixty years had done to him, turned him into an old codger, and how he hoped his family would help him totter gracefully through the rest of his days. Of course, he said nice things about Polly, but what I liked best was that he didn't forget to mention Emily and what a wonderful help she'd been to him when he was blind. Polly didn't seem to mind, I think Boots probably told her he was going to include a mention of Emily.'

'Am I hearing all this, or is it disappearing

into me fog?' said Sammy.

'Well, you must've heard Boots's funnies,' said Susie, 'because you kept chortling.'

'Well, I'm not chortling now,' said Sammy, 'I'm going to spend the rest of the day doing a slow expiring job.'

'No, don't do that, Sammy love,' said Susie. 'Think of the business. I'm going down to make some tea for us and Phoebe. I don't suppose she's up yet.'

Sammy blinked his suffering eyes.

'Who's Phoebe?' he groaned.

'Your darling daughter,' said Susie, slipping from the bed.

'In my present condition, I ain't up to remembering that,' said Sammy. 'Would you mind telling me who's standing up?'

'Me,' said Susie, out of the bed.

'Well, stay there and keep the light out of me eyeballs,' said Sammy.

In her own bed, their daughter Phoebe was still sleeping the sleep of a young lady who had enjoyed a swinging party that included rock 'n' roll and the heady delights of wine and champagne. Her clothes, scattered over her bedroom floor, testified to her first-ever condition of careless rapture on her arrival home at two in the morning. Well, lovely Uncle Boots wasn't sixty every week.

She slept on, dreaming of Philip, Aunt Annabelle's entertaining son, who was gone on her. At least, she hoped he was. At nineteen, a girl was more than ready to have a bloke as dishy as Philip knocking on her door, especially when he looked smashing in the uniform of an RAF pilot officer.

Chapter Three

'Vi, I don't feel so good,' said Tommy, Chinese Lady's middle son. He also was still in bed, and he also had had one too many for the road. Well, good old Boots stocked good Scotch, and was always generous with it.

'Tommy,' said Vi, who was up and dressed, 'you once promised me you'd never get one over the eight again.'

'I think me promise got interfered with last night,' said Tommy.

'Oh, well, I'll excuse you,' said placid Vi. 'My, imagine Boots being sixty.'

'Sixty?' groaned Tommy. 'Well, I feel like ninety meself.'

'I must say you sound a bit like it,' said Vi. 'Still, wasn't it a lovely party, and there was Boots, not looking half his age, and all that champagne fizzing about while he was making his speech. Did you notice that your mum actually looked proud of him? She told me he'd grown up a good boy, after all. Isn't she funny about all of you? She still says Sammy's heading for purgatory on account of liking money too much.'

'Vi, are you talking to me?' asked Tommy, who, along with Sammy and other related males, really had celebrated in style. In a manner of speaking, it could be said it was the spirits of the occasion that had put paid to his promise. 'Vi?'

'Yes, Tommy,' said Vi, 'I'm talking to you.'

'Well, I don't want to offend you,' said Tommy, 'but would you mind talking to the cat down in the kitchen?'

'All right, lovey,' said Vi.

'I'll come down meself in a while,' said Tommy, 'say in about four hours.'

Smiling, Vi went down to the kitchen. The house was quiet, with Tommy still in bed, and no sounds coming from the room occupied by daughter Alice and her husband, Fergus MacAllister, who were staying for the weekend. Alice and Fergus had been the focus of family interest last year when, at Bristol Crown Court, a gang of four bank robbers had been prosecuted. Alice and Fergus, having tangled with two of the men, the two who had actually done the deed, were prime witnesses, along with the bank clerk forced to hand over the money at gunpoint. The trial proved to be quite straightforward, the prosecution case easily overpowering a flimsy defence, and the four men were convicted and sentenced to long terms of imprisonment.

Alice and Fergus dined out in happy fashion at the end of the trial. Fergus, who had been conducting a subtle, low-key courtship of Alice, became more positive in his campaign from that point on. Alice, who had always felt a scholastic career would be more suitable for her than marriage, found her preference was changing. Fergus had proved himself a stalwart and far less brash than when she had first known him. Her feelings towards him climbed from a modest level to a high one.

She became engaged to him in the spring of 1955 and married him two months later, from her family home on Denmark Hill, much to the pleasure of Vi and Tommy. They had both thought their daughter would end up, in Sammy's sympathetic words one day, as an unmarried spinster.

'You don't have to say unmarried,' said Tommy at the time.

'Why not?' said Sammy. 'A spinster is unmarried, ain't she?'

'Well, yes,' said Vi, 'but–'

'There you are, then,' said Sammy, which closed the brief dialogue. It wasn't much good arguing with Sammy's own kind of verbiage.

Fergus woke up in his in-laws' house. It was nine thirty. He'd enjoyed more than a few

25

wee drams at Boots's sixtieth shindig, but his years of soldiering had given him an armour-plated stomach, and he was quite sober. Sober enough, in fact, to note that Alice's fair hair dappled her pillow with brightness. He lightly touched her shoulder.

'Will you no' come out of your dreams, Alice?'

That woke his wife. She turned. Fergus, beside her, was unshaven, blue-jawed, and eyeing her with a smile. A pirate speculating on his prize captive, she thought.

'Fergus, are you sober?' she asked.

'As a judge,' said Fergus. 'But when it comes to a fine celebration, I canna fault Boots and Polly. D'you have a head?'

'Yes, my very own,' said Alice, looking relaxed. She had slept well, having drunk no more than she knew she could take.

'I'll wager there are some heads that don't feel too clear,' said Fergus. 'I like it fine, Alice, that yours isn't suffering. Will you be wanting a wee celebration of our own just now?'

'What?' Alice gave him a suspicious look. Her piratical Scot smiled. 'Oh, no, you don't,' she said, 'not at this time of the morning.'

'Whisht, my bonny, we'll be as quiet as two bairns in their cot,' said Fergus.

'Well, you have your own quiet time while I take a bath,' said Alice, and slipped from the bed.

Fergus smiled indulgently. Alice still had

some reservations, some moments of modesty. But she was a fine wife, and he would not have wanted her to be other than she was, a little different from her extrovert and outgoing cousins. The Adams families lived life exuberantly. /

Boots's son Tim was up. He'd been down to the kitchen in his dressing gown. There, Maggie Forbes, the live-in maid, had mixed him the hair of the dog. It took the weight off his hangover. After which, he carried a cup of tea up to his wife, who had a hangover of her own, although only a slight one.

'What's that?' she asked. She was sitting up and peering.

'Tea,' said Tim, close to thirty-five and very much like his father in his tallness and looks.

'Oh, good show,' said Felicity, just thirty-five and a very photogenic brunette. 'Some husbands earn their medals.' She reached for the cup and saucer, and Tim placed the combination in her hand. He had a never-failing admiration for his blind wife, who, having lost out on her arranged consultation in New York with a Dr Rokovsky, due to his violent death, was now exclusively in the care of Sir Charles Morgan, a noted ophthalmic surgeon of London. Sir Charles had become convinced nature was doing that which he confessed he could not do himself by an operation. Felicity was now at a stage where her eyes, which had previously known brief moments of partial vision, gave her longer intervals, although still only of a blurred kind. On those occasions, she saw everything and everyone through a misty fog. But that was more than enough to make her believe the fog would clear one day, and she would see Tim and their daughter Jennifer with clarity and not as misty beings. Sir Charles was encouragingly hopeful about that, especially as her damaged cornea showed signs of natural healing. But he refused to commit himself to a time factor when she asked how long he thought it would take for healing to be complete. Be patient, he said. He wondered, of course, if perfect sight would ever come about.

As for the death of the Ukrainian ophthalmist, Dr Paul Rokovsky, the news that had come out of America suggested there were positive grounds for believing he had indeed been an SS doctor at the notorious Auschwitz concentration camp. Defence lawyers insisted they could call on witnesses who would swear in court that they had identified his mortuary corpse as such. First, however, the assassin, Wilhelm Kleibert, who had escaped custody, had to be found, rearrested and brought to trial. Until that happened, witnesses could not be brought to court to testify.

With Felicity enjoying the cup of tea, Tim asked, 'What's on your mind this morning?'

'Only the fact that there was a rattling fine get-together of family and friends for your father's sixtieth,' said Felicity. 'If one couldn't see, one could positively hear. And even if I did have a little too much bubbly, I'm wide awake now and ready to take a shower.'

'Need any help?' said Tim.

'None, lover,' said Felicity. She could always cope with the familiar. 'Where's Jennifer?' Jennifer was their eleven-year-old daughter.

'Still buried under her bedclothes,' said Tim.

'I'm not surprised,' said Felicity. 'A two o'clock bedtime for a girl her age was a bit much.'

'No time at all for a girl as lively as all the other young ones,' said Tim. 'Who'd have thought my stepma would have allowed Gemma's record player to turn the happy home into a Teddy boys' dance hall?'

'I think Polly was outvoted by Gemma and James,' said Felicity. 'Listen, lover, isn't it time the American cops caught up with their runaway prisoner?'

'You'd like the trial to take place?' said Tim.

'Yes, I want to know all about Dr Rokovsky's history, and that will come out then, won't it?'

'Good point,' said Tim. 'I'm with you in wanting to know if he really was one of those fiendish German doctors who carried out infernal experiments on Auschwitz inmates. As we've said before, that trial won't take place until the American police do catch up with Kleibert.'

'Send them a cable,' said Felicity, 'tell them to get a move on.'

'I'll underline it,' said Tim, although he thought that if Dr Rokovsky really had been the German doctor of Auschwitz infamy, then most people would consider Kleibert deserved a row of medals, not a trial.

At ten o'clock in the home of Bobby Somers, his French wife Helene, and their children Estelle and Robert, Helene was downstairs, dressed, Bobby still in bed. So up she went.

'Ah, look at you, you great log,' she said, 'what are you doing just lying there?'

'I'm doing a recovery job from last night's orgy,' said Bobby, 'and that's not lying.'

'What? Ah, I see, another of your terrible jokes.' Helene shook a finger at him. 'Are you still not sober?'

'I'm a lot better,' said Bobby, 'but I'm still not sure about my legs. Where am I, by the way?'

'At home.'

'That should be a help,' said Bobby, 'I

30

don't think my legs would make it here if we were still in France.'

They had returned only recently from a holiday fortnight with Helene's parents, but in good time to enjoy Boots's sixtieth.

'Well, never mind your legs, *chéri*,' said Helene, decorative apron covering her summer dress, 'the children are waiting for you to take them to the park, as you promised. So up, up, Bobby Somers, up, up.'

'Eh?' said Bobby, languid. Along with others, he'd had a great time at the party.

'Up, up,' said Helene, firm of body and firm of intention, and she whipped the bedclothes away. Bobby, pyjamas rumpled, considered that a touch of foul play. And said so. In response, Helene took hold of his ankles, pulled him sideways and yanked him off the bed. Bobby hit the carpeted floor with a bump.

'Strewth,' he said, 'who did that?'

'I did,' said Helene.

Bobby grinned, sat up, reached, took hold of her hands and pulled her down beside him. Helene stifled a shriek.

'Now I do feel better,' said Bobby, 'come here, you French doll.'

'Bobby – oh, you brute – don't you dare!'

'I think your dress is coming undone,' said Bobby.

'Mummy!' Estelle was calling. 'The phone's ringing!'

31

'Coming,' sang Helene, and jumped up.

'You can call that saved by the bell,' said Bobby, as she ran from the bedroom and down the stairs.

Estelle called again.

'Daddy, when are you going to take us to the park?'

'Give me ten minutes, sweetie,' called Bobby, on his feet, 'and then I'll see if my legs are working.'

While he was shaving, and while his eyes were still a little bleary, he and others of Chinese Lady's male clan might have said Boots had a lot to answer for in his over-generous dispensation of wine and champagne. And whisky for the road.

At ten thirty, in a good-looking terraced house in Wansey Street, Walworth, Mrs Cassie Brown turned from the sink as her daughter Maureen entered the kitchen in her dressing gown. Cassie, now forty-one and motherly, was a sister-in-law of Sammy and Susie Adams. Her husband Freddy, Susie's younger brother and a veteran of the Burma campaign, was at work. He'd risen at his usual time in order to open up the Adams clothing store by the Elephant and Castle for Saturday trading. Like Tommy and Sammy, he'd acquired a thick head at Boots's birthday romp. Unlike Tommy and Sammy, and their heads, however, he'd taken his out and about.

Cassie, regarding her daughter, said, 'So there you are, my girl, but not dressed.'

'Oh, man, what a jig,' said Maureen, eighteen and as richly brunette as her mother.

'That's double Dutch to me,' said Cassie.

'I'm talking about Uncle Boots's sixtieth, Mum,' said Maureen.

'Your dad said it would have been a lot quieter if you young people hadn't taken it over,' said Cassie. 'What's more, I must say you went a bit over the top. All that jiving with your skirt flying about, you saucy minx.'

'But the other girls, like Phoebe and Clare, were doing it as well,' said Maureen. Clare, twenty, was the wife of Jimmy, Susie and Sammy's younger son.

'Never mind that,' said Cassie. 'Me and your dad didn't bring you up to do a French cancan at a birthday party.'

'Oh, but Uncle Boots's sixtieth was great,' said Maureen, 'and isn't he still the sexiest man ever? At sixty, would you believe. I don't know no-one like him at that age.'

Cassie smiled. Neither she nor Freddy would ever do a Victorian act of remonstration with Maureen or their son Lewis. Cassie was happy-go-lucky, Freddy good-natured and tolerant, even if he was never going to lose his acquired hatred of the Japs, whose honourable principles as so-called soldiers embraced cruelty and sadism. His memories of their savagery still gave him nightmares.

'Oh, well, I suppose you'll only be young once, Maureen,' said Cassie. 'D'you want some breakfast?'

'Just some cereal and tea,' said Maureen, her dressing gown concealing a distinctly appealing figure. 'Where's Lewis?' she asked.

'He's gone out to meet some friends,' said Cassie, putting the kettle on.

'What, already?' said Maureen. 'Wasn't he tired?'

'Not like you are,' said Cassie, 'but of course, he didn't go wild like you did.'

'No, well, he was getting really thick with Gemma,' said Maureen.

'Your brother's sixteen now, and he's got a growing boy's natural liking for girls,' said Cassie.

Maureen, filling her breakfast dish with cereal, said, 'Well, Dad liked them when he was only fourteen, so Aunt Susie told me.'

'Girls liked him, you mean,' said Cassie. 'Bless me if I didn't have to pull their hair out.'

'Crikey, Mum, was Dad really your one and only at that age?' asked Maureen, giggling.

'Never you mind,' said Cassie, 'and d'you have to put nearly half a pint of milk on your cereal?'

'It's good for me,' said Maureen. She

meant it was good for her figure, of which she was proud.

'All right, love, if you say so,' said Cassie. 'Are you going out today?'

'Not till this evening,' said Maureen, 'then I'm going to the dance hall at Brixton. I did ask Phoebe if she'd like to go with me—'

'Phoebe?'

'Yes, we made friends last night,' said Maureen, pushing back her untidy black hair and spooning milk-soggy cornflakes into her mouth. 'She's ever so nice. But she's going to spend today and Sunday with her cousin Philip, who's on weekend leave.'

'Yes, I know,' said Cassie, 'but what about Billy Rogers?'

'Oh, I'm going off him,' said Maureen, 'he's always chewing mints and only ever wants to take me to a milk bar or the pictures. He's dead on his feet at dancing. Still, I'll get him to take me to Brixton tonight.'

'Billy's a nice-looking boy,' said Cassie.

'Not much good being nice-looking but only half-alive,' said Maureen.

'Is Phoebe going really steady with Philip?' asked Cassie.

'Well, they were all over each other last night, so I suppose so,' said Maureen. 'He's a smasher. Oh, wouldn't I like him as me steady.'

'None of that, my girl,' said Cassie. 'Hands off, if he's going that steady with Phoebe.

And just behave yourself tonight. Don't do Billy down by getting picked up by some fast bloke.'

'Mum, you're just not with it,' said Maureen. 'It's not fast blokes any more, it's groovy guys.'

'Well, never mind what they're called these days,' said Cassie, 'they're all the same, so don't bring one of them home with you, or your dad will make him run a mile.'

Two other people were having a late breakfast, Boots's sister Lizzy and her husband Ned. Lizzy, at fifty-eight, was now indisputably plump, and not even her most expensive corsets could disguise it. Still, she'd reached the stage of not letting it bother her, although she'd cut potatoes and desserts like syrup puddings from her diet. However, she still had a lustrous crown of chestnut hair, and her large brown eyes never lost their appeal for the beholder.

Ned, sixty-one, had thinning grey hair and the look of a man well past his best. He had a troublesome heart murmur, and Lizzy watched over him with long-established affection, never having had cause to find any major flaw in him as a husband and father. Of course, there had been ups and downs, but none of any serious nature or consequence.

She and Ned had both slept long and well

after returning home from the rousing party, and it was nearly mid-morning when she eventually released herself from their bed.

'You lie in, lovey,' she said, 'and I'll bring your breakfast up.'

'Kind of you Eliza,' said Ned, 'but that'll make me feel I'm a failing old crock. I put myself in the same class as Boots, who told us all last night he'd reached the stage of being an old codger. I'm that myself, which is a sight better than being an old crock.'

'Still, after a party like last night, I know you must be a bit tired,' said Lizzy. 'I don't know how Mum kept going.'

'Your mum could probably have seen us all off if it had lasted right through to dawn,' said Ned, whose best moments were always after a good night's sleep. His drawn look usually arrived at the end of a day. At this precise moment there was colour in his cheeks.

'Mum's a walking marvel,' said Lizzy, 'and so's me lovely stepdad. Anyway, I'm sure you'd like breakfast in bed, wouldn't you?'

'Breakfast in bed is for the legless,' said Ned, 'and I'll be up in ten minutes.'

'Well, don't rush, love, take your time,' said Lizzy, invariably the guardian angel.

'I'll tell you something,' said Ned.

'Go on, then, tell me,' said Lizzy.

'The best day of my life was the day I married you,' said Ned, which turned Lizzy's eyes a bit misty. Some of the flippant young people of these changing times would have called her a sentimental old biddy.

And sentiment was going out of fashion.

Chapter Four

Late August.

On an afternoon in Beamish Landing, a small American township on the bank of the Colorado river, the phone rang in the sheriff's office. He picked it up.

'Sheriff Gimbell. Who's this?'

'Jack Dodds, visiting from Denver,' said a man's voice. 'I'm at Parker's gas station right now. Listen, man, I've just seen Willy Kleibert.'

'You what?' Sheriff Gimbell alerted.

'Believe me, Sheriff. He was with two other guys, but standing with his back to me while their truck was filled up. It was when they all got back into the truck that I saw his face. Knew him at once. Willy Kleibert, the kraut on the run. They took the dirt road to the freeway. If you're set on getting after him, Sheriff, the truck's a white Ford. I noted the number.' He gave it. 'Sheriff–?'

Sheriff Gimbell was on his feet, the phone slammed down.

'Ross!' He bawled for his deputy. 'Git your

backside outside! We gotta go hunting. Pronto.'

Five minutes later they were on the dirt road, heading fast for the freeway in their patrol car.

'Hey, hold on,' said Deputy Ross, 'what did you say the number of the truck was?' Gimbell quoted. 'Sheriff, that's Barney Flanagan's truck.' Barney Flanagan was a local farmer. 'And I calculate the two guys with him are his sons, Danny and Patrick. And Patrick don't look unlike Kleibert. Sheriff, we got egg all over our shirts.'

'Goddammit!' Sheriff Gimbell, remembering there'd been scores of false alarms in so-called sightings of the escaped prisoner all over the USA, brought the patrol car to a stop and swore violently.

Such incidents were throwing officers of American law and order into confusion, and the FBI had become convinced that these red herrings emanated from Mossad agents determined to land Kleibert in Israel, even if it took them years to get him safely aboard a plane or a ship. And there was little doubt that sympathetic American Jews were helping to lay the red herrings. So all airports and seaports were still being watched.

At Toronto airport, two wiry, brown-faced men were talking to a third man and a woman. The third man and the woman were both young, both twenty-two. They were waiting to board a flight to New York.

'Once more, who are you?' asked the first man.

'Mr and Mrs Joseph Phillips,' said the young man, black hair styled in a Tony Curtis quiff. His nose looked broad and fat, his body looked stout. He had large cotton-wool pellets securely stuffed up his nostrils, and wore a kind of quilted corset next to his skin, stretching from his armpits down to his thighs. His light summer suit bulked. The effects of quiffed hair, fat nose and stout frame completely changed his normal appearance. Further, the nose pellets made him sound nasal. 'We're Canadian citizens, born in Toronto. I'm in the music business and going to New York with my wife to prospect for outlets.'

'Good,' said the second man, 'let us say you've learned your alphabet. Who's got the joint passport?'

'I have,' said the young woman.

'Good. Hang onto it, Leila.'

'Don't take me for an idiot,' said the olive-skinned young woman. She was singularly attractive of face and figure, but steely of character.

'It's a question of no slip-ups,' said the first man. He addressed the young man. 'Remember you'll be met in New York by a friend of ours.'

40

'Will he know us?' asked the young man, slightly pale of countenance, due to his time in Auschwitz concentration camp. But his nerves were under control.

'He'll know Leila. He'll give you your British visitors' visas and the air tickets for an overnight flight to London. You already know all this, but I'm emphasizing it. You'll be contacted at London Airport and taken to your lodgings smack in the heart of south London, where you'll be just two more people in a teeming crowd until you receive new identity documents and air tickets to Nice.'

'From where we'll be ferried across the Med?' said the young man.

'Yes, you know this too,' said the young woman.

'I have to ask these questions to be sure of myself,' said the young man.

'You can be sure of one thing,' said the first man, 'once you're where you belong, you'll be safe for the rest of your life.'

'As well as being received warmly but with no publicity, and privately honoured for that which you accomplished so efficiently,' murmured the second man.

Over the public address system came an announcement that passengers for the flight to New York could now begin boarding. The young woman extracted boarding cards from her shoulder bag, and the young man took charge of their small cabin bag. The

41

two brown-faced men shook hands with them, wished them luck and watched them depart to the flight gate.

Twenty minutes later the plane for New York roared down the runway, took off, climbed into the sky and disappeared. Among the passengers were Wilhelm Kleibert, wanted in America for homicide, and Leila Herschel, a Mossad agent.

On Monday, Mr Humphrey Travers, senior official at London's Foreign Office, buttonholed his assistant, Bobby Somers, son of Lizzy and Ned Somers. For his distinguished service with the French Resistance movement during the war, Bobby had been offered an excellent position at the Foreign Office, and was now an established and valued official. His wife Helene thought that in his bowler hat and very correct suits, he was most unlike the man with whom she had shared hair-raising dangers in Occupied France. She much preferred him in weekend casuals, such as an open-necked sports shirt and slacks. Then he looked much more like the Englishman she deeply loved, even if he still made idiotic jokes. His bowler hats offended her eye, and she had ruined one of them during a typical fit of Gallic temperament.

'Kindly explain why you did that, my French filly,' Bobby had said.

Helene, predictably, put her foot down on the bowler hat and added to its ruin.

'That hat is not you, it makes you look stuffy, like all the men at your office. I have seen them.' She had been to a reception, the kind to which wives were invited.

'Appearances can be deceptive,' said Bobby, who was never upset by her tantrums. He found them amusing. He found Helene amusing, which made her jump up and down, in a manner of speaking, although she refrained from tearing her hair, thick and dark, with auburn tints. She was much too proud of her wealthy crown to turn it into a ragged mop.

'Appearances? Bah,' she said. 'It is not you, I tell you.'

'Shall I go and live in a London club for stuffed fogeys?' suggested Bobby.

'If you did, I would blow it up,' said Helene. She laughed then. 'Ah, well, you must live with me as you are, your bowler hats also.'

Thinking of that, Bobby looked at Humphrey Travers, a slender man of fifty, impeccable in his grey suit, starch-collared white shirt and grey tie. But stuffy? Yes, people might have thought him so, but there was more to old Humph than that. The Foreign Minister himself knew it.

'Something on your mind?' said Bobby.

'Only that I fancy Kleibert has slipped his leash,' said Mr Travers.

43

'He slipped it months ago,' said Bobby.

'I mean it's possible he's no longer confined within the borders of North America,' said Mr Travers.

'He's on the outside?' said Bobby.

'It's possible,' said Mr Travers.

Bobby knew from where he'd received that piece of news. From Intelligence. Old Humph had a friendly relationship with that close-chested fraternity.

'Who's worried?' asked Bobby.

'The Minister,' said Mr Travers. 'Kleibert, of course, will be heading for Israel and the protection the Israelis will give him. They'll turn him into the invisible man.'

'So why is the Minister worried?' asked Bobby.

'Because, my dear fellow,' said Mr Travers, 'of the possibility that Kleibert will use the UK as a stepping stone to Israel. It would be our responsibility to pick him up and extradite him to the USA.'

'Now I see,' said Bobby.

'Yes,' said Mr Travers, 'the public in general are sympathetic to Kleibert, since they've been convinced by the press that the man he shot dead was a classified war criminal of an exceptionally loathsome kind. Should we lay our hands on Kleibert, it'll be headline news and there'll be protests and demonstrations against extradition. And no doubt directly outside our front door and that of the Home Office. Most unpleasant. We simply aren't used to all those aggressive banners protesters get hold of these days.'

'There's one solution,' said Bobby.

'Which is?'

'If Kleibert should be spotted entering this country on his way to Israel,' said Bobby. 'Turn a blind eye.'

'My dear chap,' said Mr Travers, 'what on earth are you thinking of?'

'A quiet life?' suggested Bobby.

'A delightful idea,' said Mr Travers, 'but quite dishonourable, of course, when one is aware that America is our closest ally. And you may be sure the CIA would become acquainted with our blind eye. I wouldn't be in the least surprised if our Intelligence offices themselves were bugged.'

'I suggest we leave these worries to the Home Office,' said Bobby. 'They'll have to deal with any extradition proceedings. And there's always the more likely possibility, that Kleibert won't enter the UK at all. He won't need to.'

'Perhaps not,' said Mr Travers, 'but I daresay Intelligence is keeping an eye open. We – ah – owe that much to our American cousins.'

'True,' said Bobby. He might have mentioned that Kleibert's dramatic public execution of Dr Paul Rokovsky had been a very personal blow to his cousin Tim's wife, Felicity.

However, there was something of a more serious nature concerning the Foreign Office. The Minister was involved in talks with Prime Minister Sir Anthony Eden about the crisis thrown up by General Nasser's nationalization of the Suez Canal. Bobby knew the talk was actually of war.

War against Egypt? We can do without that, thought Bobby. Mr Humphrey Travers had refused to comment. He had a knighthood in prospect, and wouldn't jump one way or another until he was sure his opinion would be regarded favourably.

Meanwhile, the people of London went about their business without giving the Suez Canal serious thought. That wasn't the case at an RAF station in Lincolnshire. The whisper was that a full squadron of fighter-bombers might be despatched to the Middle East sometime or other in the near future.

This was the station where Bobby's nephew Philip, son of his sister Annabelle, was based. His squadron was on standby.

Chapter Five

In the office of his junk yard in Camberwell, Mr Eli Greenberg sighed as he opened up the morning post. At the venerable age of seventy-six, he might have been sighing over his advancing years. Certainly, his beard was liberally sprinkled with white, and his broad-chested, sturdy frame had shrunk just a little these last twelve months.

He was still sighing when his younger stepson, Jacob, arrived.

'Old husband of my mother, do I hear you groaning?' asked Jacob.

'Groaning?' said Mr Greenberg, round black hat rusty. 'I ain't, no, but I vell might be.' His own kind of London English was the same as when he first began to speak it, after the arrival of his family from Tsarist Russia well before the First World War. It was his friend, his communicator, and he rarely used Yiddish. Also, he ignored the example set by his stepsons, Michal and Jacob, who both spoke clear English, if with a slight cockney twang. 'Yes, so I might. Vasn't I up all night vith a sick stomach, and didn't your mother give me a medicine that cured my stomach but did my head no good?'

'Old one, was the medicine out of your whisky bottle?' asked Jacob, solid of body and strong of character at thirty.

'How do I know, my son?' asked Mr Greenberg. 'Vasn't my eyes shut? Ain't I sighing for my head, vhich still ain't in good condition. It ought to be in the sun and air of a kibbutz, vhile the rest of me stays at vork, ain't it?'

'Why not take all yourself there for six months?' suggested Jacob.

'Vhat, and leave the business?'

'It's time you fully retired,' said Jacob. 'Michal and I can cope. Go to Israel for six months.'

'I ain't that old yet,' said Mr Greenberg, 'but I still ain't young enough to put up vith life in a kibbutz. Vhich reminds me that I ain't too happy about the friends you and Michal picked up vhen him and you did a kibbutz year.'

'Good friends, old father, and they've been over once or twice.'

'Don't I know it, ain't I seen them?' said Mr Greenberg sorrowfully. 'Hard noses, hard eyes. Vhich ain't the mark of good men. Vhere is Michal, might I ask?'

'At home with Judith,' said Jacob. Judith was Michal's wife. 'They're expecting friends.'

'Kibbutz friends vith hard noses?'

'Friends, just friends,' said Jacob. 'They'll

48

be staying for a little while.'

'I should believe Michal ain't vorking today?' said Mr Greenberg.

'He'll be in later,' said Jacob.

'My life, ain't that kind of him, seeing there's goods to shift and load?' said Mr Greenberg.

'Old man of my heart,' smiled Jacob, 'take an aspirin for your head that's still suffering from my mother's medicine.'

'Now vhere's your respect?'

'Here,' said Jacob, touching his heart.

'Vell, I believe you, my boy, I believe you,' said Mr Greenberg, whose eldest stepson had died for King and country while serving with the Royal Navy during the Battle of the Atlantic. The old boy was proud of the young man's sacrifice, but still sad to have lost him.

'Yes, this will do,' said the young woman, whose smooth olive skin and dark, sultry looks appealed to men who liked that type. The old-fashioned but good-looking house in Camberwell Grove was roomy, its interior modernized in that there was a tiled bathroom, carpeting had replaced linoleum, well-chosen paint had replaced ancient wallpaper throughout, and gas lighting had given way to electricity. It was situated in the crowded heart of southern Camberwell, South-East London, and although not far from the more open area of Denmark Hill,

49

its immediate eastern neighbour was densely populated Peckham. Looking for a lost soul in Camberwell or Peckham was on a par with looking for a needle in a haystack.

'Yes, here will do,' said the sultry woman's companion, a young man of lean body, dark hair and pale face. He wore horn-rimmed spectacles of plain glass. He and the woman were on the landing, having inspected the upstairs rooms.

'Good,' said Michal Wirthe, elder stepson of Mr Eli Greenberg. Broad, muscular and handsome, he was in his early thirties and the driving force of his ancient stepfather's second-hand furniture business. The firm of Greenberg and Sons Ltd was the successor to the old rag-and-bone venture, although Mr Greenberg still stabled his horse and cart.

'You'll only be with us for a few days, I believe?' said Michal's wife Judith, a full-bodied woman as handsome in her way as her husband, and grateful to God for her existence as a born subject of Queen Elizabeth the Second. That had saved her and all Britain's Jews from the terrible fate of millions of their European cousins.

'A few days, yes, until a friend arrives,' said the young woman. The conversation was in Yiddish.

'Well, whether for a few days or a little more,' said Michal, 'I thought it was understood we should speak only English, as Judith and I always do, unless Judith gets overexcited at my domestic failings.'

'My life, once a year counts?' said Judith.

'This house has solid walls,' said Michal to their guests, 'but words can still escape.'

'English, yes, very well,' said the young woman, but so curtly as to suggest she did not think much of English people. 'There will be no visitors while we are here?'

'We'll invite no-one,' said Michal, 'but there'll be callers.'

'Callers?'

'The milkman for his weekly payment, the dustmen to pick up the dustbin and the postman to deliver letters and parcels,' said Michal.

'One dustman will come into the house to collect the bin from outside the kitchen,' said Judith.

'Is this a joke?' asked the young woman.

'Not to us,' said Michal, 'we need these services. But they won't climb the stairs. The friend you say will call, is he the man who negotiated with me concerning your stay here?'

'Yes.' The young woman was not given to wasting words.

'He left this for you,' said Michal, and handed her a brown paper parcel. She took it without thanking him. 'Judith and I hope you'll enjoy your board and lodging.'

'Shall we now leave you to yourselves?'

suggested Judith.

'Thank you, thank you very much,' said the young man, much friendlier than the young woman.

Michal and Judith went down to their kitchen. Judith closed the door.

'Husband,' she said, 'the woman I don't like, the young man I do like.'

'We should let the woman's manners upset us?' said Michal.

'We should hope she won't be here too long,' said Judith.

'If questions come to be asked, remember we have two old friends of mine staying with us.'

'Well, I'm glad I won't have to say the woman is an old friend of mine,' said Judith. 'But there, we must do what we can to help.'

Michal smiled.

'You look after our child,' he said, 'and I'll look after any little problems.'

'Such a thoughtful husband you are,' said Judith, who, at twenty-seven, was four months pregnant with their first child. They had been married for two years.

'Fortunately, there's been nothing in the papers recently,' said Michal.

'Nothing about him?'

'Nothing.'

'Well, everyone is bored by now, including the press.'

'Which takes the spotlight off our guests,'

said Michal. 'Look, I must get to work, or my dear old stepfather, who likes to know everything, will begin to ask too many questions. See that my old friends enjoy a good lunch.'

'Is that a request or an order?' asked Judith.

'I should give you such an order?' said Michal.

'You would if you were strictly orthodox,' said Judith.

'If I were, I'd sport a beard,' said Michal.

'Don't even attempt it,' said Judith. She saw him off with a kiss, and away he went to the Camberwell yard.

Upstairs, in the main bedroom, which overlooked the street, Leila Herschel, unfortunately born without a sense of humour, had opened the parcel. It contained a note and a perfect wig of mousy brown hair, together with a matching beard and moustache. The note was for her, the wig and facial adornments for the young man, Wilhelm Kleibert. His own hair was thick and black, symptomatic of his race.

'If I must wear all that stuff, I must,' he had said.

'You must and you will, for the wig alone won't be enough. Your five o'clock shadow contradicts it.' Leila's response had been uncompromising. Her admiration for his deed of assassination was secondary now to the task of getting him to Israel.

53

'OK,' he said. His acquired English was excellent, with an American accent.

Now she said, 'Let me remind you that the note instructs us to have passport photographs taken.'

'Why do you remind me?' Wilhelm Kleibert was not a mere cypher, he was a young man of character, and of revived spirit in having avenged his dead brother and sister for all they had suffered at Auschwitz.

'I remind you because it's necessary for both of us to be doubly sure of every step we take,' said Leila.

'So, we're to go looking for a photographer?' said Wilhelm, his unnecessary spectacles now discarded.

'No, to go to a photographer named in this note. His address is at Camberwell Green.'

'And where is that?'

'Wirthe will tell us.'

'Good. I like him. And her.'

'Be careful of your liking for her. She has inquisitive eyes.'

'Must you mistrust everyone?'

'Until we reach Israel, I will trust no-one except our agents here.'

'But we would not be in this house if Wirthe and his wife could not be trusted.'

'You must go along with my instincts, not your own.' Leila was curt. Wilhelm shrugged and glanced around the well-furnished bedroom. The bed, with its colourful counterpane, looked inviting.

'Leila, I need help,' he said.

'You are getting maximum help from our organization,' said Leila, a navy blue dress with white trimmings gracing her fine, firm body.

'I mean a different kind of help,' said Wilhelm.

'Ah? How different?'

'I need the help of a woman to find out if I'm a man,' said Wilhelm.

'That is crazy talk,' said Leila.

'Not when spoken by a concentration camp survivor, one who was reduced to little more than five stone, and lost all sense of being male.'

'I see.' Leila softened a little. 'I'm sorry, my friend, but you are in no position to go out and look for a woman on the streets.'

'My life for the devil,' said Wilhelm, 'am I thinking of that? No, I'm thinking of you. Here is a bedroom, there is a bed–'

'This is my bedroom, and that is my bed while we're here,' said Leila. 'Yours is adjacent. You can forget any idea of sleeping with me.'

'I can't forget you're a woman who could give me the help I desperately need,' said Wilhelm.

'To find out if you're a man?' said Leila. 'That is not for me, that is for a woman you will come to meet in Israel one day.'

'How am I to know I won't disappoint her?' asked Wilhelm.

'That is a worry for you, yes, I understand,' said Leila, 'but iron tablets taken twice daily could prove a simple help.'

'What a cold woman you are,' said Wilhelm.

Leila's face suffused with an angry flush.

'How dare you talk to me like that!'

'You bully me,' said Wilhelm, 'and I would have smacked your face many times if I hadn't known you to be brave as well as overbearing. Yes, I owe you much for all you are doing for me, but I still think you a cold woman.'

'And I think you pathetic!'

'No, you don't, because you know I'm not,' said Wilhelm. 'But there, I've asked and been refused, and that is the end of it.' He smiled wryly. 'When we go to this photographer, perhaps I'll find a chemist's shop that will sell me some iron tablets, although I don't actually know if I need them or not, do I? I'll go to my room now and unpack.'

He left Leila fuming.

'Michal, my good son, vhy are you so late coming to vork?' asked Mr Greenberg.

'Didn't Jacob tell you Judith and I have some old friends staying with us for a while?' said Michal.

'So he did, so he did,' said Mr Greenberg,

cash ledger in front of him. It was one of his favourite pieces of office equipment. His old friend, Sammy Adams, had a similar liking for a cash book. 'But vhy did they keep you?'

'They didn't,' said Michal. 'Out of courtesy, I waited until they arrived.'

'They are friends from the kibbutz?' enquired Mr Greenberg.

'No, just friends.'

'Vell, Michal, I vant you to know I ain't partial to any friends that ain't friendly to our Queen's country,' said Mr Greenberg, who had been very upset by what went on in Palestine immediately after the war, when Jewish terrorists caused the untimely deaths of British soldiers. The old rag-and-bone man was solidly loyal to the country of his adoption. 'You understand, my boy?'

'Believe me, old wise one,' said Michal, 'Judith and I know our true loyalties.'

'I'm believing you, Michal, don't I alvays?' said Mr Greenberg. 'Now help Jacob to see to vaiting customers vhile I keep hold of my head, vhich is trying to float avay on account of your mother's stomach medicine, like I've told Jacob.'

Michal departed from his valiant stepfather's cramped office with a smile. The old boy was supposed to be semi-retired, but wasn't likely to vacate that office and his cash book until he dropped into the arms of heavenly Moses. Nor was he likely to refuse help to a man who had ended the filthy life of a depraved doctor of Auschwitz. But best not to tell him what was happening. He was too old to have to concern himself.

Chapter Six

At mid-afternoon, a car entered the yard. Out stepped Sammy Adams, long-standing friend to Mr Greenberg, with whom he had done more useful business deals than he would ever remember.

Michal and Jacob, with the help of an assistant, newly taken on, and of the driver of a standing van, were loading furniture from a house clearance into the vehicle. The van belonged to a customer who was buying most of it. Good business it was, second-hand furniture, among the working people of south London. Handsome new stuff was expensive and only now were manufacturers beginning to place it extensively on the market. What the war had done to all kinds of manufacturers meant, in Mr Greenberg's eyes, that Hitler still had a lot to answer for, even if the second-hand market was thriving.

'Your dad's in his office?' said Sammy, his suit a light summer grey, his trilby hat jaunty.

58

'He's in,' said Jacob.

'As ever,' smiled Michal.

'Thought so,' said Sammy, and went on to the office, an old green-painted timber shed with dusty windows. He knocked, opened the door and put his head in. 'Afternoon, Eli old cock,' he said.

'Vhy, if it ain't you, Sammy.' Mr Greenberg, despite his floating head, beamed. 'Vhat a pleasure, ain't it?'

'How's your old self?' said Sammy.

'Vell, I tell you, Sammy, I'm suffering from an upset stomach that Mrs Greenberg cured vith a medicine that vent straight to my head, like Boots's vhisky on his sixtieth birthday. My head, Sammy, it ain't vhat it vas yesterday.'

'Nor was mine after Boots's party,' said Sammy, 'so Susie gave it a friendly tap with her egg saucepan last thing the following night, and there you are, Bob's your uncle, an old-fashioned bump instead of a head complaint. Has Mrs Greenberg got an egg saucepan?'

'Vould I point her at it?' sighed Mr Greenberg. 'And might I mention Mrs G. her very own self didn't recover from Boots's party for many days? Vhat a shindig, eh? It's as vell Boots ain't sixty again next veek. But vhy am I having the pleasure of seeing you?'

'I've got another house-clearance job for you,' said Sammy. House clearances were a

59

very profitable part of his old friend's present business. 'Neighbours of mine on Denmark Hill. Number forty-one. Mr and Mrs Collins. I've recommended you, so make 'em a fair offer and get Michal and Jacob to arrange the collection day – oh, and tell 'em to wear their best suits. Mrs Collins is a nice lady, but fussy about who she lets into her prime residence.'

'Sammy, vhat a fine day, after all, ain't it?' said Mr Greenberg, head suddenly a lot better. 'You vant commission?'

'No, I want something for Susie,' said Sammy. 'A high-class stone cherub, say about two feet high, for the front garden. You know, one with wings and a big smile. It's to let visitors know they're welcome. Have you got one in stock?'

'Vhy, Sammy, ain't I got the very thing, vhich I'd say is thirty inches high and genuine oriental alabaster?' said the beaming merchant.

'Listen, Eli old cock,' said Sammy, 'if you're talking about a Chinese buddleia–'

'Chinese Buddha, Sammy?'

'Susie's not after one of those, just a good old-fashioned stone cherub,' said Sammy.

'Alabaster, Sammy, is high-class stone, and it's a cherub, don't I give you my vord? Come, I vill show you.'

What he did show Sammy, after Jacob had unearthed it from under a pile of cushions,

60

was, in Sammy's own words, a bit of all right, not half, which would make Susie feel like Christmas had come.

'That is, once I've got the dust off, Eli.'

'Sammy, Jacob vill deliver it shining bright.'

'No, I'll put it in my car boot, and take it home to Susie meself. How much?'

'Say vun green smacker, Sammy?'

'A quid? Eli, I'm not here to rob you. Give you two and a half, how's that?'

'Happy, Sammy, happy, ain't it? Now have a cup of tea vith me, eh?'

Sammy stayed for that, and when he eventually drove out of the yard, the cherub, wrapped in a sack, was in the boot.

Earlier, after a light lunch prepared and served by Judith, Leila and Wilhelm were up in their rooms. Leila had phoned the specified photographer, Amos Anderson. Expecting the call, he was friendly and co-operative in his response, arranging an appointment in his Camberwell studio for three thirty that afternoon.

Leila, gazing thoughtfully at her reflection in the dressing-table mirror, smoothed the dark lines of her dark eyebrows with a moist finger.

Someone knocked. She came to her feet, crossed the bedroom and opened the door to reveal Wilhelm wearing the wig of light brown hair and the matching beard and moustache. She stared in shock, certain at once that his appearance was impossible. She took hold of his arm, pulled him in and closed the door.

'Something wrong with my get-up?' said Wilhelm.

'Everything's wrong,' hissed Leila.

'Well, don't blame me,' said Wilhelm, 'it wasn't my idea.'

'Look at you, you fool,' breathed Leila, 'light brown hair and beard, and eyebrows as black as mine. But that's not the only thing that's wrong. It all is. I see that now. There'll be British security officers at London Airport, you can rely on it, even if not necessarily looking for you. The cold war is throwing up Soviet agents by the dozen. So how do you think airport security staff will regard a man in spectacles and as hairy as you? They'll see everything as an obvious disguise, especially if we do nothing about your eyebrows.'

'Don't think that didn't occur to me when I saw myself in the mirror,' said Wilhelm. 'I've been on the run far too long not to be aware of searching eyes at bus stations, railroad stations and airports.'

'I must phone Stargazer,' said Leila. Stargazer was the code name of their present Mossad contact, the man who had left the note and the wig in the hands of Michal

Wirthe. 'I must tell him he's crazy to have thought up such an absurd disguise. London has made him soft and addled his brains. I'll phone him from the photographer's studio.'

'He's another fool, is he?' said Wilhelm, ripping off the wig, beard and moustache.

'Shut up,' said Leila.

'You should stay in London and get yourself softened up in company with Stargazer,' said Wilhelm.

Leila gave him a look. He responded with a smile. Yes, she thought, I'm coming to know why he blew holes in that doctor. He has guts. But I don't like his insolence.

'Despite all I've just told you, bring that stuff with you to the photographer,' she said.

'Oh, sure,' said Wilhelm. 'Sincerely, I'm going to be grateful all my life to you and your colleagues if you get me safely to Israel, but I hope I don't end up working for a female boss.'

'Your gratitude isn't asked for,' said Leila, 'but it's more welcome than your sense of humour.'

Her relationship with Wilhelm, a hero in the eyes of the people of Israel, had changed from being pleasant, if unemotional, to one of distinct coolness. She was still angry with him.

Sammy, approaching the traffic lights at Camberwell Green, slowed as green turned to orange. He stopped at the advent of red. People stepped from the kerbs to negotiate the pedestrian crossing. From the left-hand kerb came three people, a young man and two women, one of whom he recognized. Judith Wirthe. He had met her at her wedding to Michal two years ago. She was what Sammy regarded as a female woman. That is, a woman with looks and a figure, and an entirely feminine rig-out with a fetching hat. No jeans. Sammy considered jeans a blight on fashion. He leaned and tapped on the windscreen as she passed his standing car. Not hearing or noticing, she carried on to the pavement with her companions. They crossed the junction in the direction of Denmark Hill.

Sammy drove forward as the traffic lights turned green. He crossed into Denmark Hill, put himself on the crown of the road and, giving a signal, veered right and pulled up outside the firm's offices. He saw Judith talking to the young man and young woman at the door of a shop a little way down. Then she turned and walked back the way she had come. Her companions entered the shop, the window of which advertised the services of a photographer. It displayed framed samples of his work.

Judith had taken her house guests there herself to make sure they didn't lose themselves.

Sammy went up to his offices by the side entrance of the firm's shop, the shop that represented the beginnings of his now expansive business empire.

No sooner was he seated at his desk than Rachel Goodman, director and the company secretary, entered his office. Rachel, in her fifties, looked as if she was still blooming. Well, she not only owned glossy raven hair and wide velvety-brown eyes, but also a sumptuous figure. She was, in Sammy's eyes, a well-preserved, high-class female woman. So, of course, was his one and only Susie.

'Sammy?'

'Well, Rachel me old friend?'

'I think you'd better have a word with Boots.'

'Might I ask why?'

'He took a phone call from the managing director of Coates an hour ago.' Coates had a West End store and branches all over the South of England, as well as one just opened in Edinburgh. All the stores had been stocking Adams Fashions' superior garments for years.

'Hold on,' said Sammy, 'don't tell me they're thinking of dropping us.'

'My life, Sammy, I should want to tell you that?' said Rachel. 'Far from it. What they do want is to take over our manufacturing factory at Bethnal Green. In fact, they're thinking of acquiring Adams Fashions Ltd if

65

an offer can be agreed.'

'Bloody hell,' breathed Sammy, 'all that's been taking place behind my back?'

'While you were out,' said Rachel. 'As I mentioned, Boots took the call.'

'Well, I hope he talked educated to the saucy geezer,' said Sammy, on which heated note Boots himself walked in.

'You're flushed, Sammy,' he said, his familiar lurking smile suggesting he was the kind of man always ready to find something amusing about life and people.

'Well, pardon me,' said Sammy, 'but I ain't exactly meself right now. What's this about selling off Adams Fashions, which I ain't too proud to say is dear to me heart?'

'Nothing has happened yet, Sammy,' said Boots. 'Suppose Rachel and I take a seat and have a three-way discussion with you?' It was gone four, but that was irrelevant.

'Now you're talking,' said Sammy, 'but d'you mind leaving out any educated stuff? Let's have it plain and unvanished.'

'Unvarnished, Sammy?' said Boots, as he and Rachel seated themselves.

'What I meant was I don't want wordage that goes over me head and vanishes up the chimney,' said Sammy.

Rachel coughed, Boots smiled, and the discussion began.

'Look at him,' said Leila to Amos Anderson,

professional photographer, 'is that a disguise or a shout for help?'

'A shout for help it could be,' said Amos, a cheerful Jewish Londoner who had the equivalent of a bedside manner when posing a sitter. He was doing very nicely in this heavily populated area, with its regular weddings and a full quota of girls wishful to be photographed as potential pin-up dollies somewhat saucier than the swimsuit beauties of the war. The modern versions were regularly featured in papers like the *Daily Mirror* and its light weekend companion, *Reveille*, as well as monthly magazines such as *Men Only*. Some archbishops thought this lurid development was hastening the disintegration of the British Empire. So did some rabbis. It hardly kept Amos awake at night; his chubby missus was comfortably relaxing to cuddle up to. 'I know little of plots and plans, don't I?' he murmured.

'It's not important, how much you know and how much you don't,' said Leila.

'Well, I tell you, I'm always ready to help the cause,' said Amos, forty, lean, and well turned out in a blue turtleneck sweater and knife-edged trousers. Sloppiness didn't impress customers dressed in their best. 'I don't ask questions, I do the passport photographs your people want. In fact, the less I know, the better I like it. Now, what shall we say is wrong with your young bloke's hairy look?'

'There's too much of it,' said Leila. 'It shrieks of a disguise.'

'I should consider that my problem?' said Amos. 'My pennyworth for the cause is to take passport photographs on the QT, which I do, don't I?'

'I must phone Stargazer,' said Leila.

'She must phone Stargazer,' said Wilhelm, sighing.

'That secretive cove tells me never to phone him unless trouble's at my door,' said Amos, 'serious trouble. Which I don't want on account of earning myself a legal living. Legal is a happy word. Trouble, I say again, I don't want.'

'There'll be no trouble,' said Leila, 'where's your phone?'

'There, on my desk, under my hat,' said Amos.

'Why do you keep it under your hat?' asked Wilhelm.

'Force of habit,' said Amos.

Leila dialled a number. A man answered. 'Atkinson's, tea merchants.' A pause. 'The manager speaking.' That was his password.

'Indian Moon here.' That was Leila's responsive password. 'You've made a mistake.'

'I never make mistakes.'

'You've made one this time. That wig and beard shriek of a disguise.'

Silence for a while, then, 'You might have a point, but he'll never clear airport security

68

as himself.'

'Tell me something I don't know.'

'Use the previous outfit. Fatten his nose, face and body.'

'Is that wise?' Leila obviously didn't think so. 'The principle is to avoid repetition. Also, the covering passport shows exit from New York. We shouldn't use anything that shows he's come from America.'

'We all know that. Haven't you been told his new passport will show entry into London Airport from Paris as an English representative of the Worth fashion house in London? And that your own will show you as his secretary and assistant?'

'No.'

'You've been told now. Use a black moustache and a small pointed black beard for your man.'

'He'll look French, not English, but he doesn't speak French.'

'Which was why we opted for brown fuzz, more English than French, but I'm willing to believe you find it too obvious. Tell the photographer to get hold of the alternatives.'

'That will mean making a new appointment.'

'Yes, but do it. Your man will be in London for several days, ostensibly on business, and then you and he will be flying to Nice, from where we'll get you both across the Med to Israel. I'll let you have the necessary documents, with the new passports, as soon as possible. Get the photographer to insert the photographs. And take care of our man. I'll see you both sometime, perhaps next week, when I hope I'll be in a position to drive you to London Airport. That's all.'

The phone went dead. It left Leila explaining the necessary adjustments. Amos said he could get the required beard and moustache by Wednesday, and take the photographs of both of them on Thursday morning at nine thirty, if they could manage that. Leila said yes. Wilhelm said as the fatty disguise made him sweat, it would be a relief to stick on only a moustache and a little beard, but he knew nothing about fashions.

'Fashions I don't know about myself,' said Amos.

'Don't worry yourselves,' said Leila.

'She's the boss,' said Wilhelm.

'I don't want to know who's which,' said Amos, 'my commitment is just to supply required photographs, and some hairpieces in this case. Anything else I don't want. See you again Thursday morning.' He shook hands with Wilhelm. 'Privilege to have met you.' He knew about the young man's heroic deed.

When they had gone, he looked at his appointments book. Ah, that was more like it. Four thirty. Maureen Brown. A lovely young lady thinking of making a name for herself in

70

a black corset and black stockings.

Who needed to do under-the-counter passport photographs? Oh, well, a small contribution to the cause from time to time was a small price to pay. How many had he supplied? Only three, all of revengeful Jewish men on the run from West German authorities for assassinating men they claimed were ex-SS officers. This new one, Wilhelm Kleibert, was the bravest of them all for his public execution in New York of a one-time SS doctor.

Chapter Seven

Miss Maureen Brown, daughter of Freddy and Cassie Brown, arrived five minutes late for her studio appointment with Amos Anderson.

'I'm ever so sorry, Mr Anderson, I worked through me lunch hour at the office so's I could leave an hour early, but it took me a few minutes longer.' She worked in the Camberwell Green branch of an insurance company as a copy typist.

'You're not late, Miss Brown, no, not a bit,' said Amos, giving her a smile. 'Five minutes is punctual, fifteen is late. Might I say punctual is a pleasure?'

'Oh, mutual, I'm sure,' said Maureen, eager to impress. She had thoughts of a glamorous career, far removed from the four walls of a boring old insurance office. Certainly, she looked highly fetching in a dress of daffodil yellow with a trim bodice that shaped her figure. The knee-length skirt of the dress was flared, her nyloned legs worth a second look. Further, she was pretty, her skin smooth and unblemished, her hair a shining blue-black. Amos classed her as a perfect example of 'the girl next door' type. Very popular as a pin-up.

'Come this way,' he said, and took her into his studio, the backcloth of which was of an unrelieved creamy-white for this particular sitting. 'There, that's the dressing room, you can change there. Take your time.'

'Thanks,' said Maureen, her eagerness touched with a hint of nervousness. Carrying a suitcase, she took herself into the dressing room, and closed the door.

Amos placed his camera on a tripod. He used a German Rolleifex with a reflective viewfinder and a push-button that operated the shutter and flashlight simultaneously.

It took a while for Maureen to emerge. Amos eyed her entrance with profound professional interest. Pin-up of the month? More like pin-up of the year. Nervous, and slightly pink about her appearance, yes, but that made her all the more delightful. She was worth special attention, faultless camera work and inspired guidance in her posing. In a figure-hugging black corset with built-in bra cups, black panties and sheer black nylons, her sex appeal was undeniable.

Maureen, ambition under attack from the nervousness of a beginner, gulped and said, 'What d'you think, will I do?'

'I'm impressed, and I can't say I'm not,' said Amos, his smile kind but impersonal. One had to be careful with some of these would-be glamour girls from the ranks of the working classes. Eager though most were, too intimate an interest was not what they wanted or liked, unless they were a bit tarty. And he himself had to be strictly principled. 'I think you'll do, Miss Brown, yes, I think you will.'

'I'd like to see meself in the *Daily Mirror*,' said Maureen. The *Mirror* sold in millions under the editorship of its go-getting editor, already a legend in Fleet Street.

'So would I,' said Amos, checking his camera, 'but hairy blokes like me they don't want.' He straightened up. 'Um, sit yourself on that bar stool, Miss Brown.'

The tall bar stool fronted the bright back-cloth. Maureen placed her round bottom on it, her long legs stretching, the tips of her high-heeled strapped black shoes touching the floor. The backcloth outlined her black-clad figure. Amos looked into his viewfinder.

Blimey, a natural, he thought, except for her hands. She was worrying about where to put them. She tried clasping the back of her neck.

'Is this all right?' she asked.

'Not exactly,' said Amos. She was all elbows and armpits. 'Try clasping the sides of the stool seat with your hands.' Maureen did so, and at once her pose took on a more natural look. 'Great. Great. A smile, say? Lovely.' He pressed the plunger the moment the smile arrived. The flash, bouncing off the ceiling, flooded the studio with light for a fraction of a second.

'Oops,' said Maureen. 'I think I blinked.'

'Not before the camera caught you. Hold that pose, lovey, but lift your chin a little. Look up now. No, not at me, at the top of the wall. That's it. Now, another smile? Fine. Lovely. Gotcher.' The shutter clicked, the flashlight bounced.

He posed her with instructive care, this way, that way, and his sitter, enthusiasm replacing jumpy nerves, fell into line with his every recommendation. And always there were words of encouragement for her.

'Great. Super. Right, just right. Lovely. My life, that's the tops, lovey, hold it.'

And so on.

Amos used two rolls of film, each of twelve exposures, his belief in what the results would be like as high as her adrenalin, for she finished the sitting flushed with excitement.

'What d'you think now, Mr Anderson, d'you think the photos will be groovy?'

'Groovy we don't want, Maureen. Top-class pictures of the girl next door we do.'

'Beg pardon?'

'Groovy is flashy. What they like, the picture editors, are happy pin-ups of what their readers see as the pretty girl next door. It's a question, lovey, of the difference between a professional model who chews gum and a shy amateur who likes ice cream and takes her doggie for a walk.'

'Crikey, I didn't look shy, did I?'

'You did in some poses, and I tell you no porkie. Shy is good, professional ain't rated, not by an discriminating picture editor. You know about discriminating?'

'I know what it means.'

'Well, all Fleet Street picture editors are discriminating about what lands on their desks. Now, get changed, then I'll talk to you in my office, won't I?'

Maureen entered his poky office as soon as she had changed. The rolls of film were already in the developing tank, and Amos was sitting at his desk, using the modern equivalent of a fountain pen, a biro, to fill in a form. He told her to sit down, then he advised her the copyright of the photographs was his, that he himself would submit the best of the selection first to the *Mirror*. If the *Mirror* turned them down, he would try *Men*

Only and then, if necessary, *Reveille*. He was confident, however, that acceptance for publication would come from one of them. In fact, he would eat an uncooked camel if that didn't happen.

Maureen giggled.

'A whole camel, Mr Anderson?'

'A whole one would kill me, lovey, so I'm laying my life on the line on your account. Now, I'm paying you three quid for your modelling–'

'You're paying me?' said Maureen. 'But I thought I'd have to pay you.'

'Not when I keep the copyright and take care of the submissions,' said Amos. 'I also pay you twenty per cent of any fees earned for publication, which I'm certain will come about, ain't I? There's papers and magazines all over the country that use pin-ups these days, especially the Sunday papers. Mind, there's not much going on around the synagogues.' Amos showed the grin of an unorthodox worshipper. 'The rabbis ain't in favour of stocking-tops. By the way, do your parents know you want to be the nation's pin-up?'

'I haven't told no-one,' said Maureen, 'but I am eighteen.'

'I should believe your parents might be church-going?'

'Oh, now and again,' said Maureen, 'but they're not prim and proper like–' She was going to say Grandma Finch of the Adams family. Instead she said, 'No, me parents aren't narrow-minded.'

'Well, you're eighteen, so it's up to you,' said Amos. 'Come in after you've finished work tomorrow evening, and I'll have contact sheets ready for you to see.'

'What's contact sheets?'

'Prints of the negatives, twelve to a sheet, each print two by two. You and me, we'll look 'em over, select the best and then I'll run off whole-plate prints, eight by six. In that size, I'll be sending one or two to the *Mirror* as starters.'

'Crikey, you're getting me real excited,' said Maureen.

'Too much excitement you don't want,' said Amos. 'Cool, that's the word. And self-belief. Now, if you'd sign this form and date it, I'll let you have your modelling fee of three quid.'

Maureen didn't argue. She scanned the form. It concerned the basics of copyright, and quoted the fee due to the sitter. Using the biro, she signed it and entered the date. Amos studied her signature.

'It's wobbly, love,' he said.

'It's me excitement,' she said.

'Didn't I tell you–'

'Yes, stay cool, but I can't just yet. Oh, thanks.' She took her fee of three pounds. 'I'll come in after work tomorrow like you said.'

'Good,' said Amos, and gave her a smiling look. It hit him then, his obvious mistake. There she was, everybody's girl next door in that pretty dress. She'd been that on arrival and so she was now, when she was about to depart. But in between he'd photographed her in a black corset. Every picture editor would see her as a sophisticated night bird. The idea of promoting her as everybody's girl next door, a sure winner, had just flown up his office chimney. He was as much of an idiot as if he'd asked for a ham sandwich at a Passover feast. What had addled his curly noddle? He knew. It was that passport photograph muddle, and the young woman with the steely air who obviously thought he ought to be more involved than was good for any English Jew who had a happy business going.

'What's up, Mr Anderson?' asked Maureen.

Amos, coming to, said, 'Well, I'll tell you, Miss Brown. We're trying to run when, rightly, we should be walking. It's my fault. I want to promote you as London's top girl next door. So, as a starter, a black corset we don't want.'

'But you said–'

'I know, but what I said we don't want, either. What we do want, as a starter, is a pretty girl in a pretty day dress lifting in the breeze. Black corsets are for later. You with me, lovey?'

'Oh, yes, you want me showing me legs

accidental, like.'

'Miss Brown, it's me pleasure to be acquainted with a young lady quick on the uptake. That's it, accidental uncoverage and, if I might suggest, a blush or two?'

'How can you photograph a blush?'

'By how you look, can't I? One hand up to your face, other hand pushing at your dress, eyes big, and mouth wide open, like you're saying, "Oh, help, me legs."'

Maureen giggled.

'Mr Anderson, d'you mean stocking-tops?'

'Such, as a starter, is classical for the girl next door. Believe me.'

'But how do we do that?' asked Maureen, willing to go along with anyone who could get her photographs published. Besides, she liked Mr Amos Anderson. He had nice eyes, an easy style and a sort of fatherly smile.

Amos consulted his desk diary.

'If you've got Saturday afternoon free, and the weather's dry, we'll motor into the countryside, find a breeze and pip, pip, click, click, who's a pretty popsie, then, eh?'

'Oh, great,' said Maureen.

'Be here by two next Saturday, then?'

'I'll be punctual again.'

'Punctual is good.'

'In this dress?'

'That is better than good,' said Amos.

'Oh, shall I still come in after work tomorrow to see the photos you've just taken?'

asked Maureen.

'We'll leave that until Saturday,' said Amos. There was no hurry. Corsets were for later in her career, he should have thought of that.

'Okey-dokey,' said Maureen, happy that her prospects were in good hands. 'Crikey, I'd better get home, it's nearly six o'clock.'

Amos saw her out, thanked her for everything, told her she was a certain winner and watched her depart. She did so on lithe legs, and the flared skirt of her dress swayed very fetchingly. She was nice, that girl, and he wasn't going to throw her to the wolves.

He thought about that woman agent and the young Jewish man, and the fact that he needed to get hold of a little pointed black beard and a matching moustache. Well, he knew where to find them.

'You're a bit late,' said Cassie when Maureen arrived. 'Your dad's beat you home for once.'

'Oh, I went to see a photographer about having some photos taken,' said Maureen, helping herself to a glass of water from the kitchen tap.

'Photos, what photos?' asked Cassie, preparing a summer supper of sliced ox tongue, hot boiled potatoes that would glisten with a smidgen of butter, and a mixed salad.

'Oh, sort of glamour photos,' said Maureen.

'What?'

'You know, Mum, pin-ups like you see in our *Daily Mirror*.'

'Like what?' Freddy, having had a wash and a brush-up on arriving home from the store, was entering the kitchen. He had changed into a light blue summer shirt and dark blue jeans. The Walworth store, part of the Adams Fashions empire, stocked a wide range of jeans, even though Sammy considered they were only for cowboys. In fact, the Adams factory at Bethnal Green manufactured them from imported denim. 'Like what, Maureen?' repeated Freddy.

'Like in the *Daily Mirror*,' said Maureen.

'Did you say pin-ups?' asked Freddy, forty-two, lean and hardened from years of jungle combat in Burma, but still a bit of a joker and regarded as a sport by his son and daughter.

Maureen, who had had no intention of keeping her mum and dad in the dark about her ambitions now that she was making a beginning, said she'd been to see Mr Amos Anderson at his Camberwell Green studio. She didn't say he'd photographed her in a new and sexy corset, because of what he'd said about it afterwards, making her aware that it was just a bit too sexy for her as a starter. But she did say he was going to take her out on Saturday and photograph her as a girl-next-door type for *Daily Mirror* readers.

Freddy fell about.

'I've got to believe this?' he said, laughing his head off.

'What's funny?' asked Maureen.

'I think your dad thinks you and Mr Anderson are,' said Cassie, smiling.

'Well, I'm serious,' said Maureen. 'I don't fancy working in any old office all me life, I want to have a career that's glamorous.'

'Like being a mannequin?' said Cassie, tipping the hot boiled new potatoes into a colander over the sink.

'Mannequin? Mannequin? Mum, that's as antique as bloomers,' said Maureen. 'You mean fashion model.'

'Let's hear a bit more about you being photographed as the *Daily Mirror*'s girl next door,' said Freddy.

'Yes, Mr Anderson's going to get me to pose in a country background with the breeze blowing me dress about and me blushing because of me legs showing,' said Maureen.

'Eh?' said Freddy.

'Honest,' said Maureen.

Freddy roared with laughter. Cassie, with the steaming, creamy-white potatoes in a tureen, was applying the smidgen of butter while trying to keep a straight face.

'Cassie, did you hear what I heard?' asked Freddy.

'I don't know how anyone could photograph a blush,' said Cassie.

'That's just what I told Mr Anderson,' said Maureen, and went on to explain how he would get her to pose so that she looked all shy and blushing. Freddy fell about again. 'Honest, Dad,' she said, 'I don't know why you're going barmy.'

'I can't help meself,' said Freddy, 'I've heard some cock-eyed waffle during me years of living, but that beats the lot.'

'Now, Freddy, don't make fun of your daughter,' said Cassie, although she was trying hard not to giggle. 'If she wants to do pin-ups, well, lots of girls do these days.'

'But our Maureen, shy and blushing?' said Freddy, cackling.

Enter Lewis, Maureen's brother, a thin and lanky young sprig, but passable in looks, cheerful by nature, and, like his dad, a bit of a joker.

'What's going on?' he asked.

'Supper, that's what's about to go on,' said Cassie, 'so call your grandpa, there's a good boy.'

'Oh, right,' said Lewis, and called up from the open kitchen door. 'Oi, Gaffer, come on down, supper's ready!'

'Coming, coming,' called Cassie's good old dad, Harold Ford, long a widower and still living with his daughter and son-in-law. He was affectionately known as the Gaffer from his working days as a ganger with the old LSER, now part of the nationalized railways. Well retired at seventy-two, his hair was grey and his face lined, but he was still sturdy of body and character. Down he came from his room, and entered the kitchen on lively legs. 'Have I been hearing a riot?' he asked.

'Yes,' said Maureen; 'me dad's got—'

'Never mind that now,' said Cassie, 'you can talk about it over supper, so sit down, everyone. Freddy, take that soppy grin off your face.'

Cassie and her family took every meal in the large, old-fashioned kitchen of their equally old-fashioned terraced house. Except Sundays. Sundays, tea was always taken around the table in the parlour, as was the long-established custom with most Walworth families. Television hadn't yet had a bad effect on table meals, but it was only a matter of time. Cassie and Freddy would fight that.

Chapter Eight

Over supper, Freddy encouraged Maureen to talk about her intention to become a pin-up dolly. The Gaffer listened to her with his mouth open, his knife and fork at a standstill.

'Eh?' he said.

'Here we go again,' murmured Cassie.

'Gaffer, wait till you hear how she's going to do country poses on Saturday,' said Freddy.

'Country poses?' said Lewis through a mouthful of ox tongue and potato. 'I can't wait.'

'If you go barmy, like Dad did, I'll tread on your model Spitfire,' said Maureen.

'I dunno I want to hear more,' said the Gaffer, recovering enough to put his knife and fork to work again.

'Well, I think you ought to, Dad,' said Cassie, 'it's sort of fascinating.'

Freddy spluttered.

'Come on, tell us, Muffin,' said Lewis. Muffin had been his sister's nickname from infancy to girlhood.

'Well, all right,' said Maureen, keen in any case to talk about her ambitions with her family. So, mainly for the benefit of her brother and grandpa this time, she gave her version of what Mr Anderson, the Camberwell Green photographer, had in mind for her, including how she was to look like the nice girl next door, shy and blushing because of her legs showing.

Lewis went overboard, in a manner of speaking. The Gaffer choked on a potato.

'What's up, Gaffer?' grinned Freddy, highly tickled by his daughter's fanciful hopes. He was not in the least the disapproving dad. 'What's up, eh?'

'I'll tell yer,' gasped the Gaffer, 'in all me years I ain't never heard the like of what I've just heard this very minute.'

'Like our Maureen all shy and blushing?' said Lewis, still a bit over the top.

'Now don't you start making fun, my lad, just because Maureen will be showing her legs,' said Cassie.

'In a kind of accidental way,' said Maureen.

'Accidental?' said Freddy. 'Oh, me aching ribs.'

Lewis went spare again, and, of all things, a grin was slowly dawning on the Gaffer's weathered face. His mouth split, his dentures gleamed, his eyes twinkled, and a throaty chuckle emerged from his tickled tonsils.

'Well, blow me over,' he said, 'it's legs and a blush, is it, young Maureen?'

'Well, yes, Grandpa,' said Maureen, who couldn't raise a blush, even for her much-loved Gaffer.

'So she naturally has to look – well, embarrassed,' said Cassie.

'Mum, if you'd ever seen Maureen at a hop, swinging it, you wouldn't have noticed no embarrassment, nor blushes,' grinned Lewis. 'Just her legs.'

'I saw her swinging it at Boots's sixtieth,' said Freddy, 'and all the other dollies too, 'swelp me, I did. And what's more, even the married ones, like Patsy, Paula and Clare. Not a blush among 'em.'

'Oh, they all looked ever so young and lively,' said Cassie, who, during her teenage years, had kept her own legs very much under cover, which was the proper thing to do in the early Thirties.

'Has everyone said their bit?' asked Maureen.

'Go on, Muffin, get with it, do your stuff as a pin-up,' said Lewis, 'and we'll order six copies of the *Daily Mirror*.'

'Laugh a minute, this is,' said the Gaffer. 'I ain't known the like since Conker Kelly's belt busted and his trousers dropped off.'

'Some young kid, was he, Gaffer?' asked Freddy.

'Not likely,' said the Gaffer, now hugely enjoying his meal. 'Gang foreman at the time, and we was all walking through Woolwich station after finishing a shift. Fell over his trousers, didn't he, arse over tip, in front of a ladies' church outing just coming

87

off the train. They all fainted.'

Everyone went spare then.

And no-one minded about Maureen becoming a blushing pin-up.

Boots, Sammy and Rachel had had a long discussion about how to respond to a possible takeover bid for Adams Enterprises Ltd. Sammy began by saying an affirmative response would be like selling his own baby. Rachel said hardly a baby, Sammy, at thirty years old.

'To me,' said Sammy, 'it's still on Cow and Gate.'

'And I should say you're not still its doting father?' smiled Rachel. 'Never, Sammy.'

'Let's think about what the offer might amount to,' said Boots.

Sammy said he wasn't keen on thinking about anything that might lead to losing their fashion company. Still, money's money, he said, which wasn't going to be exactly peanuts in this case, so what figure did Boots have in mind? Boots said Coates would probably know, for a start, what the balance sheets of the company were like over the last few years. There were ways and means of finding out. That meant Coates would know Adams Fashions Ltd was consistently in handsome profit. And even if they didn't know, they were capable of making a good guess.

'So?' said Rachel, addicted heart and soul

to her position in this family firm of Gentiles dear to her.

'We call in our auditors and get them to estimate the worth of our private company to a corporation long gone public,' said Boots.

'Well, all right,' said Sammy, 'but I asked you what you personally think it's worth.'

'A hundred thousand to a keen bidder,' said Boots.

'A hundred thousand?' gasped Rachel.

'A hundred thousand?' Sammy sat up. 'Would you do me the favour of repeating that?'

'Consider what's on offer,' said Boots. 'Shops, store, stocks, factory, machinery, outlets, goodwill, turnover. Our auditors will make something of all that. I'm making something of it. I'd quote £100,000, yes.'

'My life, £100,000?' breathed Rachel. 'But, Boots, aren't you forgetting the shops, store and factory are owned by our property company?'

'So the property company gets its share,' said Boots.

'Heavens,' said Rachel, quite flushed, 'all that much is money, Sammy.'

Sammy said that kind of money in the bank would be highly agreeable to the shareholders, but they'd be minus a business which he personally had brought up from its East End cradle, and he'd miss it. And how many shareholders were there?'

'We three,' said Boots, 'along with Lizzy, Ned, Tommy, Vi, Susie, Polly and Chinese Lady.' All these family members now held shares in each of the three companies, Adams Enterprises, Adams Fashions and Adams Properties. Rachel counted as family because her younger daughter Leah was married to Lizzy's son Edward.

'A ten-way family split?' said Sammy.

'With variations according to each one's holding,' said Boots. 'But, of course, we'd up the asking figure to £200,000.'

'Do what?' said Sammy.

'Boots lovey, did you have a liquid lunch?' asked Rachel. 'I mean, my every life, £200,000?'

'Pick me up, someone,' said Sammy, 'I think I've fallen off me chair.'

'I fancy you're still with us, Sammy,' said Boots, and went on to point out that as a private company, the share value wasn't quoted on the Stock Exchange and they could put their own value on the company. Further, he didn't think any of the shareholders would sell if the directors advised against it. If Coates backed off, nothing would be lost. If they actually went for it, then the recipient shareholders could invest their windfalls in the property company. That would give it a capital huge enough to turn it into a major development corporation.

There'd be new and worthwhile jobs for Tommy and Jimmy, both of whom were presently running the Bethnal Green factory.

'Blind O'Reilly,' breathed Sammy, '£200,000 capital? We could buy up every undeveloped site for miles around.'

'And wait for the developers to come running when the economy's really on the turn,' said Rachel.

'Or go in for development ourselves by acquiring an established firm of contractors,' said Boots.

Sammy thought long and hard.

'Boots,' he said, after some while, 'I've got a feeling we could be overreaching ourselves. Look at it this way. What we've got now is what we've built up over thirty years. It's all been gradual, and we ain't ever been out of control. Up to now, nothing's ever been too big for us to handle. Then there's the factory and all the staff, all the machinists and seamstresses who've been working for us for years, a lot of them all through the war. I know some have retired, and some are coming up for retirement, but all of 'em are used to Adams management. How will Coates management treat 'em? Not like Tommy and Jimmy do, I'll bet on it. Tommy's their mother and father, and Jimmy's their uncle. Then there's Susie's brother Freddy, running the Walworth store. Didn't know the first thing about shop-keeping when he came back from Burma, but look what he's done for the store. I ain't keen on telling him we might sell it. Boots, we've got to think long and serious.'

'No need,' smiled Boots, 'who wants ulcers? We can make our decision now. We simply refuse to sell, whatever Coates offer.'

'Boots, is that what you'd like?' asked Rachel.

'I set out the possibilities, I know,' said Boots, 'but I favour the simple option – that what we have we hold. Sammy's right, we're in control and always have been. What are your feelings, Rachel?'

'The same as yours and Sammy's,' said Rachel. 'I love what we have and how it's been achieved. I don't want ulcers and I don't need a windfall. Money, Boots, isn't the same as happiness.'

'A little helps, an excess is for the greedy,' smiled Boots, and Rachel thought how cool he was. She herself had experienced hot little flutters about the proposition and what it could mean, and Sammy had actually shown agitation. Boots hadn't blinked an eyelid. If anyone was in control, he was, always. These brothers, Boots, Tommy and Sammy. She knew no other trio of men quite like them. Not one of them looked his age. She wondered, not for the first time, how their Victorian mother had produced such sons. Their father, the man who, as a corporal in the army, had been killed on the North-West Frontier fifty years ago, had he been as remarkable a character as Boots, his eldest? He must have been.

'Well, Sammy?' she said.

'If I might say so,' said Sammy, looking as if a dud penny had turned into a genuine coin of the realm, 'I'm highly gratified that you two coincide with me.'

'Coinciding we all like, Sammy,' said Rachel.

'I'm particularly gratified that Boots ain't turning me upside down any more,' said Sammy. 'Upside down makes me feel I'm falling ill. D'you know, Susie does that to me sometimes when I'm talking to her. It's the way she talks back. All me married life I've done me best to let her know I'm the one wearing the trousers. And what happens? She turns me upside down, if you get me.'

'I get you, Sammy,' smiled Rachel.

'Knew you would,' said Sammy. 'Anyway, this special board meeting is agreed we give Coates an affirmative negative if they make an offer?'

'A firm negative, Sammy?' suggested Boots.

'Same thing, Boots old cock,' said Sammy.

'I'll put my hand up to the same thing,' said Rachel fervently.

'All agreed, Sammy,' said Boots. 'We three constitute a quorum.'

'Sometimes,' said Sammy, 'I'm in favour

of your educated talk, Boots, and you're still king of the family castle.'

'Don't mention it, old lad,' said Boots, 'it's all done with mirrors.'

Rachel laughed. Boots and Sammy, two lovely blokes. How she would have liked to have been the wife of either, if only her religion hadn't compelled her to marry a man of her own race.

Something else went Sammy's way when he arrived home. That was Susie's happy approval of the alabaster cherub. In fact, her approval stretched to the point of giving him the kind of kiss that touched his heart and made his waistcoat quiver a bit.

Bust my braces, he thought. I'm lucky with Susie, and lucky with me well-preserved corpuscles. I wonder if Boots's are still in working condition? You can never tell with Boots about this, that and the other. Mind, if he's still enjoying the other with Polly, Chinese Lady wouldn't label it as proper, not at their ages. Oh, well, I'm lucky all right with Susie.

Next: 'Sammy – Sammy – be your age.'

'Believe me, Susie, you've still got class.'

'Yes, I know, Sammy love, but kindly don't muck about with it in the kitchen.'

Chapter Nine

'Well, old love,' said Polly to Boots that evening, 'I agree with Sammy. Much jollier to hang onto what you've got than give up a large slice of it for filthy lucre. Sammy's one love, outside his family, is the business. And let's face it, old sport, he's been the driving force from the time he opened up that first shop.'

'All of us who benefit from the business owe Sammy,' said Boots.

'As for that shop, grotty though it was in those days, I've tender memories of it,' said Polly. 'It was where I first met you. I haven't been inside it for ages, but it's still sacred to me.'

'Like a church?' said Boots.

'Hardly. You were never a verger, and I was never one of God's heavenly souls.'

'A wild flapper, if I remember right,' said Boots.

They were having one of their companionable evenings, sitting on the swing hammock on their patio and looking out over the garden, the late August evening russet and balmy under the setting sun. They were perfectly relaxed, with no urge to be other than where they were, and no wish to be rushing about in pursuit of excitement. The restless generation these days was that of the teenagers, perhaps the equivalent of Polly and her flappers who had gone on crazy searches for the fruits of victory during the years immediately after the First World War. Those fruits, when found, had been bitter. The fruits of the Second World War had hardly proved sweet, and so the teenagers were creating their own pleasures. These related to music, music, dancing, dancing, and rock and roll concerts featuring up-and-coming young bands. If some austerity still existed, at least there was not the disillusionment suffered by the young people of the Twenties.

Polly and Boots, of course, had reached the age when they could be philosophical about every turn of the tide. The twins, Gemma and James, lived life with all the ardour and eagerness of their teenaged contemporaries. At the moment, they were with Polly's widowed stepmother, who loved having them.

Thinking of that, Polly said, 'By the way, Step-mama would like a photograph of Gemma and James.'

'We've scores of snapshots,' said Boots, 'and she's welcome to take her pick.'

'Snapshots, no,' said Polly, 'a formal photograph, yes.'

'Formal?' said Boots. 'A studio job? Who's going to tie them down? If I do, they'll tell their friends that their father's turned into a Victorian sadist, as per Wackford Squeers. Now mothers, of course, can do no wrong.'

'Mothers, of course, get taken advantage of by backsliding fathers,' said Polly. 'Oh, well, heigh-ho, I'll take them to a studio while they're still on school holiday and still have a Cornish tan.' The family, along with Susie, Sammy and Phoebe, had spent two weeks in North Cornwall and its foaming rollers. 'Stepmama wants a large portrait photograph of the two of them together, and in a large frame. It's to hang on her living-room wall.'

'Happily, Polly old girl, I'll leave it all to you,' said Boots.

'In return for which, I'd like a drink,' said Polly.

'It's a warm evening,' said Boots, 'so would you like a large gin and tonic with a large amount of ice?'

'Love it,' said Polly.

'I'll have one with you,' said Boots, 'and we'll make love to them together.'

'That'll be worth seeing,' said Polly. 'It'll let me into the secret of how a man makes love to a glass of iced gin and tonic. As far as mine is concerned, I'll just drink it.'

She watched him as he rose to his feet and entered the house, his movements still of the same easy long-legged kind as ever. She sighed for the years that had gone, the years that were now pointing her at sixty, the age of a definitely old woman.

Come back, the days of my wild heartbeats, come back.

She remembered again Sammy's grotty shop, and the moment when she first came face to face with Boots, tall, grey-eyed, masculine and whimsical. That was the moment when her first wild heartbeats began.

But there was a bright smile on her face when Boots returned with the drinks.

'Here we are, Polly.'

'Yes, here we are, old scout, two of a kind.'

'What kind?'

'A happy ever after kind,' said Polly, and laughed as she took the glass. 'Out of one of your mother's Victorian novels.'

'Are we as old-fashioned as that?' asked Boots.

'We would be,' said Polly, 'if we weren't about to down our twentieth-century gin and tonics.'

'Here's to you, Polly.'

'Here's to you, old darling.'

After supper with Leila, Michal and Judith, Wilhelm said, 'I think I'll go out.'

'Where to?' asked Leila.

'I thought I'd take in a movie,' said Wilhelm.

'Then you're an idiot,' said Leila, 'you could be recognized.'

'Not in a cinema,' said Wilhelm, 'cinemas are dark, aren't they?'

Leila turned to Michal.

'His photograph has been seen in many of your newspapers, hasn't it?'

'Yes, but not so much lately,' said Michal. 'Why don't you go with him? He'll attract less attention if he's with a woman who could be his wife.'

'I see most films as trivial,' said Leila.

'The trivial can be a form of escapism,' said Judith, 'and we all need an occasional helping.'

'I guess I'll help myself to some this evening,' said Wilhelm.

'You have orders not to show yourself unless by special arrangement, such as going to have your passport photograph taken,' said Leila.

'Look, he's bottled up,' said Michal, 'so go with him to the cinema. I'll drop off both of you in my car. Then neither of you will be seen except by the girl in the ticket office, and not even then if you get the tickets, Leila.'

Judith thought how patient he was with this touchy woman from Israel. It looked as if her responsibilities as an agent at this particular time were making her edgy. Certainly, it was going to be a great coup for Mossad if the man wanted by America for murder could be safely landed in Israel. Michal had been more than willing to help.

He had friends in Israel, friends he had made during his sabbatical year in a kibbutz. One of them had been a security man.

'Very well,' said Leila, 'I will go with him, but I hope the film won't be one of those absurd American Westerns, with every cowboy talking out of the side of his mouth.'

'And just saying either "yup" or "nope"?' said Michal with a smile. He thought Leila should show more empathy with America, for America had provided the greatest help to the Palestine Jews in the establishment of their independent State.

'We shall see when we get there,' said Leila. She softened. 'I must thank you and Mrs Wirthe for taking good care of us.'

'Oh, you're very welcome,' said Judith.

'I shall be forever grateful,' said Wilhelm in his generous way.

Michal looked at his watch.

'I'll drive you to the cinema in ten minutes,' he said.

'Come along, bless you,' said Polly's stepmother, Lady Simms, to the twins, 'time for Thomas to drive you home.'

'Oh, can't we stay the night, Grandma?' said Gemma, on her way to fifteen, and an entrancing image of her vivacious mother at that age. Her looks were deliciously piquant, her slender body taking on a convex curvature, and Gemma was very pleased about what nature was doing for her. Well, thin flat-chested girls were just a little bit freakish, poor things.

'Yes, could we stay the night, Grandma?' asked James, the same age as Gemma, of course, but already taller. Twins they were, with similarities, but just one glance at the pair told the beholder that while Gemma resembled her mother, James was like his father, with his dark brown hair, his grey eyes and his firm mouth. Already susceptible young schoolgirls were sighing over him. Cathy Davidson, who lived with her mother in Paris, wrote regularly to him, frequently reminding him that during their time together in Dulwich they had made promises to each other. James sometimes wrote to say he was too young to make that kind of promise to any girl, but she never took any notice. James had long thought girls were a bit of a problem.

Well, there was Cindy, daughter of Harry and Anneliese Stevens, friends of James's parents. Talk about a girl dynamo. She phoned him frequently, gave him orders about when to meet her and where to take her, and all this while she was beginning to bring other young men into her social round. His dad said it was known as playing the field until she settled on whoever she considered was her best prospect. James reckoned she was more likely to settle on being the coun-

101

try's first woman Prime Minister.

Lady Dorothy Simms regarded the twins affectionately. There they were, asking to stay the night after being with her since lunchtime. She loved having them. As a childless woman, she considered herself blessed in her happy relationship with stepdaughter Polly and her loving relationship with Gemma and James, firmly referring to them as her grandchildren. At seventy-six, she was still an elegant, aristocratic woman, daughter of a Yorkshire landowner, and still permanently involved in charity work. She was a rich woman, with a butler/chauffeur, two house servants and a gardener. The butler, Thomas Hillier, had succeeded the previous incumbent years ago, and was devoted to her.

'Darlings,' she said, 'you have no night things with you.'

'Oh, I can sleep in my pants,' said James airily, 'and Gemma can sleep in her knickers.'

'Grandma,' said Gemma, 'can you believe that boy can be so common? Mind, I don't mind sleeping like that.'

'Oh, I think we can find both of you some nightwear,' smiled Lady Simms, 'but first I must phone your parents.'

She phoned. Boots answered.

'Hello?'

'Hello, Boots, dear man. How are you?'

'Fairly normal, but Polly's a little high.'

'High?'

'Yes, she's just finished her second large gin and tonic.'

'I'm astonished she can manage even one after all that which went down our throats at your sixtieth last month.'

'Dorothy, not much went down your throat.'

'Oh, I'm a modest drinker, Boots. Listen, the twins are here, as you know.'

'I do know,' said Boots. 'This house is remarkably quiet. Is yours in need of repair yet? They've been with you since noon.'

'Yes, and good as gold,' said Lady Simms. 'They'd like to stay overnight and have breakfast with me. Do you mind?'

'Not a bit, except they've no pyjamas.'

'I can find them nightwear,' said Lady Simms.

'If you put James in a nightshirt,' said Boots, 'take some snapshots and send me one. Which reminds me, Polly says you'd like a formal photograph of them for framing, so she'll be popping in on a photographer and making an appointment for them.'

'Well, thank you, Boots, and Polly too.'

'Just thank Polly, I'll be ducking out.'

'I can't think why. Gemma and James are adorable.'

'How adorable is adorable if the walls of this house fall down one day?'

'Energy, dear man, allow them energy,' said Lady Simms.

'Could prove expensive,' said Boots. 'Anyway, say goodnight to them for me and Polly.'

'Yes, of course. Goodbye, Boots, I enjoyed every moment of your sixtieth.'

'Polly's of the opinion that if it had gone on any longer, only the fittest would have survived. Goodnight, Dorothy.'

When Boots put the phone down he thought what a splendid woman Polly's stepmother was. He knew she missed Sir Henry, her late old warhorse of a husband, but she was as resilient as Chinese Lady and a figure of warmth and compassion to the unfortunate souls she helped through her charities.

How old was she? Seventy-six, yes. And old Aunt Victoria, living with Tommy and Vi, was seventy-seven. And Chinese Lady was coming up to eighty. Most women outlasted most men. Which suggested that, all in all, they were tougher.

On that reflective note, Boots rejoined Polly, a woman as brightly alive as ever.

It was dark when Leila and Wilhelm left the cinema to find Michal waiting for them in his car. Driving them home, he discovered the main film had not been an American Western but a British comedy, featuring Will Hay as an eccentric and hopeless headmaster of a boys' school.

'Was it funny?' he asked.

'It was to Wilhelm,' said Leila. 'Myself, I

didn't understand a word.'

'But you laughed at times,' said Wilhelm.

'At the visual content, not the dialogue,' said Leila. 'However, it was not too bad, no.'

'A small helping of escapism?' said Michal, then drew a breath as a uniformed constable stepped from the pavement and held up a restraining hand. 'Damn,' said Michal, bringing his car to a stop. In the back, Leila and Wilhelm sank in an attempt to make themselves more invisible. The constable advanced and tapped on Michal's window. Michal, noticing a second constable watching from the pavement in the glow of a street lamp, wound his window down. 'What's up, officer?' he asked lightly.

'Good evening, sir,' said the policeman, 'would you mind telling me where you've come from?'

'The cinema,' said Michal. 'A Will Hay film.'

The constable peered at the vague outline of the passengers, studying them for long seconds, then asked, 'What's the number of your car, sir?'

'CYV 853.'

The constable checked, came back and said, 'Would you mind stepping out, sir, and opening up your boot?'

'Is there a reason?'

'Step out, sir, would you, please?' The constable opened the door. Michal shrugged and alighted. In the back, Leila and Wilhelm were tense. Michal walked round the car and opened up the boot. It was empty save for a spare wheel. The constable took a brief look. 'Thank you, sir, you can go on your way now. Sorry to have inconvenienced you.'

'But what's it all about?' asked Michal.

'A break-in. A jeweller's shop by the Elephant and Castle. We think a stolen car was used.'

'I see. Well, good luck and goodnight, officer.' Michal eased himself back into the car and resumed his drive home. He heard Leila tell Wilhelm in sibilant Yiddish that he'd just been shown how dangerous it was to appear in public. And he heard Wilhelm say they would have to do that when they kept their new appointment with the photographer. In response, Leila told him to muffle the lower half of his face with a scarf.

'It's summer, not winter,' whispered Wilhelm.

Michal spoke up.

'I've told you both it isn't wise to speak Yiddish. It's a foreign language in Camberwell. You must get into the way of always using English.'

'I guess you're right,' said Wilhelm the amenable.

'You need not remind us again,' said Leila the unbendable.

Michal brought the car to a stop outside

his home, and they were all greeted by Judith minutes later.

'And how was the film?' she asked.

'Funny,' said Wilhelm.

'A mystery to me,' said Leila.

'We were stopped on the way home,' said Michal, and told Judith of the inquisition.

'Perhaps you were lucky that the constable didn't ask Leila and Wilhelm to step out with you,' said Judith.

'There, you see?' said Leila to Wilhelm.

'I see,' said Wilhelm, 'but the film was still funny.'

'I'll make a bedtime milk drink,' said Judith, 'and offer everyone a slice of my honey cake, the kind I bake for Passover.'

'You are very hospitable,' said Wilhelm. 'Yes, thank you,' said Leila, and since she followed that by being almost mellow over the little bedtime repast, Judith, Michal and Wilhelm felt the long day had ended quite pleasantly.

Chapter Ten

'Are you awake, young sir?'

James opened his eyes. The morning of the first day in September was flooding the pleasant bedroom with light, and beside his bed stood Jane Hillier, sixteen-year-old daughter of Thomas Hillier, the butler. The girl was Lady Simms's parlourmaid, three months into the position. In her maid's uniform of royal and blue and starched white front, she was demure in appearance and expression. Not many girls were choosing to be in service these days. The Labour Party had conditioned most young people into avoidance of menial work. That is, slaving for the nobs. In any case, employment opportunities were now improving.

Jane held a cup and saucer as she regarded James with eyes that were not quite as demure as her smile.

'Oh, hello,' said James, dark brown hair ruffled from its night-long contact with the pillow. He looked warm from sound sleep.

'I've brought you a cuppa,' said Jane.

James sat up and she placed the cup and saucer on the bedside table.

'Thanks,' he said.

'Her Ladyship said breakfast in half an hour.'

'Kippers?' said James.

'Kippers? Kippers?' Jane giggled. 'Her Ladyship don't allow the smell of kippers around the house. It's eggs and bacon. My, you're a cheeky boy, aren't you, young sir?'

'Not specially,' said James, stretching his arms. 'I've decided on a serious life.'

'Serious? Crikey, what a one,' said Jane,

and sat down on the edge of the bed. She regarded him again. She knew he wasn't yet fifteen, but already he seemed more grown-up than any of the boys she knew. 'Would you like a present?'

'Before or after I've had my tea?' smiled James.

'Now,' said Jane, 'but you've got to promise not to tell no-one.'

'OK, fair's fair,' said James, as airy-fairy as his dad, despite his declared intention to live a serious life.

'Close your eyes, then, and I'll give it you,' said Jane at her demurest.

'All right, try me,' said James, and closed his eyes in the expectation of receiving a dead frog in his hand.

Almost at once an eager pair of rosebud lips connected with his unready mouth. All demureness departed from the young parlourmaid, and James could hardly believe the kind of kiss it was. Certainly, it was nothing like the boy and girl kisses he'd exchanged with Cathy and Cindy. Even the tip of a girlish tongue pushed into his mouth. This kind of kiss took his breath and his body seemed to flush. The ardent, lingering contact broke eventually. He opened his eyes, and there was Jane, standing up and looking as pure as an unopened rose.

'Don't tell now,' she said, 'drink your tea. My, you're a nice boy, really, young sir.' And out she whisked.

James lay back, eyes blinking, face hot. Well, blow me, he thought, I'm lucky she didn't catch me in the dark. Saucy minx. If Mum knew, she'd yank me back home and pull the drawbridge up. What goes on with girls? Blessed if I know. I thought they were all innocent at her age. Oh, well, not a word to Grandma Simms. I'll just talk about her rose garden over my eggs and bacon.

After breakfast, he and Gemma said goodbye to their loving grandmother, and were driven home by butler/chauffeur Thomas, Jane's dad. Jane herself waved them goodbye, hankie fluttering demurely. Lady Simms, beside her, also waved.

'If you don't mind me saying so, ain't they sweet children, Yer Ladyship?' said Jane.

'Hardly children,' said Lady Simms. 'In no time at all, Gemma will be a young lady, James a young man.'

'Will they be coming to stay again?' asked Jane.

'I hope so,' said Lady Simms.

Her demure parlourmaid smiled the smile of the flighty.

James was thinking that when he started living his serious life, he'd have to pay serious attention to what made girls a puzzle to fellers, or he might end up falling overboard out of sheer ignorance.

Boots, if consulted, would have said, 'James old lad, in certain cases, and at certain times in one's life, ignorance is bliss.'

It was the kind of wrinkle he'd given James during the time when young Cathy's attentions were turning his good-natured son upside down.

Vi's mother, now living with her daughter and son-in-law Tommy, was known to the family as old Aunt Victoria, although no-one referred to Chinese Lady as old Grandma Finch, even if she was senior by two years. The difference, of course, was that Chinese Lady was still comparatively vigorous, while Aunt Victoria kept mostly to her armchair like a woman content to slowly fade away. She was, however, much mellower than in her former years, when her main interest – even recreation – had been finding something to complain about.

She was frail of body now. Her seventy-eight years were showing, her memory faulty. She kept asking Vi where Tom was. Tom, her husband, had died a few years ago. Vi, compassionate, liked to answer in the best way she could.

'Oh, he'll turn up sometime today, I expect.'

'Well, I must say I can't think where he's got to.'

She was no trouble, she really had

mellowed, and was quite content with the two rooms Vi and Tommy had put at her disposal. But she was definitely fading.

Vi spoke to Tommy.

'I'm worried about Mam.'

'So am I, Vi, I think our old lady is feeling dead tired,' said Tommy.

Vi said she hoped he didn't mean her mum was tired of living. Tommy did mean that, but didn't say so. However, he did say he'd get Dr Jerribond to call. Dr Jerribond, he said, was the kind of GP who could cheer up someone suffering appendicitis and two broken legs all at once. Perhaps that was what the old lady really needed, a bit of uplift from the kind of doctor who'd go as far as to prescribe a reviving tonic of two glasses of port a day.

'Tommy, are you being funny?' asked Vi.

'On me honour, Vi, no,' said Tommy, 'it's what they call being talked into feeling better, along with a drop or two of your favourite tipple. You and me, we can't talk our old lady into feeling better, because she's listening to us every day. But good old Dr Jerribond, he could do the trick.'

'Tommy, you could be right,' said Vi. 'I mean, it's not as if Mum's really old. Not really old.'

'Just getting on a bit, Vi. I'll phone the doctor tomorrow morning.'

That resulted in the arrival the following

afternoon of Dr Jerribond, bright and encouraging, if a bit portly for a medico who was forever busy on his afternoon rounds. Although Aunt Victoria said she wasn't ill, and that her son-in-law was fussing, the breezy GP gave her an examination and a fund of cheerful adjectives, and spoke to Vi on his way out.

'Slightly anaemic, slightly, Mrs Adams, but there's life in the old lady yet. Here's a prescription for vitamin tablets. See that she takes one a day, would you?'

'She's not actually ill, doctor?' said Vi.

'Ill? No, just a little aged, and she seems quite perky at the moment. Let me know–'

'Perky?' said Vi.

'At the moment. Let me know as soon as you feel she needs me again.' That was a hint that an emergency might arise. It didn't register with Vi, simply because she refused to believe her mother's fading condition was terminal. 'As it is, perhaps I'll call in once a fortnight, anyway.'

'Oh, thanks, doctor,' said Vi.

'Goodbye now, regards to Mr Adams.'

'Goodbye, doctor, and thanks ever so much for calling,' said Vi gratefully.

'Don't mention it. Must get on.'

No sooner had he departed than Vi's mum made herself heard from upstairs.

'Vi? Vi? You there?'

'Yes, Mum.'

113

'Well, I wonder, could you get me a little glass of port, dear?'

When Tommy arrived home, Vi gave him details of the doctor's call, then asked him a question.

'Did you tell Dr Jerribond that a little drop of port would do Mum good?'

'Me?' said Tommy. 'Now would I tell any doctor how to treat a patient, how to do his job? Not much. What makes you think I did?'

'Because as soon as the doctor had gone, Mum called down and asked if she could have a glass,' said Vi.

'Of milk?' said Tommy.

'Port,' said Vi.

At that, Tommy showed a grin from ear to ear. Well, almost.

'Port?' he said.

'Well,' said Vi, 'I told you the doctor mentioned she was feeling a little perky.'

'Well, I'm blowed,' said Tommy, 'good old girl. I'll treat her this evening.'

'What to?' asked Vi.

'Another glass of port,' said Tommy.

On Wednesday afternoon, Mr Geoffrey Piper, a director of Coates, was keeping an appointment, arranged yesterday, with Mrs Rachel Goodman, secretary and director of Adams Enterprises and its associated companies. He sat facing her on the other side of her desk. He was finding her not just a handsome woman, but an intelligent and lucid one.

He was there to lay before her a general outline of his board's possible proposal to acquire Adams Fashions Ltd. So far, Rachel considered his outline not too precise.

'You realize, Mr Piper, that before I submit details to our senior directors, Mr Sammy Adams and Mr Robert Adams, I need to have a clear-cut presentation. You've spoken of your interest in taking over our Bethnal Green factory, and you've also indicated an interest in our store and our shops. Tell me, what exactly will the possible proposal cover? A hundred per cent purchase of the shareholdings, which will give you complete control of the company? Or do you have merely a majority holding in mind? Or an offer that will give you full ownership of everything?'

Mr Piper, an appealing gentleman in his late forties, raised a hand.

'My dear madam, I've no wish to be vague, indeed not, and forgive me if I haven't made myself reasonably clear. This, of course, is a preliminary and informal meeting intended to lead to an official discussion between your senior directors and ours.'

He's sounding me out, thought Rachel. He wants to discover if I'm eager to present a favourable case to Sammy and Boots. Little does he know what a couple of wise old owls they are.

'Carry on, Mr Piper,' she said.

'Shareholding could give us control,' he said, 'but I imagine your board would resist a move that might result in their being voted out. Therefore, I think I should tell you we have in mind outright ownership of the company and its assets.'

'Ownership of our factory, our shops, our Walworth store and all shares?' said Rachel, velvety voice delightfully pleasing to Mr Piper.

'The freeholds of all these properties are yours?' he said.

'Oh, yes,' said Rachel, but refrained from informing him that the freeholds of the factory, the Walworth store and most of the shops belonged to Adams Properties Ltd. Adams Properties was as solidly established as Adams Fashions, so much so that Boots's son Tim, and Sammy's son Daniel, co-managers, were still sold on the idea of building an American-style supermarket in the not too distant future. 'Yes, these freeholds are ours, Mr Piper.'

Mr Piper mused and looked Rachel in the eye. Rachel smiled. Mr Piper blinked. Undeniably, Rachel was still a very comely lady, and Mr Piper probably put her in her mid-forties. Next month she would be fifty-four, the same age as Sammy, but she was very much like Susie and Polly in the resistance she offered to the persistent sorties of Father Time, not a gentleman in the unpitying war he waged on ladies.

'Well, Mrs Goodman,' said the impressed representative from Coates, 'let me be frank at this point and say that we definitely have full ownership in mind.'

'On my life,' murmured Rachel, 'a total acquisition? That's clear-cut indeed. Am I to be informed of what offer your company has in mind, or will that remain confidential until the official meeting?'

'You'll probably understand it won't be made known until then at least,' said Mr Piper, 'when I presume your auditors will supply us with a copy of your latest balance sheet.'

'There's no chance you can whisper a guess to me?'

'I'm afraid not.'

'Well, I can at least let my senior directors know that the official meeting should be extremely interesting,' said Rachel. 'So thank you for coming, Mr Piper.'

'My dear madam, it's been a great pleasure,' said Mr Piper cordially. 'I hope we shall meet again. Um – perhaps over lunch one day?'

'Who knows?' smiled Rachel, and saw him to the door. He shook her hand, said goodbye, put on his bowler hat, picked up his rolled umbrella, and left. The bowler hat and umbrella made him look what he was, a City gent. Rachel, smiling, popped into Sammy's office. Sammy used the house line to call Boots in, and the brothers listened to what Rachel had to say, all of which was highly interesting, and no error.

'All right, it means they're keen,' said Sammy.

'It means they'll make an offer,' said Boots.

'At the meeting?' said Sammy. 'What's the point of going, if we intend to turn down any offer?'

'To turn it down without meeting them wouldn't be good manners,' said Boots.

'Come again,' said Sammy.

'A lack of courtesy, Sammy,' said Rachel.

'I've heard of that, and I'm all for it,' said Sammy. 'I was brought up on showing me manners and keeping me shirt tucked in. So all right, we go, and I daresay we'll get a cup of tea and some biscuits. That's if they don't fall out of their waistcoats and watch chains at hearing our sale price of £200,000.'

'Sammy, we still need Coates's custom,' said Boots, 'they still buy in large quantities from the factory. So let's have the meeting and let's tell them, without mentioning £200,000, that whatever their maximum offer is, we'll give it consideration. Unless, in some way, they corner us and we're compelled to drop a bombshell, our figure of £200,000 need never be mentioned. In any case, our balance sheet will speak well enough to make them realize we're worth more than a pound of peanuts.'

'Boots,' said Rachel, 'I must point out that the balance sheet won't show the assets owned by the property company.'

'We'll explain that,' said Boots, 'and I fancy they'll ask for them to be included by special arrangement with the property company. It'll be then that we say we'll give the whole proposal consideration.'

'As a matter of courtesy?' smiled Rachel. 'I'm for that, Boots.'

'Agreed,' said Sammy. 'You mean negative consideration, of course, Boots?'

'Yes, as we decided,' said Boots. 'Eventually, we'll come up with the information that at a meeting of all shareholders, the majority voted against the proposition on the grounds that, as family members receiving excellent dividends, they insisted on the family retaining the firm.'

'All that counts as good manners?' grinned Sammy.

'It will allow you and Boots to sound like very courteous gents,' said Rachel.

'Stuff my old socks,' said Sammy, 'when you think what it's done for Boots, don't you consider education highly recommendable, Rachel?'

'Highly, Sammy,' said Rachel.

'I wish I'd had some meself,' said Sammy.

'Sammy old lad,' said Boots, 'what you did have was a grounding. And in your case, what you didn't have was never necessary. You've been a man of the world since you were fourteen.'

'I'm tickled, Boots old cock, tickled,' said Sammy. 'And might I say, Rachel, what a helpful meeting you had with Mr Diaper?'

'Piper, Sammy.'

'Yes, something like that,' said Sammy. 'Anyway, good on you for your performance.'

'Well, thank you, Sammy,' said Rachel.

'Can't do without you these days,' said Boots.

'Boots, my dear, I'm the happiest of women in all I'm able to do for our companies,' said Rachel.

Boots looked at his watch. Mid-afternoon. Office teatime.

'Rachel, have two extra biscuits with your cup of tea,' he said, 'you've earned them.'

Chapter Eleven

Earlier that afternoon, Patsy, the American wife of Daniel, elder son of Sammy and Susie, came out of her house in Kestrel Avenue with her children, eight-year-old

Arabella and six-year-old Andrew. They walked to the bus stop at the lower end of Herne Hill before it joined Denmark Hill. Patsy was taking her children to Lyons at Camberwell Green to treat them to ice creams and milk shakes, a promised outing.

There, waiting at the bus stop, was Emma, younger daughter of Daniel's Aunt Lizzy and Uncle Ned, and the wife of Jonathan Hardy. With Emma were her nine-year-old daughter Jessie and her two-year-old son Mark. They lived close to Patsy and Daniel.

'Hi there,' said Patsy, outgoing and as lively at twenty-nine as she'd been at seventeen, when she'd first met Daniel. 'Hi, kids.'

'Hi,' said Jessie, while little brother Mark stared shyly, and Emma said hello to Patsy's two. Then she addressed Patsy.

'Where are you off to with yours?'

'Lyons, for ice creams and milk shakes,' said Patsy. 'I've told them it'll make them fat, but at their age, do kids care?'

'I'm taking mine to the park,' said Emma, who, like her mother and her sister Annabelle, was a chestnut-haired, brown-eyed brunette. She was coming up to thirty-four, and considered by Jonathan to be a prime example of how to promote continuous sex appeal with the minimum effort. Come to that, Daniel thought much the same about Patsy. Both ladies accepted these compliments as their fair due, and both kept their sex appeal up to the mark with attractive make-up, well-chosen clothes and healthy bodies.

'How's Daniel, Patsy?' Emma asked.

'Believe me, Emma,' said Patsy, with the kids mixing it, 'I'm still waiting for that guy to grow up. By the way, Uncle Boots's sixtieth was just great, wasn't it?'

'How great was great, Patsy, when Jonathan's hangover laid him out all the following day, and I spent the same amount of time trying to find out where my head was?' Emma delivered this in a confidential whisper, in case the three elder children heard and carried a tale of drunken grownups into the ears of their schoolfriends.

'Daniel likewise,' said Patsy. 'And me. Whoops, break it up, kids, the bus is coming.'

The red bus was coming down the hill quite fast towards the stop, and for a moment Emma thought the driver was going to ignore his waiting passengers and pass them by. However, he did pull up, although not without putting a strain on his tyres.

'Here we are, ladies,' called the conductor, 'all aboard, little 'uns. Nice day, eh?' He helped the kids to step up. 'Hope you're in a hurry, because me driver is,' he said to the ladies. 'I think he wants to get home to his missus. She's baking a cake.'

'How sweet,' said Emma.

'Cute,' said Patsy, shepherding the

children. 'Move along, you guys.'

The conductor rang the bell and the bus, with about a score of passengers on board, moved off. It quickly gathered speed.

'Here, he's going a bit fast, what's his hurry?' complained a woman.

Patsy, Emma and their children had hardly settled into their seats before the bus entered Denmark Hill and rushed towards the next stop at the corner of Ferndene Road, where two people were waiting. It thundered past them.

'Hey, Joe!' The conductor shouted at his driver and rang the bell. The driver took no notice. He seemed to be crouched over his wheel, hugging it. 'Joe!' Again the conductor rang the bell. There was no response, and the bus continued its fast descent.

The conductor moved forward, shouting, and his obvious agitation communicated fright to the passengers. Some panicked, especially when the heavy vehicle slewed as it rounded the bend at the bottom of the hill. It charged on, passing Ruskin Park and King's College Hospital, and headed at unchecked speed towards the junction at Camberwell Green. People crossing the road ran for their lives. The bus driver, not using his horn, was sounding no warnings. He was simply going pell-mell into the heart of Camberwell.

'Oh, my God,' gasped Emma. She had little Mark on her lap, and Jessie next to her.

She clasped them both, her eyes staring as she saw the junction traffic lights coming up horrendously fast. They were red. By the grace of God there was no traffic immediately in front of the careering bus, and it shot the lights, missing only by inches a car coming out of Camberwell New Road on the left. From the pavements, transfixed people screamed at the bus driver.

Seated with her children behind Emma, Patsy gasped, 'Emma, oh, Jesus, Emma!'

Passengers were hysterical as the bus thundered along Camberwell Road, charging in the wake of a small van forty yards ahead. The conductor was banging on the window dividing the driver from the passengers, and he was almost hoarse from shouting.

'Joe! For Chrissake, man! Pull up, pull up!'

No response emanated from the hunched driver. Emma, frightened out of her life for the four children, prayed between clenched teeth. It was all too obvious now that the driver had gone off his head. He was driving straight for the back of the small van as it made a sedate progress towards Walworth Road.

The passengers, mostly shopping housewives, were clinging to whatever they could get hold of, and either shrieking or screaming. A middle-aged man came out of his seat, staggered along the reverberating floor of the aisle to join the conductor in hammering on the window and bawling at the driver.

'Stop! Stop, you crazy bugger, you'll kill us all!'

Everyone walking the pavements came to a halt as the bus, charging like a runaway, swerved with a hideous screech of tyres, and overtook the van. Now its mighty weight was on the wrong side of the road. An oncoming car spun out of the way by mounting the kerb. The bus rolled by at a suicidal speed, taking up a position in front of the van and reaching Walworth Road. Ahead were a couple of cars, and a little over half a mile further on were the traffic lights guarding the crossing from Manor Place to Browning Street. A man pushing an empty barrow heard the noisy, drumming approach of the bus. He turned his head, saw the charging monster, let go of his barrow and rushed onto the pavement. The bus hit the barrow and smashed it aside amid screams from women passengers.

Jessie was clinging to her mother, and her mother was holding fast to her frightened daughter and her bewildered little son. And Patsy was holding onto Arabella and Andrew for dear life. Like Emma, she was praying, her body trembling from the vibrations of the thundering bus. Her eyes, mesmerized, were staring at the car immediately ahead. It seemed then as if its driver had glimpsed the raging bus in his mirror, for he overtook the second car at speed, giving quick warning toots on his hooter. And as he passed he made a hand gesture. The driver of the second car turned his head and saw the terrifying apparition of a red juggernaut almost on his tail. He put his foot down and his speed reached that of the other car. They sped away hell for leather.

In the distance, Patsy and Emma saw the traffic lights. Oh, great God, thought Emma, all kinds of images flashing into her distraught mind. The bus roared past the East Street market, which was teeming with shoppers. Everyone visible on the pavements and at the market entrance stopped moving, except for a turn of every head. Many looked dumbstruck, others yelled at the bus driver. But on he went, the middle-aged man and the conductor still thumping frantically on the window.

It seemed as if the traffic lights at Browning Street suddenly began to race towards the speeding bus. They were at red, and the red appeared to glare angrily. Jessie buried her face against her mother, her young body shaking, while Arabella gasped to Patsy, 'Mummy, Mummy.'

A parked car, fortunately empty, was hit and tossed onto the pavement like a heap of old iron. The bus passengers were white-faced and stricken as their public vehicle thundered at the traffic lights. The red turned green at the last moment, and the bus charged on in pursuit of traffic ahead. It passed shops, it passed the stately town hall, and it passed Wansey Street, where Cassie Brown lived with her family. It reached the railway bridge, rushed under it and careered towards the busy junction of the Elephant and Castle, around which were still signs of some post-war development. Not far ahead was another bus.

We're going to die, thought Patsy, all of us, Emma and me and our darling children. And Emma thought in a kind of devastating and mesmerized way that there was going to be mayhem at the Elephant and Castle. This bus is going to hit that bus ahead by the time we reach the junction, and we're all going to be crushed to death.

With unimaginable fright and hysteria prevailing on both decks, the driver, suddenly slumped. His hunched shoulders collapsed, his hands came off the steering wheel, his foot off the accelerator, and with the clutch out the gears ground, the rudderless bus slewed, slowed, bumped heavily against the kerb, rolled onto the pavement and came to a stop outside shops like a red colossus devoid of all motion. Its engine stalled.

'Oh, merciful God,' gasped a woman passenger.

The conductor, expelling hoarse words of reassurance, ran down the aisle, jumped onto

127

the pavement and rushed round to wrench open the driver's door. A crowd of stunned pedestrians had already gathered. The collapsed driver was huddled and inert, his face blue, his lips blue, and spittle issuing from his mouth.

'Gawdalmighty,' breathed the conductor, 'you near done for us all, Joe. But now I'm looking at yer, I can see you've had a bleedin' brainstorm, so I forgive yer, so help me I do. You're never going to taste your old lady's cake, not this side of Christmas, if ever.'

Chapter Twelve

A policeman on the beat had taken charge of the incident. A summoned ambulance had carried the brain-stricken driver to hospital, and a second ambulance had arrived to deal with any passengers suffering severe shock. A crowd had massed, and a second constable arrived to keep the gawping bystanders clear of the bus and the shaken, disgorged passengers.

Freddy Brown, manager of the Adams store close to the Elephant and Castle junction, emerged from the premises, saw the bus, the crowd and the ambulance, and crossed the road. Among the first people he spotted were Emma and Patsy, their children around them. He broke through the crowd. A constable checked him.

'Stay back, sir.'

'I know those two ladies and their children,' said Freddy, 'they're relatives of mine. Let me talk to them.'

'Very well, sir.'

Freddy made his way to Emma and Patsy.

'Emma? Patsy? What happened?'

'Freddy? Where did you come from?' asked Emma, pale, and with little Mark up in her arms.

'From the store. What happened, Emma?'

'The bus driver went crazy,' said Emma.

'Crazy, crazy,' said Patsy, biting her lip.

'It was awful, Uncle Freddy,' said Jessie. She, Arabella and Andrew were all shaken.

With the ambulance crew ministering to distraught women, Freddy said, 'Look, Patsy, let me get all of you out of here. There's a cafe across the road near the store where we can get hot milk drinks for the children, and some strong coffee for you and Emma.'

'What about the store?' asked Emma.

'I can leave that to my two assistants,' said Freddy, 'and there are no customers at the moment. They all left, one after the other, to join this crowd, I suppose. Let me get all of you out of it. Come on.'

He took them across the road to the cafe, Italian-owned. There, Emma and Patsy gratefully seated themselves at a table with the children, Mark on Emma's lap. Freddy went to the counter and ordered coffees and hot milk drinks.

'That bus, eh?' said Victor, the agreeable proprietor. 'On the pavement, yes? That is no place for a bus.'

'God knows exactly what happened,' said Freddy, 'I've only been told the driver went crazy.'

'The war, perhaps, eh, Mr Brown? It did many things to men.' Victor had served with Mussolini's army in the Western Desert, been captured by the British, and stayed in England after his release from a prisoner-of-war camp. 'The bus driver, yes, perhaps was a soldier left with a sick head. You think a sick head can blow up? Yes, I think too. You sit, Mr Brown, eh? I will bring the drinks.'

'Ta muchly,' said Freddy, and joined his relatives. Together, in spasms, Emma and Patsy began to give him the details of their frightening experience. Halfway through, Victor arrived with the tray of drinks. He gave a chocolate biscuit to each of the children with their hot milk.

'You like, eh?' he said to them, beaming.

'Oh, thanks,' said Jessie.

'A present from me, yes?' said Victor.

'So kind of you,' said Emma.

'We were going to have ice creams,' said Arabella.

130

'So?' said Victor, beaming again. 'I have ice cream. You like when you have finished your hot milk?'

'Crumbs, yes, not half,' said Jessie. 'Can we, Mummy?'

'Of course,' said Emma, and Freddy nodded at the proprietor.

'We'll all have ice creams, Victor,' he said, 'they'll cool us down.'

'Good, eh?' said Victor, and went back to his counter. Other customers had arrived, all talking about the bus.

Over their coffee, Emma and Patsy resumed giving details to Freddy. At the end, only the presence of the children stopped him from expressing his reactions in some elementary language. All he could acceptably say was, 'Well, thank God the poor devil collapsed before he reached the junction. It's always crowded with traffic. Something very nasty could have happened.'

'I was ever so frightened,' said Arabella.

'Well, you're safe now,' said Freddy, giving her a pat on her knitted woollen hat that was topped with a bobble. 'We're all safe, and there'll be ice creams coming soon.'

'Yummy,' said Andrew.

Freddy looked at Emma, then at Patsy. They smiled, a little weakly, but their colour was back. Freddy chatted to the children, telling them that the bus driver had been showing off, that he'd get the sack for it, and

131

so it wouldn't happen again.

'We need our buses, don't we, eh? Tell you what,' he said, 'when we've had our ice creams, I'll bring my car round, squeeze all of you into it and drive you home.'

'Freddy, that's real sweet of you, it really is,' said Patsy, 'but there's your store, and I'm sure we can raise a cab, can't we, Emma?'

'Of course,' said Emma.

'Not many taxis whizz up and down Walworth Road,' said Freddy. 'And my assistants can manage until closing time. So crowd into my car and I'll drive you.'

'Are you sure, Freddy?' asked Patsy, not too keen under the circumstances about going home on another bus. And the kids would probably take some time to regard bus rides as harmless adventures, although Freddy had been a wise guy in telling them the show-off bus driver would be fired. Actually, the poor guy was probably dead by now. 'You'll bring your auto round?'

'I insist,' said Freddy. 'You young 'uns would like to squeeze in, wouldn't you?'

'Hooray,' said Andrew, as bright as his mother and as lively as his dad. 'I'd like to.'

'Me too,' said Arabella.

'And me,' said Jessie. 'Could I squeeze in next to you, Uncle Freddy?'

'You and Arabella both,' said Freddy, 'I'm a fan of young ladies.'

Jessie giggled, the ice creams arrived, and

Patsy thought how rewarding it was to be married into a family as diverse and tribal as that presided over by its matriarch, Grandma Finch. Everyone looked out for everyone else. Help and affection arrived quickly at one's door in any crisis. Polly had asked her once if she ever felt hemmed in by the manifold Adams brood. Patsy had said no, do you? My dear, said Polly, I'm one of the brood.

'Jesus Christ,' breathed Daniel, having been given details of the incident on arriving home from the office, 'is this true or are you recounting a nightmare, Patsy?'

'It's true, honey, it sure is,' said Patsy, 'and it's also a nightmare. A nightmare in broad daylight. I'm still suffering grisly shakes.'

Daniel asked how the children were, and Patsy said that fortunately, they'd been so bucked by their hot milk, chocolate biscuits and ice creams that they'd emerged from the cafe with contented tummies and happy faces. Daniel asked where they were, and Patsy said in the garden, where Arabella was teaching Andrew how to play baseball.

'Rounders?' said Daniel.

'Rounders?' said Patsy.

'Don't you know by now that that's what it's called in this country, and that it's a game for girls?'

'Well, you cutie,' said Patsy, 'it's played in

133

America by men six feet tall and four feet wide, and it's called baseball.'

'You win,' said Daniel. He put his arms around her, kissed her and said, 'Love you, Patsy, and thank the Lord you and the kids weren't losers.'

'Hey,' said Patsy, overbright, 'don't you know there are no losers in the Kirk and Adams families?' Her pa was a Kirk.

'I'll hang onto that,' said Daniel.

Jonathan, on being told of the nightmare bus ride by Emma, expressed himself in the honest fashion of a country-born man, very much to the effect that the Lord Himself could bear witness to his sense of gratitude that no harm had come to anyone.

'That's a little dramatic, Jonathan,' said Emma.

'Yes, it is a bit, Daddy,' said Jessie.

'Nothing of the kind,' said Jonathan. 'I be expected to show my relief by a tiddly old grunt, like old Farmer Diprose and his pigs? More specially, like his old sow, Henrietta? That Henrietta, she were the best grunter in the country, second only to Farmer Diprose himself. And I should know, I were born not far from his pig farm. See here, young Jessie, you and your mum, and little Mark too, Providence took a hand in delivering you from calamity, and I'd be a fair old lump of wood if I didn't think so or say so. Emma, have you had a brandy?'

'No, coffee and ice cream, as I mentioned,' said Emma.

'Well, you need a shot of brandy, and so do I,' said Jonathan with all seriousness, 'and young Jessie here, she needs a cuddle. And where's Mark?'

'In bed and asleep,' said Emma.

'Daddy, could I have a cuddle and some brandy?' asked Jessie, curly-haired, fond of asking questions and sharing things with her mum and dad.

'Not brandy, no,' said Jonathan, outwardly cheerful now for the sake of reassuring his daughter, but inwardly still appalled at what might have happened if that mind-crazed bus driver hadn't collapsed. And even then, the bus could still have crashed. He looked at Emma, and opted for continued lightness. 'Gin?' he suggested.

'Gin? For Jessie? Don't you dare,' said Emma, at which point she saw through his cheerful mask. 'Jonathan, we're all right, we're at home, and we're with you. So we're very safe, love.'

Jonathan swept Jessie up into his arms, hugged her, let go with one arm and put it around his wife. He held wife and daughter tightly and closely, and they both saw that his eyes were cloudy and moist.

Jessie gulped.

'Daddy?'

'That old Henrietta,' said Jonathan, 'she were nearly as big as a bus herself.'

'Boots, you really think Coates will make an offer?' said Polly over supper.

'I think so,' said Boots.

'After they've recovered from your suggested figure of £200,000?' said Polly. 'That's if you need to drop the bombshell.'

'I think so,' said Boots.

'Some hopes, Dad,' said James. He and Gemma both knew something about the family business. Gemma, in fact, had said she'd go in for modelling the firm's fashion designs when she was old enough. All fashion designers used models to show off their clothes, she said, didn't Uncle Sammy know that? Boots said yes, but thanked her for her reminder.

'What d'you mean, some hopes?' asked Gemma of her brother.

'No-one could recover from being asked for that amount,' said James. 'It could even bring on heart failure.' James was adept at putting words together, which trait Gemma referred to as showing off.

'Oh, I think the firm of Coates is made of stern stuff,' said Polly.

'We're not selling out, in any case,' said Boots.

'Thank goodness for that,' said Gemma. 'Mind, if you did sell for thousands and thousands, Daddy, how much would I get?'

'How much?' said Boots.

'Discuss,' said Polly.

'What, now?' said James.

'No, not now,' said Polly. 'When it happens, if it ever does.'

'I don't mind it not happening,' said Gemma. 'I mean, I don't want my chance of being a fashion model to die before it's even been born.'

'You've got to be tall to be a fashion model,' said James.

'Well, I'm going to grow,' said Gemma. 'It comes naturally, growing.'

'Of course, you could be stretched,' said James.

'What, on the rack?' said Gemma.

'Well, Uncle Sammy knows a lot of useful people,' said James, 'and he could even know someone who'll sell him a rack that stretches but doesn't hurt.'

'You'll come to a dotty end one day,' said Gemma darkly.

'What happens, Boots old thing,' said Polly, 'if Coates go dotty and actually agree to your asking price?'

'We'll recommend an asylum with a sympathetic staff,' said Boots. 'No, whatever, it won't alter our decision not to sell. Now, who wants second helpings of Flossie's bread and butter pudding while it's still hot?'

'Not me,' said Gemma. 'Oh, wait a bit,

though, I think I will have seconds, Daddy.'

'Tomorrow,' said James, 'I think I'll ask Flossie if her bread and butter pudding helps to stretch girls.'

And what was Gemma's response to that? A giggle.

Gemma could take a joke.

Chapter Thirteen

Boots drove Polly to the offices the next morning. She climbed the stairs with him to say hello to Sammy and Rachel. Sammy told her about the crazed bus driver who had given Emma, Patsy and their children the fright of their lives yesterday. He'd had the story from Daniel only five minutes ago, and was about to tell Boots. Polly, aghast, looked in on Daniel, who shared an office with her stepson Tim. Daniel assured her that Patsy and the kids had recovered, but were off bus rides for the time being. Polly offered every kind of commiseration, then said she would tell Boots to phone Emma and find out how she and her children were.

'Yes, do that, Mama,' said Tim, which Polly did and then left to walk to the premises of the photographer a few doors down. Her friend, Mrs Anneliese Stevens, was picking her up there at nine thirty. They were going shopping up in town, and among their purchases would be new baby clothes for Anneliese's one-year-old infant son, Harry. At her insistence the child had been named after its father, whom she considered the kindest man ever born, in total contrast to those she knew to be unforgivably monstrous. Himmler's SS. Anneliese, once a German army nurse, had witnessed unimaginable cruelty on the Russian Front.

Polly entered the premises and admitted herself into the poky office through its open door. The photographer was absent, so she pressed the button of the bell fixed to the desk. Its ring brought the photographer out of his darkroom and into the office via an inner door. He was fortyish, had a mop of curly black hair and a very appealing smile. Polly knew him. He had once taken a portrait photograph of her for her late father, and of her father and stepmother for herself.

'Well, hello, Mrs Adams,' said Amos Anderson, 'good morning to you.'

'Good morning,' smiled Polly, 'I want to make an appointment for my son and daughter. A portrait photograph of them together. Say sometime next week, before their summer holidays come to an end, if you can fit them in?'

'Sometime next week you want?' said Amos, and opened up his appointments book. He studied it. 'Sometime next week I can do, can't I? Wednesday, at two thirty in the afternoon, how is that, Mrs Adams?'

'Fine,' said Polly, and made a note in her pocket diary. 'I'll see you then, Mr Anderson, with my children.'

'A pleasure, won't it be?' smiled Amos.

'I hope so,' said Polly. 'Thank you, Mr Anderson. Goodbye.'

Leaving his office, she walked to the front door. The time was coming up to nine thirty. As she reached the door it was pushed open and she came face to face with a good-looking young man and a handsome young woman.

'Oh, so sorry, madam,' said the young man, his accent American, and he stepped aside to allow Polly to pass him. She took another look at him, and noted his polite smile while being conscious that the young woman's expression was stony.

'Thank you,' she said, and emerged onto the pavement. By the kerbside was a car, Anneliese at the wheel. She waved, and Polly entered the car, slipping with silky grace into the passenger seat.

'I've just arrived,' said Anneliese, 'so we are well met, Polly. And I am very free. Harry and Cindy are looking after my little one.' Cindy was her stepdaughter. 'Polly?' Boots's elegant wife, still a fashion plate, was sitting in silence.

140

'I think,' said Polly, 'I think I've just seen a face I know, but can't put a name to.'

'It was an unpleasant face?' said Anneliese, blonde and smiling.

'On the contrary,' said Polly. 'It was the face of a good-looking, dark young man. Well, I fancy the name will come to me eventually, so let the horses rip, Anneliese, and we'll sample the delights of the West End shops.'

'And have lunch before we return?' said Anneliese, setting the family's Austin car in motion. She and Polly were the closest of friends. She thought they each had the kind of husband most women could only dream about.

'Yes, we'll have lunch,' said Polly, settling down. The car travelled the same route as yesterday's careering bus, but at the modest speed required by reason of the traffic. Anneliese drove through the green lights of the Camberwell Green junction, and headed for the Elephant and Castle and Westminster Bridge via Camberwell Road and Walworth Road. She loved the West End of London, now recovering well from the prolonged and austere consequences of a hugely expensive war, and she was becoming fond of her adopted country. Germany no longer had any appeal for her, although she admired the people of West Germany for the way they had rebuilt their devastated cities and their ruined economy. She little knew that Boots's

141

stepfather, Sir Edwin Finch, was German-born, and Sir Edwin certainly had no intention of telling her.

Polly asked how Harry was. Anneliese said he had just completed his second novel, a thriller like the first. It was now in the hands of his agent, and he was waiting for her opinion. The sales of the first book had been good rather than exciting, but the advance and royalties had put enough money into his bank to make him feel reasonably happy. Further, his publishers had encouraged him to write the second thriller.

'He deserves encouragement, Polly.'

'My dear,' said Polly, 'deserving husbands cause us to wonder how deserving we are ourselves, a condition that puts us at a disadvantage. I avoid being at a disadvantage with Boots. Much better for me to always be one up on the old soldier.'

'In my case, it's my old sailor,' smiled Anneliese, travelling in the wake of a laden bus. Harry had served in the Royal Navy.

'No difference,' said Polly, as they passed the East Street market, 'they all wear trousers.'

'Heavens,' said Anneliese, whose English was perfect, if touched with a faint accent, 'don't tell me you've come to the end of your best time with Boots.'

'End? My dear woman,' said Polly, 'I've known that man of mine for thirty-six years, and if I could have my married life with him all over again, I'd start on the waking moments of our wedding day. I adore the old darling.' She laughed. 'That's disadvantage enough, in the nicest way, of course – oh, pull up, Anneliese, I'm seeing someone I know.'

'Someone whose face you can put a name to?' said Anneliese, and brought the car to a stop. Polly wound her window down and called.

'Cassie?'

Cassie Brown, waiting to cross the road to her home in Wansey Street, was carrying a shopping bag. She turned her head, saw the car a few yards away, and spotted Polly's gesturing hand. Up she came.

'Gracious goodness, hello, Polly, where you off to?'

'The West End, with Anneliese Stevens,' said Polly.

Cassie, who had met Anneliese and her husband at Boots's rousing birthday party, dipped her head, smiled at Anneliese and said hello.

'Hello too,' said Anneliese, returning the smile.

'Wasn't it a gorgeous party?' said Cassie. 'Freddy said all that champagne kept making him go pop all day Saturday in the store. Oh, he told me about Emma and Patsy having a terrible journey on a bus that finished up on the pavement by the Elephant

143

and Castle. Are they and their children all right, Polly?'

'Apparently,' said Polly, with traffic passing by, 'but a dreadful experience for them. How are your children, Cassie?'

'Oh, fine,' said Cassie, 'except while Lewis is sort of level-headed, Maureen's kind of up in the air. She wants to be a pin-up, would you believe.'

'Must I believe?' asked Polly.

'That's what me old dad says,' smiled Cassie. 'Can anybody believe it he says. But it's a fact, Maureen's going to be photographed with hopes of seeing herself in the *Daily Mirror*.'

'Great balls of fire,' said Polly, 'don't let Grandma Finch know, or she'll want Boots to blow up the paper's printing works. Oh, well, life's still fun, Cassie, for us and the young. Happy to have seen you, love to Freddy. Bye.'

'Bye, Polly, tell Boots how much we enjoyed his party,' said Cassie. 'Bye,' she said to Anneliese, who gave her a parting smile. Cassie, watching the car move off, thought Polly was still ever so vital. And blessed if she won't be sixty herself later this month. Imagine her saying don't tell Grandma Finch about Maureen being in the *Daily Mirror*, or she'd get Boots to blow the paper up.

Laughing to herself, Cassie crossed the road and carried her shopping home.

'Now,' said Amos, 'do we like that or don't we?'

He and Leila regarded Wilhelm with mutual interest. Wilhelm was sporting a little pointed black beard and a black moustache, with pince-nez spectacles. The combined adornments gave the young man the spruce professional look of a doctor.

'What I cannot see is a representative of a fashion house,' said Leila.

'It's the glasses, they are too fussy,' said Amos. 'Fussy we don't want.'

'You supplied them,' said Leila.

'It was a thought,' said Amos. 'Let Wilhelm take them off.'

Wilhelm took them off. Immediately, he looked more the part. Further, the hirsute pieces changed his normal appearance very effectively.

'Better, much better,' said Amos.

'I agree,' said Leila.

'You do?' said Wilhelm. 'Break open a bottle, Amos, the lady agrees.'

'Agreement is good,' said Amos.

'Disagreement we don't want, eh?' said Wilhelm, taking off Amos, and looked in surprise at Leila. There was actually a faint smile softening her face.

'What's causing that?' he asked.

'Sometimes idiots are amusing,' she said.

'Shall I take the photographs now?'

suggested Amos. 'I have a sitter in half an hour.'

Wilhelm and Leila followed him into his studio. His camera was set up, and he did not take long to photograph them in plain passport fashion. When did they wish to collect them? Leila said she understood he always fixed them to the passports, that it was a job for professionals, not amateurs at home.

'So I'll bring the passports when I receive them from Stargazer,' said Leila. 'Wilhelm can remain under cover.'

'I hear you, Indian Moon,' said Wilhelm.

'Clown,' said Leila, but not unkindly.

'My God,' said Wilhelm, as they moved back into the office, 'what I'd give for being able to take a simple walk around the shops would make a Brooklyn down-and-out rich for the rest of his life.'

Leila pointed to Amos's soft trilby hat. As usual it was covering the phone.

'If you will lend that to Wilhelm, Mr Anderson,' she said, 'I will let him have his walk. He can wear it well turned down.'

'My hat he wants?' smiled Amos. 'It is his for as long as he wishes, isn't it? What is a hat when I have others?'

Five minutes later, with the brim of his hat pulled well down over his forehead, and the wrapped beard and moustache in Leila's handbag, Wilhelm began his walk around the shops of Camberwell Green. Leila accom-

146

panied him. He said she need not, that she could trust him to get back to the house before lunchtime. Leila reminded him she was not going to trust anyone outside of her fellow agents until he was safe in Israel. Also, she was as much in need of some exercise and fresh air as he was.

'OK, guardian, be my guest,' said Wilhelm.

'Don't strain my good nature,' said Leila.

'Strain it?' said Wilhelm, happy to be out and about among the people. 'I'm only too pleased to know you've got some – no, I shouldn't have said that. Sorry. You're doing a great job on my account, and I mean that. I guess being on the run for such a hell of a long time is finally shredding my nerves.'

'Cool down,' said Leila, 'you're doing a great job yourself. We'll get you there.'

'That,' said Wilhelm, 'is what keeps me going.'

They walked, they strolled, they stopped to look in shop windows, and when they reached a fruiterers, Wilhelm went in. Leila stayed outside, keeping watch. She did not want him to step out into the path of a patrolling policeman. In this populated area, one man was just another among crowds, unnoticeable unless he was wearing or doing something absurd. A policeman was different. No-one could be certain he did not have an image of a wanted man in his mind.

She knew Wilhelm Kleibert's public execution of an Auschwitz doctor had attracted worldwide attention, and that America was still after him. The hunt might not have been so persistent if there'd been proof that the victim really had carried out inhuman experiments on children at Auschwitz. But that proof could only have been established at a trial, which Wilhelm so far had escaped. Leila had no doubt that the FBI's agents in Britain, France and other European countries were still on the lookout for him. Perhaps, she surmised, it was more to do with establishing the facts about the murdered man in court than with conducting a heavy prosecution of Wilhelm, who commanded any amount of sympathy in the West. Nevertheless, she intended to keep risks to a minimum.

Out of the shop came Wilhelm, a brown paper bag containing a bunch of black grapes in each hand. He gave one bag to Leila.

'Grapes,' he said.

'To carry back to Mrs Wirthe?'

'No, to eat while we're walking.'

'And what do we do with the pips?'

'I'll eat mine with the grapes,' said Wilhelm. 'You can spit yours out, if you wish.'

'On the sidewalk?' said Leila. 'How disgusting.'

'Not nearly as disgusting as what was done at Auschwitz,' said Wilhelm.

'Of course, yes, you are right,' said Leila.

'Well, grapes are refreshing and I will eat mine, and the pips.' She looked at him. He was already enjoying his fruit. 'That hat suits you,' she said.

'So does yours,' said Wilhelm. She was wearing a navy blue beret with a plain but quite smart beige dress. 'I guess I mean it suits you.'

'I am not mad about fancy hats,' said Leila, as they resumed their leisurely exercise.

'Fancy hats we don't want, eh?' said Wilhelm, taking off Amos again, and once more Leila surprised him, this time by emitting a little laugh, even if it did sound like a cough with a bit of a gurgle to it.

They went along, two people among busy shoppers, each holding a bag of grapes and eating the fruit, grinding the pips to destruction with strong molars and swallowing them. Wilhelm said this part of London was hardly like New York's Broadway. Leila responded that he was far less at risk here than in any part of New York. Here, in fact, they were two thousand miles nearer Israel.

When they had gone some way along Camberwell Road, they turned back and began to retrace their steps. A uniformed policeman appeared, a solid figure of the law, deliberate in his steps as he came towards them. He eyed them. Too keenly, thought Leila. His observation of Wilhelm alarmed her. Nor did she like the way he

149

transferred his searching gaze to the young man's bag of grapes. Did he think there was a gun in it?

Wilhelm, the idiot, spoke.

'Would you like a grape, officer?' he said, and Leila could only hope his Americanized speech would disguise the fact he'd been born a German Jew. He'd been accepted as an immigrant in 1947, along with other young concentration camp survivors.

'Well, don't mind if I do, sir,' said the constable, and Wilhelm put his hand in the bag, broke off a sprig from the bunch and handed it to the law. 'A nice day for a grape or two,' said the law. The day was warm, although the sky was full of floating white clouds. 'Where you from, sir?'

'Canada,' said Wilhelm. 'We're staying with relatives here.'

'You don't say,' said the constable, eating a couple of grapes. 'I've got relatives in Canada. An aunt and uncle in Vancouver. Emigrated in the Thirties. Would you know Vancouver?'

'Sure,' said Wilhelm, 'but we've never been there, we're from Toronto.'

'Well, have a nice time, sir,' said the constable, giving Leila a smile and a nod as he resumed his beat. He hollered at a boy who had just discarded an empty sweets bag.

'That was dangerous, opening your

mouth,' said Leila.

'He'd have thought it suspicious if I'd kept it shut,' said Wilhelm.

Leila said she meant he shouldn't have started a conversation, so Wilhelm said he thought the guy was going to start asking questions. Leila mused on that, and decided this resolute survivor of Auschwitz had an inherited intelligence, except it had deserted him when he shot the SS doctor in broad daylight. He should have contrived the execution at night, and then disappeared into the darkness.

'Well, yes, I understand,' she said, 'perhaps it was more natural to say something.'

'Leila, I think you're human, after all,' said Wilhelm.

'Of all things, I dislike being patronized,' said Leila.

'Well, can I patronize you by buying you a coffee?' asked Wilhelm.

'I would not dislike that,' said Leila, 'but find a cafe where you don't have to take your hat off.'

'Sure,' said Wilhelm, 'no hat we don't want, eh?'

The little smile ghosted over Leila's face again.

Chapter Fourteen

They found a cafe in Camberwell Road, where Wilhelm kept the hat on, their conversation was murmured and minimal, and the Italian coffee good. London had proved a safe and promising haven for many one-time soldiers of Mussolini's armies with a penchant for running the kind of cafes the citizens liked, which mostly meant no spaghetti, thanks, mate.

When Leila and Wilhelm eventually left, they began to walk to the enclosed green at the junction. Almost at once, Leila slipped an arm around Wilhelm's left elbow and even lightly rested her head on his shoulder, so that they were sauntering like lovers.

'What's this for?' he asked.

'For showing we are lovers who have no worries,' whispered Leila, as an approaching old lady gave them a smile. It was the smile of old age remembering young days. 'That policeman is behind us.'

'Well, cuss it,' breathed Wilhelm, 'is he following us or there by accident?'

'Walk on,' whispered Leila, keeping lovingly close.

They walked on. They reached the inviting

oasis of Camberwell Green, turned and sauntered through the open gate. The policeman kept straight on. Leila breathed with deep relief.

'I guess I like that cop,' said Wilhelm. 'Yup, and I think I've heard about the good old London bobbies.'

'We're at risk,' said Leila, 'so spare me more jokes.' Usually cool and controlled, the gradual onset of nerves these last few days was irritating her. Worrying her. But her fixed determination to get herself and Wilhelm aboard a plane for Nice was unwavering. This young man deserved the safe and protective haven of Israel, his natural home. Her natural home.

'I've a feeling,' said Wilhelm.

'What feeling?' Leila was no longer close to him.

'That luck's walking with us.'

'My God, we need it to be,' said Leila.

'Perhaps it's you,' said Wilhelm.

'What do you mean?'

'Perhaps you're Lady Luck,' said Wilhelm.

'Why do you say such silly things?' Leila was a practical woman, a first-class agent, who considered sentiment or gallantries totally irrelevant in a world in which Israel was still fighting to establish itself while almost fully ringed by hostile Arab nations. She was not asexual. She had a healthy and normal body, and she also had a lover back in Tel Aviv. She allowed him to sleep with her occasionally, but she did not allow him to whisper absurdities into her ear or to think she was a marrying woman with a wish to raise a family. That was for other women. For herself, her ambition was to become Chief of Police or the top name in Mossad. 'Yes, why do you say such silly things?'

'I guess it's because I'm an idiot,' said Wilhelm.

Leila could hardly believe she wanted to laugh out loud. Life for Palestine Jews had always been far too serious for laughter, and it still was for them as citizens of Israel.

'Oh, well, perhaps you're not such an idiot as others,' she said.

It was gone twelve thirty by the time they arrived back at the home of Judith and Michal Wirthe. Judith at once asked them where they had been, since she'd begun to worry about what might have happened, that Wilhelm might have been recognized and arrested. Leila apologized, and Wilhelm explained. Judith said her nerves had taken a beating, but that she could understand their need for exercise and fresh air. However, if they intended to repeat such an outing, please to let her know beforehand.

'Yes, we'll do that, Judith, so sorry,' said Wilhelm.

'Yes, I am sorry too for worrying you,' said

Leila, realizing, as did Wilhelm, that trouble for the two of them could very well lead to consequent trouble for their hosts. She and Wilhelm were under strict orders from Mossad's chief London agent, Stargazer, to remain under cover except when vitally necessary.

'Well, it's all said and done now,' smiled Judith, 'and lunch is ready. Oh, have the photographs been taken?'

'Yes,' said Leila.

'Good,' said Judith, hoping that would mean the guests would soon be leaving.

'My son,' said Mr Greenberg to Michal, who was handing him money from a cash transaction, 'you are not a happy man.'

'Old one,' said Michal, 'I have a good wife and the prospects of being a father. I also have a good job in our new business. So I should not be happy?'

'But I've seen you arrive for your vork vith a look not happy,' said Mr Greenberg kindly. 'Is it that your friends ain't too friendly?'

'My life,' said Michal, 'would Judith have them in the house if they weren't?' The truth was, of course, that the visitors were putting a strain on himself and on Judith in particular. The woman, Leila, had no social graces, and was interested only in her work for Mossad.

'Vell, my good son, I believe you,' said Mr

155

Greenberg, 'but I am here and vill alvays listen if you vish to talk to me.'

'Who better to talk to than you, old wise man?' said Michal. He smiled and went back to his work.

Over lunch in the select atmosphere of Fortnum and Mason's restaurant, something returned to Polly's mind.

The face of the dark young man at the door of Amos Anderson's premises.

She was sure it was familiar to her. Not in an important way, or she would doubtless have immediately identified him. Perhaps she had at least met him under interesting circumstances, since that would explain why he was on her mind. Perhaps at one of her stepmother's charity functions, although they weren't always vitally interesting. One met many people on those occasions, but never saw them again. Anyway, she could still not put a name to the dark young man, or recall when it was she had met him. She supposed she had met him, sometime or other.

'Two pennies for your thoughts, Polly?' said Anneliese, her summer hat fetching enough for Ascot, never mind the West End.

'Two?' smiled Polly, her own hat delightful. Some women were beginning to dispense with any kind of hat, but that would have disqualified them from entering the Ascot enclosure, or the West End's more exclusive restaurants. Of course, London's fish and chip shops welcomed any old hat or none at all. 'Hardly worth one, my dear, let alone two. Allow me the pleasure of paying the bill.'

'No, no, it's my turn, I'm sure,' said Anneliese, whose frequent trips to the West End with Polly gave her immense pleasure. She had much in common with Boots's aristocratic wife, for she came of an aristocratic family herself. The fact that Polly could be very down-to-earth only entranced her. That trait, of course, came from Polly's time as an ambulance driver in the First World War. Polly, indeed, when provoked enough, could swear as profoundly as any bitter Tommy of the trenches. But then, so could the country's leading blue bloods. 'Yes, I will settle, Polly.'

'You are providing the buggy ride,' said Polly. 'Therefore, ducky, I'll provide the wherewithal for the lunch. Only fair, you know.'

'This is a happy argument,' smiled Anneliese.

'A discussion,' said Polly, lightly lifting a hand.

'A discussion, yes, of course,' said Anneliese. 'Very civilized, Polly.' And very English, she thought, as the head waiter arrived with the bill. Polly settled and included a handsome tip. 'I'm thinking perhaps we should each buy a jar of caviare on our way out,' said Anneliese. 'As a special treat for Harry and Boots.'

'Dear girl,' said Polly, as they came to their feet, 'Boots considers caviare highly over-rated. He much prefers fresh oysters, swallowed with Guinness, a frightful gourmet punishment to which my late papa introduced him in 1950.'

Anneliese's blue eyes sparkled.

'Ah, so?' she said. 'Is that why he looks so virile?'

'Looks can be deceptive,' said Polly, as they left the restaurant.

'But not in all cases?' said Anneliese.

'No, not in all cases,' said Potty, thinking of her years of sheer magic with Boots.

They picked up their shopping, and in the store Anneliese did stop to buy a jar of caviare for Harry. The assistant was serving a tall gentleman in a fine-tailored Savile Row suit of charcoal grey, with a black homburg. His features were clean-cut. Chiselled, the English would have said. Impressively handsome and fit, he looked to be in his early forties. Anneliese, glancing at him, glanced again, in a much more positive way. Her spine turned icy.

She knew him, and she knew she was not mistaken. She recognized him as Colonel Neumann, commander of a disintegrating group of Waffen SS troops, who, during the pell-mell and disorganized German retreat in March 1945, had used his men to shoot

158

hundreds of Russian prisoners and scare-crow refugees on the elementary grounds that they were in the way. From a vehicle belonging to her retreating medical unit, she had seen him shoot desperate and starving refugees himself. Colonel Neumann then, and Colonel Neumann now, represented to Anneliese all the horror and cruelty unleashed by Himmler, Hitler and Goering, all that had made her weep and despair for a Germany she had once loved.

She watched him now while his order was made up and packaged, and she listened as, in polished English, he instructed the assistant to debit his account.

'Sir?'

'Professor Knox.'

'Yes, of course, Professor. Thank you.'

He left, carrying his purchase, and Anneliese's spine thawed a little, but her request for a jar of the best caviare sounded slightly strained. Polly, waiting, decided to buy Boots a jar of delicious preserved ginger. She did so, and she and Anneliese left the store together. They stepped into an afternoon bright beneath large patches of blue sky and rolling white clouds.

'Anneliese,' said Polly, 'what happened at the counter?'

'My God,' breathed Anneliese, her foot-steps quick and angry, 'that man.'

'Handsome enough,' said Polly.

'Yes, as handsome as the devil himself,' said Anneliese. 'I cannot believe how many have escaped the courts of justice. That one, yes, that one, I saw him murder starving refugees fleeing from the Russians. I saw him shoot them in cold blood and without a quiver, or a prayer for his soul. I know him, even though he was unshaven and had a bearded growth when I saw him. I know his name, his real name. Colonel Neumann of the Waffen SS. And now he is living here, in London, and posing as a Professor Knox. What is he a professor of? Death?'

'Anneliese, calm yourself,' said Polly.

'Because of the German Nazis, I would like to have been born English, as my grandmother was,' said Anneliese, 'but I can't be English, not today, not now. I can't be calm, I can't be calm, cool and collected, as you English say. I practised years of being that for the benefit of hideously wounded soldiers, not wishing them to know I knew they were going to die.'

'You can be calm now, and you will,' said Polly. Then, 'Oh, very well, ducky, let storm and tempest rage. Who cares that we're in the middle of the pomp and circumstance of Piccadilly? On the other hand, dear girl, I think we should talk about this in the car.'

Anneliese drew a long breath and eased her angry stride. A faint smile broke through.

'Polly, you are so typically British, and

perhaps many foreigners would think you absurd and even arrogant,' she said, 'but I know you better. Yes, let's talk in the car.'

It was parked in Duke Street, and as soon as both women, and their parcels, were in the car Anneliese drove away, heading for Whitehall and Westminster Bridge. Traffic was thick until she crossed the bridge, when she then spoke.

'I'm furious that that man has escaped hanging.'

Polly was well aware that this German woman was totally unforgiving of the countless Nazis who had brought her country to destruction and shame, to render it unspeakable in the eyes of the world.

'What are you going to do?' she asked.

'What should I do?'

'You could run to the police, but that would involve you in a hundred interviews and questions,' said Polly. 'You've a small child, a stepdaughter and a husband taking up your care and time. So let me speak to Boots. He has a way of solving problems.'

'Would you do that for me, Polly, speak to Boots?'

'Happily,' said Polly. 'How strange that you should see a face you recognized and could put a name to, while I saw a face this morning that I'm sure I know, but simply can't put a name to. Heigh-ho, such is life. Drive on, ducky.'

When Anneliese brought the car to a stop outside Polly's house in East Dulwich Grove, she said, 'I'm sorry I was so angry.'

'My dear, you had a right to be,' said Polly, 'although it's the first time I've seen you in a temper. Tim always insists you were the coolest woman ever during the time you nursed him as a wounded prisoner of war.'

'I had to be.' Anneliese smiled. 'Otherwise, he would have cracked me wide open. Already, at that time, early in 1942, I was doubting my faith in Hitler, and I think Tim suspected it.'

'Water under the bridge, Anneliese,' said Polly, slipping out of the car.

Anneliese leaned.

'Polly,' she said, 'you are the loveliest kind of friend I could ever wish for.'

'Oh, when you see me indulging in a fit of storm and tempest myself, you'll change your mind,' said Polly. 'Pip-pip, old thing.'

Pip-pip? What did that mean? Some kind of goodbye, supposed Anneliese, not knowing only one-time flappers would have used it, and not many of them these days. Certainly not those approaching sixty. Polly was unique, still a flapper at heart in Boots's opinion.

'Goodbye, Polly.' Anneliese waved and drove away.

Chapter Fifteen

On arrival home, Boots found Polly in the living room, waiting to switch on the television set to catch the six o'clock news. Flossie was in the kitchen, preparing supper, and the twins were sitting in the garden, enjoying an unusually civilized talk about their recent holiday in Cornwall.

Boots was carrying an evening paper, which he tossed onto the settee. Polly was relaxing at one end, legs curled up under her like those of a lithe young woman. Her knees, nylon-clad, peeped like shining round caps. They might have been bony by now, but they weren't, and her legs were still shapely and slender.

'Hello, darling,' she said as he bent and kissed her. Even now, she still offered her lips to her husband, not her cheek.

'Had an economical day, shopping?' said Boots.

'Are you kidding?' said Polly. 'You throw economy out with the cat when you shop in the West End. Otherwise, you might as well patronize Petticoat Lane. Uneconomically, I treated myself to some exquisite new lingerie. Uneconomically means fantastically expensive.'

'Age, I suppose, has nothing to do with adorning your well-preserved self in a fantastically expensive way,' said Boots.

'Absolutely not,' said Polly. 'My well-preserved self is my own work and deserves Bond Street adornment. I still have a figure, you know.'

'Have I seen it lately?' mused Boots.

'Think of my dignity,' said Polly. 'I never asked for it, it's a sign of wanting to be respected, and having bus drivers call me madam. I prefer them to call me love or dearie. But there you are, old fruit, dignity has crept up on me and I can't flaunt myself without a blush.'

'A blush?' said Boots.

'An old lady's blush,' said Polly.

'That,' said Boots, 'I can't wait to see.'

'You'll be lucky,' said Polly. 'Listen, dear man, I've something to tell you about Anneliese.'

'Fire away,' said Boots, and Polly told him of Anneliese recognizing an ex-Waffen SS officer in Fortnum and Mason's store, and how it opened up old wounds for her. What should she do that would still enable her to live her happy-ever-after life with her family?

'I'll think about it,' said Boots.

'Seriously?'

'Seriously,' said Boots.

'There's a good old sport,' said Polly. 'Sit,

and we'll watch the news together.' She moved his evening paper, and as she did so she saw a photograph on the front page of Prime Minister Anthony Eden, the man who, with his Cabinet, had to decide whether or not to allow Egypt's nationalization of the Suez Canal to stand. The Prime Minister looked dark and handsome.

It came to her then, the reason why she was sure the face of the dark young man at the photographer's door was familiar to her. Of course, she had seen it in a newspaper, with a report of how the young man, a Jewish survivor of Auschwitz, had escaped custody while awaiting trial in New York for the murder of a Dr Rokovsky. Dr Rokovsky, a brilliant ophthalmic surgeon, purporting to be a Ukrainian immigrant, had been due to examine Felicity's blind eyes with a view to a possible operation. The escape of the young Jew had happened well over a year ago, since when it seemed he had disappeared from the face of the earth.

This was something else to tell Boots, and she did so while he was helping himself to his usual pre-supper whisky and mixing her a gin and tonic.

'Are you dreaming, Polly?' he asked, handing her the gin and tonic. 'It's certainly the stuff of dreams.'

'What is?'

'The suggestion that on the same day you

could have seen the executioner of a man he claimed to be an ex-SS doctor, and Anneliese could have seen a man she claims was an ex-Waffen SS officer. Well, is it possible, Polly?'

'Possible, you old doubter?' said Polly. 'It happened.'

'That's what I call the coincidence of a lifetime,' said Boots, enjoying his finger of Scotch.

'You can call it once upon a time there was an elephant with wings, if you like,' said Polly. 'I know Anneliese saw a Nazi fiend she recognized, and I know I saw Wilhelm Kleibert. Yes, that's his name.'

They heard Flossie calling Gemma and James in for supper. And they heard her next call.

'Supper's ready for the table, Mrs Adams. Coo-ee!'

'Coming, Flossie,' sang Polly.

'Polly,' said Boots, 'do we want to go after a young man who came out alive from Auschwitz, caught up with a hellish SS doctor and sent him to join Himmler and the other mad dogs?'

'You clever old Chinaman,' said Polly, coming to her feet, 'of course we don't. Aren't you a walking Solomon? Now I'll enjoy my supper. Oh, by the way, James received a picture postcard by the late post this morning. He showed it to me when I arrived home

166

from town. It's a postcard of the Folies-Ber-gère. From Cathy Davidson, the saucy minx.'

Boots laughed.

'Now I'll enjoy my supper, too,' he said.

Over supper, of course, he put a question to his youthful, growing son.

'James old chap, is it true you've had a postcard from Cathy today?'

'Not half he hasn't,' said Gemma. 'It's my belief she's got a whacky crush on him. And you ought to see the picture, Daddy. It's of dancing girls showing their undies.'

'Yes, it's sort of classical,' said James.

'Some hopes,' said Gemma. 'Sexy, you mean.'

'Classically French,' said James.

'I wonder the postman was allowed to deliver it,' said Gemma.

'Might I remind you that at Dad's party your dress was mostly up in the air?' said James. 'And that you were showing your frillies?'

Gemma blushed a little, thought a little, and came up with a triumphant riposte.

'Still, I haven't been sent through the post on a card,' she said.

'You certainly haven't,' said Polly, 'and you certainly never will. Dear, dear, what was I doing in allowing your father's big day to turn into a spectacle of saucy minxes?'

'Just like the days when you and the

flappers in frilly garters were doing the charleston, Mum,' said James.

'Heavens,' said Polly, 'what have I done that my own son should let me down in such a way?'

'James,' said Boots, keeping his face straight, 'let me inform you that your mother has recently acquired dignity and should therefore be respected.'

'Eh?' said James, a forked lump of baked parsnip halting halfway to his mouth.

'Dignity?' said Gemma through chewed parsnip. 'I blessed well hope not. Old Mrs Wooderson's got dignity and it makes her blow her blouse out. Daddy, I won't know where to look if Mum's dignity does that to her blouses. I mean, what a giggle, and you can't respect a giggle.'

'I think the answer's a lemon,' said Boots.

'No, I think dignity would suit Mum,' said James, 'especially at Sunday church, Dad, or when you both come to the school on speech days. I'd expect some of the fellers would ask who that dignified lady was, and I'd be able to say she's my noble mother. Imagine that.'

'If I could imagine it,' said Gemma, 'I'd fall off my chair.'

Polly laughed. The two of them, Gemma and James. In their capacity for being comical, each was an Adams more than a Simms, although happily enough, there was some of her father's resolution about James.

He was resolute when up against the odds in sport, and just as much in a crisis.

'If that's all over,' smiled Boots, 'could I hear what Cathy said on the postcard, James?'

'You won't like it, Daddy,' murmured Gemma.

'Well, Dad,' said James, 'she hoped I was in good health, and remaining faithful to her. Oh, yes, and would I like to spend Christmas in Paris with her and her mum. That was all.'

'That was enough,' said Gemma. 'It made Mum quiver all over and say shocking things. It was like–' Gemma paused for a giggle. 'Like she'd lost her dignity.'

'I'll fight any Christmas trip to Paris,' said Polly determinedly.

'It's Cathy's soppy crush on James,' said Gemma.

'It'll be last year all over again, when her mother had a crush on your father,' said Polly. 'We had to lock him away from her, you remember. If James goes to Paris, there'll be no-one there to lock him away from Cathy. So Paris is out, James, out, and kindly understand that out out is final and absolutely definite.'

'Oh, righty-oh, Mum,' said James, 'I'll stay home and respect your dignity. It won't cost me any pain. Could I ask what's for afters?'

'One of Flossie's creamy rice puddings,'

said Polly.

'Great,' said James. 'Give Gemma two helpings, Dad, and let's all watch it stretch her a bit.'

'Daddy, it's time your son got with it,' said Gemma.

'Right, James, get with it,' said Boots, 'fetch the rice pudding.'

Later that evening, Boots thought about phoning his stepfather. But Sir Edwin was close to eighty-three now, and not quite as brisk as he had been. Would he want to be involved? Boots supposed he could still effect contact with British Intelligence, with whom his reputation, built up over many years, would always mean something special. But he was living a very quiet life these days.

So Boots phoned Lizzy's son Bobby instead.

'That's you, old soldier?' said Bobby. 'I'm honoured.'

'You will be when the Foreign Office recommends your elevation to the peerage as Lord Somers of Camberwell Green,' said Boots.

'In which case, I'll get to be known as Lord Mouthful,' said Bobby, 'but thankfully and confidently I can state I'll never be in the running. Your flattering suggestion tells me you want something.'

'Just a talk,' said Boots. 'I'll drop in on you

on my way to the office in the morning. Say at eight thirty.'

Bobby said that since he would be leaving for town at his usual time of eight fifteen, would it do for Boots to talk to Helene instead? Helene, he said, would undoubtedly be delighted, and probably receive her favourite English uncle in her best French two-piece. Boots said he didn't doubt that Helene in that get-up would be delightful to talk to, but it was Bobby's ears he was after, not Helene's.

'It's going to be a confidential chat?' said Bobby.

'An interesting one, I promise you,' said Boots.

Bobby said in that case he would opt for being late at the office, which wouldn't matter too much since he wasn't yet head of his department, just another cog a little higher up in the wheel. Boots said he'd been a cog in various wheels himself during his lifetime, but there were no scars.

'You're a one-off,' said Bobby. 'Fair enough, I'll expect you at half eight tomorrow morning, then.'

'Much obliged,' said Boots.

To pass the evening in an entertaining way, Michal and Judith were playing Monopoly with Wilhelm and Leila. Leila was hardly a lighthearted conversationalist, since she was

171

always inclined to dwell in serious vein on the struggles of the Israelis in founding their State and stabilizing it in the face of Arab hostility. Michal and Judith accepted it was a serious matter to her, but too much of it dulled one's ears. And Wilhelm only sighed each time Leila began another dissertation.

So this evening, Michal had contrived for all of them to sit around the living-room card table and seek their fortunes at Monopoly. He joked that it had its appeal to all the children of Moses. It was, however, very much a game of chance that always became a contest for possession of the Mayfair and Park Lane properties. Once they were both in one player's hands, the end was inevitable.

Leila said there was not enough skill involved, that a superior brain was no more necessary than an inferior one. Judith said that that was the fun of the game. Leila said that life in Israel was not a game, nor was it fun for many of its citizens. She said that at the moment when her throw of the dice landed her symbol on Piccadilly, owned by Judith with a complement of houses. Judith asked for rent payment.

'There, you see,' said Leila, 'it's all silly chance.'

'Yes,' said Wilhelm with a wide grin, 'that's the fun of it.'

Quite a happy moment arrived then.

Leila laughed. And she paid up.

'Now I am almost broke,' she said.

'That's serious,' said Michal.

'Oh, well, it is only a game,' said Leila. 'Who will lend me a thousand pounds?'

'A thousand?' said Judith.

'Yes,' said Leila, 'just for the fun of it.'

It could be said then that little gusts of laughter ran around the table, like titters round a court. This encouraged Michal to call a temporary halt to the game while he uncorked a bottle of wine.

When the game was resumed, four glasses of wine gleamed redly in the light.

'Here's your thousand, Leila,' said Wilhelm, who was doing exceptionally well.

'Ah, thank you,' said Leila.

'At twenty per cent interest,' said Wilhelm.

'Twenty per cent?' said Leila. 'Twenty per cent?'

'Sure,' said Wilhelm. He smiled. 'Just for the fun of it.'

Leila actually laughed again, and for the first time since the arrival of the Mossad agent and her charge, a sociable element made its welcome entrance.

In his well-appointed ground-floor Mayfair apartment, the man calling himself Professor Knox, a practitioner of psychiatry mainly for the benefit of wealthy women with emotional problems, slept the sleep of the just.

Such a sleep was not difficult to come by for any man who had no conscience.

Not that anyone had ever pointed a finger at Professor Knox. Since his arrival from Communist East Germany in 1946, with documents recording his anti-Nazi activities during the war, and a certificate of his professional qualifications, he had quickly found his niche, in the form of consulting rooms in Mayfair Close. Adjoining these were his living quarters.

He was excellent as a psychiatrist.

Well, so thought most of his women patients.

Professor Knox also did other work quite unrelated to psychiatry.

Chapter Sixteen

The following morning, at the open door of a house in Thurlow Park Road, West Dulwich, two people met.

'Ah, how nice,' smiled Helene, splendidly French in a dark blue shirt-blouse, open at the neck, and a summery white skirt. Thirty-four, she had reached the stage of being handsome. 'Come in, come in.'

Boots stepped in.

'Apologies, Helene, for intruding at this

time of the day,' he said.

Helene turned her cheek and he kissed her. She surveyed his tall, long-legged frame clad in a fine summer-weight grey suit. Conservative he might be in his choice of clothes, but then, she did not think him a man for outlandish or popular garb. He was at his best as a well-dressed and distinguished figure. She always thought of him as an English gentleman of instant masculine appeal. Had she delivered that opinion into his ear, Boots would have considered her slightly off her Gallic chump. However, as a farmer's daughter, she had never been greatly impressed by the outward charm of Parisian men, noted for the art of seduction. Husband Bobby had come into her life as a rugged, breezy and infuriatingly obstinate British soldier during the Dunkirk evacuation in 1940, and turned her existence upside down. She belaboured him with words, all of which bounced off him. So, of course, she fell in love and told herself she was mad to do so, for the man was an idiot and made terrible jokes.

'No apologies, *chéri*,' she said. 'Always, at any time, it's good to see you. Bobby will be with you any moment. But first come and say hello to the children, yes?'

'Kids are my weakness,' said Boots, and followed her into the kitchen where Bobby, on his feet, was washing his last mouthful of toast down with his last gulp of coffee, and his son and daughter were sitting at the table.

'Hi, pickles,' said Boots, adaptable enough to use the modern vernacular.

'Hi, Uncle Boots!' shouted nine-year-old Estelle and seven-year-old Robert. The boy, at Helene's wish, had been named after Boots, the girl after Helene's mother.

'Hi!' shouted Robert, as an encore.

'Who's shouting?' asked Helene.

'I am!' shouted Robert.

'He is,' said Estelle. 'He's hardly ever quiet, Uncle Boots.'

'We've all got problems,' said Boots.

'Well, Helene will look after ours,' said Bobby, 'so come on, Boots, let's talk.'

Helene shook her head. To call one's uncle by his nickname was not what happened in France. Good family manners prevailed there in that respect. But most of Boots's nieces and nephews addressed him by his nickname. So unconventional.

But rather nice, in a way.

In his downstairs study, Bobby listened as Boots outlined the story given to him by Polly.

'Familiar bells are ringing,' said Bobby.

'How familiar?' asked Boots.

'Well, old soldier,' said Bobby, 'nearly everyone in London claims to have seen a dodgy German war criminal working as a waiter or a doorman or doctor. Or whatever. But most are walking about with Mexican

176

moustaches in Argentina or Peru, or some other place as far away from Europe as they can get.'

'That's from the horse's mouth?' said Boots.

'It's from Intelligence, and that's not a horse, it's a mine of reliable information,' said Bobby. 'Some horses are duds. Of course, it's nothing to do with the Foreign Office, but little titbits are sometimes picked up over lunch at a club, and such titbits are passed to the right quarter. However, are you sure Anneliese was positive in her identification of this professor?'

'I'm not sure myself,' said Boots, 'but Polly is. 'She's convinced that Anneliese made no mistake.'

'About this bloke being responsible for murdering refugees?'

'Apparently,' said Boots.

'Of course, if I could claim diplomatic immunity I could hunt the bugger down and chop his head off myself,' said Bobby.

Boots said that that was perhaps excessive, and unlikely to meet with the approval of Grandma Finch, who was against anyone in the family using a chopper, except to chop wood. Why not simply use his position as a Foreign Office official to see that the information reached a friend in MI5?

'That seems the obvious thing to me, Bobby.'

'I thought you'd come to that,' said Bobby, 'but if Anneliese is wrong, I'll have soft-boiled egg all over my face.'

'I see your point,' said Boots, 'Anneliese could be wrong. But she could also be right. Polly and I would simply like to save her having to go to Scotland Yard, which I fancy she would do, if there was no alternative. I suggest we do our best to help her live a quiet life after all she went through during the war.'

'Fair enough, Boots old chap,' said Bobby. 'I'll have lunch with somebody.'

'Leave it to you, then,' said Boots. He returned to the kitchen, said goodbye to Helene, gave her children ten bob each for holiday pocket money, and departed for his office.

'What did he want?' asked Helene, as she saw Bobby to the front door.

'A favour,' said Bobby.

'What kind of favour?'

'The loan of one of my bowler hats,' said Bobby.

'Ah, very funny.'

'I'll tell you tonight,' said Bobby. 'Right now I must get off to the asylum.'

'Ah, yes?' said Helene. 'Please to remember not to send all the other inmates mad with your terrible jokes.'

But she was silently laughing as she watched him begin his short walk to West Dulwich railway station, his Foreign Office

178

bowler hat at a jaunty angle.

Bobby did not have lunch with somebody. He made a phone call. The impersonal person at the other end became less impersonal.

'Interesting, very. Do you know the lady well?'

'Well enough.'

'And she's German herself?'

'She served as a German army nurse and one of her patients during the desert campaign was a wounded British prisoner of war, who happens to be my cousin.'

'Interesting, very.'

'You've already said that.'

'I'll see a doctor about it. The lady's reliable?'

'As reliable as my grandmother, and there's no-one more so.'

'I see. Well, I suppose we could find out if there's a file on Professor Cox–'

'Knox.'

'Knox, yes. We'll look into it.'

'I'll leave it with you, then.'

'It seems worth a look.'

'Yes,' said Bobby, 'interesting, very.'

That evening, he phoned Boots and told him that action was under way. Boots said he was much obliged. Bobby said he only hoped the investigation wouldn't put Whitehall on a false trail. Boots said if it led to a cold kipper,

179

Polly would be very surprised, since she was sure Anneliese had uncovered a hot potato.

'Your metaphors slay me,' said Bobby.

'You're welcome,' said Boots, 'and I'm still much obliged.'

'Pleasure, old soldier,' said Bobby, who then put Helene in the picture.

Helene visibly swelled with temper.

'Kill that German swine,' she hissed.

'Steady,' said Bobby.

'Men like that! Not just murderers, but cold-blooded sadists, and every one of them should die a lingering death!' Helene's wrath was in full flow. 'Do you know they made slave labourers of thousands of Frenchmen, and sent thousands of French Jews to the gas chambers? How glad I am that Anneliese has recognized one of Himmler's butchers. When will you arrest him?'

'Personally?' said Bobby.

'Why not? I know that in this country there is such a thing as a citizen's arrest.'

'Would you mind if I left his arrest to the authorities?' said Bobby.

'To men in bowler hats?' said Helene.

'Does it matter what kind of hats they wear?' asked Bobby.

'Not if they can take action instead of filling in forms,' said Helene, firm bosom calming down a little. 'It is the same in Paris. Hundreds of government officials filling in forms all day every day, even officials of the

Sûreté. I know. My father tells me so in his letters. And yes, even as a farmer, he now has to fill in forms.'

'Well, my French lily,' said Bobby, 'I'll do what I can to expedite action and cut out the paperwork. Not that I can do much. I'm a Foreign Office body of diplomatic charm, not the active head of the Home Office.'

'Ah, but you will do something, eh, *chéri?*' said Helene. 'Think of poor Anneliese, memories of terrible war crimes brought back to her, and she the one German we can all like. That man must be hanged. Slowly.'

'If he's guilty,' said Bobby, 'he'll almost certainly be sent back to West Germany for trial.'

'But the Germans will only give him a few years in prison, as they have with other war criminals,' said Helene. 'You must arrange his assassination before he leaves this country, yes, you must.'

Bobby said he thought that was a bit out of his league. Helene said no, not at all, that he and she had been happily responsible for acts of sabotage that had blown up Nazis during their time with the French Resistance. Blow this man up, she said.

'I can't do it now,' said Bobby, 'it's time for supper.'

Helene gave him a look. A bit of a critical look. But it resulted in a smile.

'Ah, you are still a clown, Bobby,' she said,

'but a better man than a thousand pro-
fessors.'

'A thousand?' said Bobby. 'You're sure
that's not an exaggeration?'

'The next time we all go to France to stay
with my parents,' said Helene, 'you and my
father can talk to each other all day about
forms.'

'Exciting,' said Bobby, 'can't wait.'

'Mummy!' Estelle called from the kitchen.
'The cooker's smoking!'

'Oh, my grilled tomatoes!' gasped Helene,
and dashed.

The supper was served without grilled,
peppered tomatoes. No-one ever had to eat
burnt offerings in a household where the
cooking was undertaken by a French
mother. On the other hand, there was sometimes a little resistance to the introduction of
garlic. A soupçon was all right, but no more
than that. More was antisocial. Estelle
averred that it made schoolfriends reluctant
to sit next to her in class. So usually, Helene
introduced only a soupçon.

Anneliese, having been informed by Boots
that action was being taken, also served a
supper with no burnt offerings, and did so
with relief. She was sure she wouldn't rest
until the man who called himself Professor
Knox had paid for his atrocious crimes. Too
few of such monsters had suffered the

extreme penalty, and others, who had been sentenced to long terms of imprisonment in West Germany, had been released after serving only five years, which angered Anneliese. Her husband, Harry, asked her a pertinent question. If Professor Knox was caught and extradited, would she be willing to go to West Germany and testify for the prosecution? Anneliese replied that she was willing to do that and to watch the man being hanged.

The next day, Mr Humphrey Travers of the Foreign Office called Bobby into his sedate-looking office. Sedate was the word for everything about Her Majesty's Foreign Office, especially its officials. Temperamental reactions to pressing affairs were frowned on and discouraged.

'Ah, my dear Somers,' said Mr Travers.

'Good morning,' said Bobby, sedate in his dark grey suit.

'Um – I understand someone has been talking to someone else,' said Mr Travers.

'Is that so?' said Bobby. 'What about?'

'I have no details, only a whisper,' said Mr Travers. 'However, a name was dropped.'

'That can be worrying, a dropped name,' said Bobby.

'Knox, I think,' said Mr Travers, 'a Professor Knox.'

'Well, of all things, someone dropped his name into my ear too,' said Bobby.

'Dear me,' said Mr Travers. 'Well, do keep him out of the Foreign Office, there's a good fellow.'

'He's not our problem, of course,' said Bobby.

'Quite so,' said Mr Travers. 'Mmm, does it amuse you?'

Bobby, guilty of letting a smile show, said, 'Not in the least. I was simply thinking of something my wife said to me last night.'

Mr Travers showed a small smile himself.

'Thoughts of domestic conversations are allowed,' he said.

Probably not when they take in a wife's demand for her husband to do an assassination job, reflected Bobby.

Somehow, nothing very much escaped old Humph, but Helene's demand should be an exception.

Chapter Seventeen

'What's that?' asked Cassie Brown of her daughter Maureen, when the ambitious young lady arrived home from her dull old insurance job that evening. She had a white carrier bag with her.

'It's me new dress,' said Maureen, looking as pretty as any girl next door in a thin summer sweater of a golden hue and a swirly-whirly flared skirt of royal blue patterned with yellow daisies.

'Another one?' said Cassie. 'You've already had about six new dresses this year. I don't know, the money you spend on them, and not saving a penny.'

'Mum, I don't have to start putting pennies away for me old age yet,' said Maureen, and took the new dress from the shop's carrier bag. She unfolded it and draped it over her blouse and skirt. It was a delightful turquoise blue with a fashionable flared skirt and a pinched waist. 'It's groovy, don't you think?'

'Me and your dad don't exactly know what groovy means,' said Cassie, 'but is it for when you have your photograph taken on Saturday?'

'You bet,' said Maureen. 'Mr Anderson said the one I was wearing would do, but I couldn't resist this.'

'Well, it's lovely, I must say,' murmured Cassie, 'but is it a bit short?'

'It's not long,' said Maureen.

'There, it is a bit short,' said Cassie.

'Mum, it's inches below the knee, actually,' said Maureen. 'You can't get anything shorter than that.'

'Oh, and you'd like to, would you?' said Cassie.

'Well, I'm supposed to show me legs for the photos,' said Maureen.

185

'You'd better make sure you wear the right kind of stockings,' said Cassie.

'Oh, I'll wear me sheer navy blue nylons,' said Maureen. 'They're really special.'

In came Lewis.

'What's that blue stuff?' he asked.

'It's your sister's new dress that she's going to wear when she's photographed on Saturday,' said Cassie, 'so don't start being cheeky.'

'What's wrong with any of her other dresses?' asked Lewis, helping himself to an apple. Biting off a lump, he chewed and said through juicy remnants, 'She hasn't given 'em to Mrs Hobday's cat, has she? It'll eat anything, Mrs Hobday's cat, did you know that?'

'Crikey, there's hope yet,' said Maureen.

'Hope for what?' asked Cassie.

'That Mrs Hobday's cat'll make a meal of me daft brother one day,' said Maureen.

Lewis grinned and bit off another chunk, of ripe apple. One a day polished up his teeth. Two a day livened up his tonsils.

'Did you buy that dress at Dad's store?' he asked.

'No, I didn't,' said Maureen.

'You'd have got a discount,' said Lewis.

'But I wouldn't have got this dress,' said Maureen.

'What's special?' asked Lewis. 'It looks like any old dress to me.'

'Lewis, didn't I tell you not to be cheeky?'

said Cassie.

'Don't take any notice, Mum,' said Maureen, 'sense never comes out of boys with wooden heads. Crikey, Lewis, imagine you going all through life with a head that's only good for knocking nails in.'

'I don't fancy that,' said Lewis, making short crunching work of his apple core, pips as well.

'I shouldn't think you would, you'd end up with a head looking like a pincushion,' said Maureen, and went up to her room to try the dress on, to swirl about in front of her mirror, and to study the effect.

Then she sat on the edge of the bed and thought of the kind of poses that would make her look like the girl next door to the readers of the *Daily Mirror*.

Downstairs, waiting for Freddy to get home before she put supper on the table, Cassie listened to Lewis saying that Maureen's chance of having her photograph printed in any newspaper was about one in five million.

Cassie asked where he got the figure of five million from. Out of his wooden head? She asked that with a laugh.

'Oh, it's me estimate of how many girls next door there are in the country,' said Lewis.

'Five million,' said Cassie.

'Well, there's Wales and Scotland as well as England,' said Lewis, as he heard the key turn in the front door to signal the arrival home of his good old dad. 'And the Isle of Wight too,' he said as a worldly afterthought.

'Well, we mustn't leave that out,' said Cassie, 'there must be at least a hundred girls living next door to people on the Isle of Wight.'

Lewis grinned. There were no flies on his mum. Nor were there on Mrs Hobday's cat. It could always track down who'd had kippers for breakfast, and get at the bones and tails before all disappeared into dustbins. Come to that, Lewis reckoned that one day it would work out how to get the lid off any kind of dustbin.

'Mrs Hobday, your cat's eating a skinned rabbit on top of your backyard wall.'

'Is it? Oh, well – 'ere, wait a bit, I bought a rabbit for me and me old man's supper tonight. Don't tell me that Pussy's eating our supper.'

'I just think you might have to make do with cheese sandwiches, Mrs Hobday.'

'Blessed if I won't drown that cat in the river one day, young Lewis.'

'You sure, Mrs Hobday? Only it wouldn't surprise me if it could swim.'

Mrs Hobday's cat was a feature of life in Wansey Street, Walworth.

You could ask anybody.

Or young Lewis Brown.

188

Jimmy Adams, twenty-six-year-old younger son of Susie and Sammy, left the Bethnal Green factory at the end of his day's work as personnel manager, which was some job these days. The factory not only manufactured garments, it also produced its own fabrics. The all-in staff numbered nearly three hundred. Order books were full for finished items, which included Sammy's bête noire. Jeans. Which the factory manufactured under licence, and which he considered responsible for taking skirts off girls and women, in a manner of speaking. Jeans were for sweating cowboys, skirts for feminine females. Jeans, he once said, made some women's bottoms look like pumpkins struggling to get out in time for Hallowe'en. However, he was able to put up with his bête noire (which he called his own white man's burden), on account of the fact that orders were rampant and profits ascending. Even so, the sight of family members wearing jeans made him sigh.

Jimmy began to motor home to Bow, where he lived with his young wife Clare, granddaughter of Bert and Gertie Roper, once prime factory stalwarts and now retired. Clare was not only an exciting wife, she was also a good cook and a very promising gardener. Their own vegetables were gracing the supper table these days.

'Look, all my own work, Jimmy.'

'With a little help from a friend.'

'What friend?'

'Me.'

'Oh, you're not a friend, Jimmy, you're my wedding present.'

Driving along Roman Road, Jimmy slowed for a left turn into a minor road that would take him in the direction of Victoria Park, close to his home. A large car, coming up behind him, gave him a shove that accelerated his turn and made a mess of his bumper. He hollered, stopped and turned his head. He saw the car, a gleaming black Austin Princess limousine, speed on. He took its number, RK 1234. He stopped a little way into the minor road, got out, examined his rear bumper, saw the savage dent, got back in and drove on. He stopped again, this time at the Bow Street police station, where he reported the incident to the desk sergeant.

'Your name, sir?'

'Jimmy Adams.' Jimmy also gave his address and phone number.

'The driver didn't stop, Mr Adams?'

'No, he bloody didn't,' said Jimmy, 'and it's upset my good nature.'

'Did you get his number, sir?'

'You bet I did. RK 1234.'

The sergeant's shrewd eyes showed a distinct gleam as he took note.

'RK 1234, right. Any witnesses, Mr Adams?'

'If there were, they'd all gone by the time I got out to inspect the damage. What I'm livid about is that he didn't attempt to stop or even say beg pardon, mate. I'm not in favour of bad manners. I want an apology from the cowboy and a promise to pay for repairs.'

'What was the time of the incident, sir?' The sergeant seemed extra keen about details.

'Ten minutes ago,' said Jimmy.

The sergeant checked the station clock. Five thirty-five. Jimmy had left the factory at ten past, motoring through the rush hour.

'Right, we'll say between five twenty and five twenty-five,' said the sergeant. 'Would that be right?'

'As near as you could get,' said Jimmy.

The sergeant studied his notes.

'Got him this time,' he murmured.

'What's that?' asked Jimmy.

'What? Oh, just a hope we can nail him for leaving the scene of an accident – in fact, for causing it and failing to stop.'

'I'll leave it with you, sergeant,' said Jimmy.

'We'll be in touch, sir.'

'Good,' said Jimmy, 'I'm off now for a helping of home cooking. Thanks for your time and attention.'

'Oh, Jimmy, what a rotter, not stopping,' said Clare, twenty years old and looking fetchingly domestic in a pretty apron.

Jimmy said very unfortunately not every bloke was Christian-minded, that there were always some who were a bit heathen. However, on this occasion the coppers were bound to nail the creep, since they had the number of his car. Clare asked her legal love if he was hurt. No, said Jimmy, but our Ford bumper's had a painful time.

'Anyway, what's for supper, Clare?'

'Lamb's liver, bacon, tomatoes, mash and runner beans, Jimmy love.'

'Good-oh, that'll help me forget our groaning bumper.'

Two police constables, one a woman, called on Jimmy at eight thirty that evening. Jimmy expected to be informed that the driver of the Austin Princess had been charged.

Instead, PC Randolph said, 'About the incident, sir, can you say if there were any witnesses?'

'Look,' said Jimmy, 'I told your desk sergeant that if there were, they were gone by the time I pulled up.'

'H'm,' said Constable Randolph, looking disappointed.

'What's the problem?' asked Jimmy.

'My husband took the car number,' said Clare.

'Well, Mrs Adams,' said WPC Sarah Musgrove, 'we're up against the owner's insistence that at the time stated, his chauffeur was in charge of the car and waiting to drive him home from the Kempton Park racecourse.'

'Eh?' said Jimmy.

'Oh, yes, a likely story, I don't think,' said Clare, who hadn't been born yesterday. 'In his dreams, more like.'

PC Randolph coughed. WPC Musgrove looked sympathetic.

'What we have to tell you, Mr Adams,' said the former, 'is that Mr Rudy Karpenter–'

'Hold on,' said Jimmy, 'isn't he a dodgy club owner?'

'Yes, with his older brother Rafael,' said WPC Musgrove.

'I've heard some funny stories about that pair,' said Jimmy.

'Yes, and so's my granddad,' said Clare.

'Funny peculiar stories,' said Jimmy. 'Listen, I made no mistake about the car, a black Austin Princess, number RK 1234. He can't have witnesses to say he didn't barge my rear, because he kept driving on.'

'He's produced witnesses confirming he was at Kempton Park racecourse all afternoon and didn't leave till six o'clock,' said PC Randolph.

'Oh, that's a fact, is it?' said Jimmy. 'Well, tell me another, a really funny one this time.'

'What it comes down to, sir,' said WPC Musgrove, 'is that it's your word against his, and his is supported by witnesses. It's a shame, sir, that you don't have any.'

'I tell you what I have got,' said Jimmy, 'a rising temperature likely to boil over any minute. Stand well back. No, come on, you know the bloke's having you on. Jump him.'

'We'd like to,' said PC Randolph, 'but–'

'We can only go by the book, sir,' said WPC Musgrove, 'which means we've got to have enough evidence to charge Mr Karpenter.' Her sympathy was still showing.

'It'll be disgusting if that man gets away with all them lies,' said Clare, 'especially as my husband's as honest and upright as me dad and me grandad.'

'I'm sure,' said PC Randolph. 'We can't do any more ourselves at the moment, but you could see your solicitor, Mr Adams.'

'I'll think about that, you bet I will,' said Jimmy, and saw the constables out. They said goodbye and wished him luck. Jimmy, rejoining Clare, grimaced and said, 'Lucky we had supper before this happened, Pussy-cat, I wouldn't have enjoyed it like I did.'

'Oh, I feel for you, Jimmy, love,' said Clare, 'let's have a pot of tea and some of me fruit cake.'

'Spoken like a winner,' said Jimmy. 'Like Grandmother Finch, in fact, and she's been a winner all her life.'

First thing on his arrival at the factory the next morning, he spoke to his Uncle Tommy, general manager of the whole works. He told him about the incident, and that he was thinking of seeing a solicitor.

Tommy, frowning, said, 'It'll cost you, Jimmy, and that's all it'll do. Those witnesses, take it from me, will stand up in court and swear their heads off in favour of Rudy Whatsit.'

'You're saying I should leave it?' said Jimmy.

'That's it, Jimmy, leave it,' said Tommy. 'I ain't ever been in favour of backing off from trouble, but in a case like this, it's what I'm advising. And I'm pretty sure your Uncle Boots would agree.'

'Would he?' asked Jimmy.

'Try the wise old owl,' said Tommy.

'I'll phone him at the morning break,' said Jimmy.

Which he did.

Boots, having listened to the tale of an honest nephew up against a character of highly dubious references, suggested that if said character had had any sense, he'd have stopped, apologized and offered to pay for the damage, thus avoiding any police investigation. But said character, brother of the same kind, preferred to exercise muscle and influence. So Jimmy would be better off claiming on his insurance for the cost of repairing the bumper, or the fitting of a new one, rather than tangling with the Kings elect of the East End.

195

'Kings elect?' said Jimmy.

'Read the papers, Jimmy.'

'Well, I'll take your advice, Boots,' said Jimmy, 'but it's going to gall me.'

'Better than getting mixed up with any East End heavies, Jimmy old lad,' said Boots. 'Live a quiet life with Clare, and give her my love.'

'That'll make her day,' said Jimmy. 'I suppose you know that Clare, Patsy, Leah and Phoebe all think you've still got sex appeal?'

'Just a wild notion, Jimmy, but I'll investigate it with Polly's help.'

That left Jimmy laughing.

In the evening, Clare served up a delicious supper to console him for losing out to the East End heavies.

Chapter Eighteen

Friday, mid morning.

In her house in Poplar Walk, Boots's daughter-in-law, Felicity, felt the walls of her lounge were closing in on her. She had a thumping headache, the kind that suggested a rubber-cushioned hammer was delivering blows to her skull, particularly her forehead. She rarely had headaches, and certainly never one like this, except during the few days immediately following the bomb blast that had blinded her.

She was sick with pain now, and at the end of her tether. For the last three weeks there hadn't been a single one of those heartening intervals when sight returned for the space of a minute or so, albeit blurred. For three weeks she had been as blind as a bat, and that seemed to have led to this sickening headache. Her fortitude and resilience were draining away, and she felt she could burst into tears. That would be a weakness hard to bear.

'Mrs Adams? Mum?'

Felicity, resting along the settee, opened her closed eyes. She saw nothing, of course, but the lifting of her lids was involuntary.

'Maggie?'

Maggie Forbes, her live-in cook and housemaid, so invaluable to her, said gently, 'Isn't your head no better, mum?'

'It's bloody worse,' said Felicity in a rush of bitterness.

'Well, I've brought you a Beecham's powder mixed with water,' said Maggie, 'and you ought to drink it, it might help.'

'If there's arsenic in it, that would be all the help I want,' breathed Felicity.

'Lord, mum, don't say things like that,' said Maggie.

'Haven't I already had a Beecham's?' said

Felicity, every word dragging.

'That was two hours ago, just after breakfast,' said Maggie. 'Come on, mum, drink this one.'

Felicity sat up, Maggie put the glass in her hand, and she drank the mixture, gagging on it a little. She sank back again, and Maggie took the glass from her.

'Thanks, Maggie.'

'You rest there nice and quiet, mum,' said Maggie, 'I won't be doing no noisy hoovering.' She tiptoed from the room, closing the door quietly, and feeling for her mistress's suffering. Daughter Jennifer was out with a friend, and Mr Adams was at work. Just as well, thought Maggie, it kept the house nice and quiet, and that was what Mrs Adams needed just now, quiet.

Miraculously, Felicity dropped off to sleep. It was two hours before she awoke at twelve thirty.

Relief flooded through her. The hammer had stopped its thumping, the headache gone. Completely. She moved her legs, slowly at first, just in case the hammer returned. Then she put her feet to the floor and stood up. No headache, no hammer. Wonderful. She heard voices at the front gate. The lounge overlooked the gate and the road. The voices were high and girlish, and she recognized that which belonged to Jennifer. A parting of the ways followed.

'Bye, Carol.'

'Bye, Jennifer.'

Moments later came the sound of a turning key in the front door and the advent of Maggie from the kitchen.

'Hello, Maggie, I'm back. Is Mummy's headache better?'

'Oh, we hope so, don't we? She's resting nice and quiet in the lounge, and asleep when I peeped in half an hour ago.'

'Let's peep in now.'

The door was pushed open, and Jennifer quietly entered. Eleven years old, she was dressed in a simple gingham frock of green and white check, her hair a thick, healthy dark brown, her body slender. She saw her mother standing beside the settee.

'That's you, Jennifer?'

'Yes, it's me, Mummy. Are you better?'

'Darling, I'm so much better that let's all go shopping this afternoon, shall we?'

'Oh, whizz-oh, Mums.'

Maggie appeared. She asked Felicity if she really was better, and, on receiving a definite affirmative, said it just might be all right, then, to go shopping later.

It was about four o'clock when Felicity, up in the bedroom on the return from shopping and the walk in the open air, felt light strike her eyes, the light from the sunlit window. She caught her breath, and the light opened up the little world of her immediate surroundings. There, through the window, was the clear sight of hedges, road, houses and a couple walking their dog. Felicity, eyes huge, stared. No moment had ever given her such a clear and sharp picture. Hazy or blurred visions were the usual thing.

This vision was unbelievable, this was what she had hoped for, what her specialist, Sir Charles Morgan, had said might happen. Tense with wonder, she stared almost greedily at the picture of the moving couple and their frisky dog. She stood there, mesmerized and lingering, watching as the couple moved in leisurely fashion out of her view. She heard the dog bark, and the sound was as much a part of these minutes as all she could see.

She wanted to turn and rush downstairs, to see her daughter for the very first time, but her feet seemed clamped to the floor. She made an effort. She turned, and the open door of the bedroom leapt to her sight. She heard Maggie and Jennifer talking downstairs. She activated her legs and moved.

It went then, that clear vision, it receded and died. For long seconds, she was sick with bitter disappointment. Then she remembered that Sir Charles had said any moments of clear sight might only be as temporary as the vague images. At the same time, he said, all such moments could be regarded as further steps and brighter steps on the road to complete recovery.

Felicity drew a breath, squared her shoulders in as firm a fashion as when she was a serving ATS officer, groped her way to the open door and made her way downstairs to tell Jennifer and Maggie of her long wonderful minutes of clear vision. Yes, long minutes.

'Bloody marvellous!' The exclamation mark put a dramatically emphatic finishing touch to Tim's heartfelt comment. He had just arrived home.

'Daddy, really,' said Jennifer, whose private schooling was making a young lady of her.

'Well, it is what I said,' insisted Tim, and took Felicity into his arms. In the kitchen, in front of Jennifer and Maggie, he kissed his wife smack on her lips. 'You're a miracle, Puss.'

'Well, she will be, Mr Adams, if she gets her eyes back,' said Maggie.

'Oh, she always had her eyes, Maggie,' said Jennifer, 'it's her sight that's been missing.'

'Oh, go on, you know what I meant,' said Maggie.

Tim, hands resting lightly on Felicity's shoulders, looked into her misty if blind eyes and said, 'It's really true, Puss, you had long minutes of completely clear vision?'

'Joyful minutes,' said Felicity, emotional with hope and optimism. 'I could even make out that the couple's dog was a spaniel.'

'Maggie, where's the champagne?' asked Tim, high spirits at this moment on a par with his physical vitality, still in as good a condition as it had been during his war years as a commando. Felicity could write a commendable reference about that. In fact, male weaklings were absent from the Adams family. If one had shown up, she was sure Grandma Finch would have regarded the birth as highly suspect. 'Come on, Maggie,' said Tim again, 'where's the champagne?'

'Champagne?' said Maggie. 'Well, we bought groceries when we went shopping, but we didn't buy no champagne, Mr Adams.'

'Pity,' said Tim.

'We'll have a bottle of wine with supper,' said Felicity. 'Or two, if you like. I'm game for a celebration.'

'Oh, help,' said Jennifer, 'it looks like someone's going to end up squiffy by bedtime.'

'I'll phone Sir Charles about this news,' said Tim, 'and if it does for him what it's doing for me, perhaps he'll tumble cross-eyed into bed himself.'

'Mr Adams,' giggled plump Maggie, 'ain't you a one?'

'Daddy's a sixer,' said Jennifer.

'Now what's a sixer, for goodness sake?' asked Maggie.

'A smash hit at cricket,' said Jennifer.

Sir Charles Morgan was delighted to hear the news, and he advised Tim to encourage Felicity to take such moments as natural and not to let her become overexcited.

But he didn't suggest he'd take steps to get himself squiffy.

The managing director of Coates, the big man himself, had been formally in touch with Sammy to say he would arrange a meeting of his board, at which he hoped Sammy and his directors would be present. Discussion on the assets of Adams Fashions could take place and a price for a full takeover agreed.

Sammy said to let him know the date, when he would then arrange for himself and the other directors, his brother Robert and Mrs Goodman, to attend. The managing director of Coates said excellent, Mr Adams, excellent.

Sammy could have said their attendance would only be a matter of courtesy, as recommended by Boots, but his good manners stopped him from chucking that banana into the arena.

He mentioned the matter to Susie during

the evening. It was always a pleasure to talk business with Susie, she being a woman who had quite a bit of sense up top.

Susie said she couldn't think why a meeting with Coates was necessary, seeing any offer of theirs was going to be turned down. So Sammy, of course, referred her to the point made by Boots, that the meeting would just be a matter of courtesy.

'If I know Boots, he's laughing up his sleeve about everything,' said Susie.

'No, it's a serious point, Susie,' said Sammy, 'on account of not upsetting Coates by just saying no without a meeting, and having them stop all further contracts for supplies.'

'I bet Boots is still laughing up his sleeve,' said Susie. 'I mean, his idea of asking for £200,000, if that's not a big joke, what is?'

'He's still a wise old bloke, Susie.'

'Well, you're not far behind, Sammy love.'

'Granted, Susie, but I like you for saying so. Is that a new dress you're wearing?'

'Only something I bought from your Brixton shop six months ago,' said Susie, looking like Sammy's favourite female woman in emerald green.

'Thought it was new,' said Sammy.

'You're dreaming,' said Susie. 'By the way, Phoebe's a bit miffed that Philip hasn't been home on leave just lately.'

'I think his squadron must be doing a lot of

practice flying,' said Sammy. 'I mean, they've always got to make sure they can get their planes off the ground. Still, Phoebe seemed all right at the office.' Phoebe, his adopted daughter, was nineteen and worked at the firm's offices as an assistant bookkeeper. She had a smart head for figures, and Sammy liked smart heads in the firm.

'Work stops her thinking about her disappointments,' said Susie.

'Listen, is she in love with Philip?' asked Sammy.

'Of course,' said Susie.

'She hasn't said anything to me,' said Sammy.

'And I don't suppose she's said anything to Philip, either,' said Susie. 'She's not the kind to admit her feelings unless Philip comes up with a ring.'

'Well, he's not twenty-one yet,' said Sammy.

'He's a fighter pilot,' said Susie, 'and if he's old enough for that, he's old enough to propose.'

'Perhaps he's shy,' said Sammy.

'Philip?' Susie laughed. 'Sammy, there's not a shy bone in any of you Adams men.'

'Philip's a Harrison,' said Sammy, who didn't actually believe that.

'Annabelle, his mother, is an Adams by her own mother,' said Susie.

'Our Lizzy? Well, I can't argue with that,' said Sammy. 'Tell you something, Susie.'

'What something?'

'I like your new dress,' said Sammy.

'Well, you don't say,' said Susie, who had been wearing it on and off for six months.

Later that evening, Leila and Wilhelm, in company with Judith and Michal, were watching the nine o'clock news on BBC TV. They were all interested in the coverage of the Middle East events, particularly items concerning Israel and Egypt. Egypt, at the moment, was Israel's most eloquent enemy.

As soon as the news switched to another matter, Leila, in Yiddish, made a fierce denunciation of all the Arab nations that were at Israel's throat. Michal and Judith refrained from commenting on the outburst.

Michal only said in deliberate English, 'I'd like to hear the cricket news.' The end of the bat and ball season was coming, but there were still some notable matches being played.

Leila stared at him in disgust.

'Cricket?' she said. 'Cricket?'

'Michal's a fan of cricket, and a Surrey supporter,' said Judith, while Wilhelm tried to hear what was being said about an investigation into a Soho murder. Police items always interested him.

'Cricket?' said Leila again, and in sheer disbelief. She rose abruptly to her feet and walked out, mounting the stairs to her room.

'Such a serious young woman,' murmured Judith, casting a sympathetic glance at Wilhelm.

'She feels for Israel,' he said, 'she feels it's still fighting for its life.'

'We should be unsympathetic?' said Michal. 'We aren't. In any case, Israel is already strong and well organized, and I'm frankly confident that if Egypt attacks, Israel will give Nasser a bloody nose.'

'Michal, my friend,' said Wilhelm, 'I'd like to be there when it happens, I sure would.'

'So would I, so would I,' said Michal, 'but I'm tied to the business.' He smiled, thinking of his watchful ageing stepfather, one of the old brigade of Jewish immigrants to Britain. 'Hand and foot.'

'Wilhelm, is the wait for your new papers trying your nerves to breaking point?' asked Judith. It's trying mine, she thought.

'I'll survive,' said Wilhelm.

'I'm sure you will,' said Michal, liking the young man for himself and for his valiant public execution of an ex-SS doctor. He had no doubt that Michal had known the true identity of the man.

When the report on the day's cricket began, Wilhelm went upstairs to talk to Leila. He recognized that the wait for papers and plane departures were putting a strain on the dedicated agent. He knocked on her door, opened it and put his head in.

'Leila–' He checked. She was lying on her bed and looking as moody as hell. But her strong, firm legs were exposed, the white hem of her slip softening the dark look of her black skirt, which had ridden up. She lifted her head from the pillow.

'What the hell do you want?' She used Yiddish.

'Oh, just a friendly word or two,' said Wilhelm in English. 'I guess I'll look elsewhere.' He withdrew his head and made to close the door.

'Come back,' said Leila, reverting to English.

'Sure?' he said.

'Come back.'

Wilhelm stepped in, closed the door and said, 'We're both getting impatient.'

"I am not,' said Leila, 'I am used to waiting for the right moment, the safest moment. But those two, the Wirthe couple, how they irritate me. They are so complacent, so smug, so bourgeoise.'

'I don't agree,' said Wilhelm.

'Did you hear Michal talk of cricket? That silly English game, for God's sake.'

'I know nothing about cricket, but how do you rate baseball?'

'Baseball is just as silly and irrelevant.'

'To you, not to Americans. I quickly found that out.'

'Sit.' Leila patted the edge of the bed. 'Sit,

and we can talk.'

'Cover your legs up,' said Wilhelm.

'My legs worry you?'

'Worry me? No.'

'What are you thinking about?'

'The plane that will take us to Nice.'

'Be patient. Sit.'

'No. I prefer the company of Judith and Michal. They are good people, worth more than your sulks and ingratitude.'

Leila sat up.

'My sulks? My ingratitude?'

'Yes,' said Wilhelm. 'It's no big deal, perhaps, but a little courtesy wouldn't be out of place. But don't think I don't understand. I guess it could happen to anybody, your kind of work making everything else look unimportant. You've forgotten that life can still be enjoyable. Try it sometime. Michal and Judith will help. I've been on the run for a year, but I've still had some enjoyable moments. Have a good night, Leila.'

Leila seethed as the door closed behind him.

When I land him in Israel, and the whole nation lines up to kiss him, she thought, I'll be the odd one out.

'How is she now?' asked Judith when Wilhelm reappeared.

'It's her work,' said Wilhelm, 'she can't think that anything else matters. I know she's a trial, but I'd like to ask you and Michal to be understanding, and to thank you for your kindness in having us.'

'There's no problem, Wilhelm,' said Michal. 'Have you any idea when your contact will turn up with your new papers?'

'No idea at all,' said Wilhelm, 'and I guess Leila hasn't, either.'

'Well, let's all be patient,' said Judith.

It was the following morning when Jimmy, coming down to breakfast, took an early phone call. It was from Police Constable Randolph, who thought he would like to know that a dubious gent by the name of Rudy Karpenter, together with his brother Rafael, and members of their gang, had been caught red-handed last night while making a raid on a warehouse in the East London docks.

'Is this a fact?' asked Jimmy.

'It's a fact all right, Mr Adams. The warehouse, stacked with spirits, was half-empty when tipped-off CID men arrived, and the Karpenters' lorry half-full. We've got 'em for sure this time – apologies for phoning you this early, but thought you'd like to know, thought it might make up for you coming off worst in that car incident.'

'Not half,' said Jimmy. 'What a good bloke you are. Accept my thanks for letting me know, and best of luck to you.'

'You're welcome, sir.'

'I'm going to enjoy my breakfast cornflakes now,' said Jimmy, 'very much I am.'

And he did. So did Clare. The news, plus
the fact that the insurance company had
agreed to pay for their car repairs, put an
intoxicating ingredient into their cereal, and
when Jimmy went off to work he was rolling
a bit.

Chapter Nineteen

Saturday afternoon, and Mr Amos Anderson, photographer, was showing a delighted
smile.

'Blue on a summer day is good,' he said.

'D'you really like it?' asked Maureen,
attired in her new creation, and sporting a
stylish hairdo. She'd been at the hairdresser's
during the morning.

Amos viewed her professionally. The dress
was perfect, its flared skirt definitely feminine. And her make-up was excellent, favour-
ing delicacy, not the bold. The bold was for
tarty girls.

'I like it, don't I, Miss Brown?' be said.

'Maureen.'

'Well, Maureen, I'm ready to go, and so
are you, don't I fancy?'

'I'm more than ready,' said Maureen, an

excited young lady.

'My car's outside,' said Amos, wearing a brown and white check shirt, open-necked, and tan trousers. Maureen thought he looked just the job. 'So let's go.'

Five minutes later, on this balmy September day, they were heading south towards the Surrey countryside. Amos said he hoped to find a nice quiet spot and a farm gate, and a farmer who wouldn't sue them for trespassing.

'Oh, I'm going to pose on a gate?' said Maureen.

'Which is what we want, don't we?' said Amos. 'A girl next door out in the country on a summer day.'

'It's cloudy, though,' said Maureen.

'But the light is good and even,' said Amos, 'better than harsh sunshine and dark shadows. We'll find a spot, you bet.'

'Oh, I know a place we could use,' said Maureen. 'It's a poultry farm that belongs to someone me mum and dad have known for years. I was at a birthday party in July, for a relative of me dad's, a gorgeous bloke.' She was referring to Boots and his sixtieth. 'And I was talking to one of his daughters, the one me mum and dad know, who runs this farm with her husband. She told me where it was, the Surrey Poultry Farm in Woldingham.'

'Woldingham I know, don't I?' said Amos. 'For the gentry and their ladies, and no synagogue. Yes, I know it, Maureen, not half.'

'Oh, great,' said Maureen. 'Rosie – that's her name – told me I could come and see the farm whenever I liked. Let's go there now, I bet there'll be a field and a gate we can use.'

'She won't mind?' said Amos, deftly weaving the car through traffic heading for Croydon.

'No, course she won't,' said Maureen, 'she's a real doll.'

'Real dolls we like, eh?' smiled Amos.

'Mind, I think she's a bit over thirty,' said Maureen, which would have tickled Rosie at forty-one.

'We should worry about that?' said amiable Amos, a rakish peaked cap pulled over his barbered head of springy black hair. Amos was a likeable bloke, in appearance as well as personality. It earned him a steady flow of engagements and studio sitters. 'Real dolls a bit over thirty we still like, don't we?'

'Oh, you'll like Rosie,' said Maureen.

Rosie and husband Matthew, together with their cheerful West Indian helpers, Hortense and Joe, were in the large shed that stood on the edge of their main field, their farmhouse at their backs. Rosie was trim and elegant, even in her workaday smock, Matthew was lean and sinewy in shirt and corduroys, Hortense was buxom in apron, straining cotton shirt and long skirt, and Joe strong-shouldered and lanky, in dungarees.

They were all plucking chickens, and the floor was covered with feathers. They had a large order that had to be ready by Monday, so Rosie and Matt were giving their workers a hand. Hortense and Joe would dress the plucked fowls in the tiled scullery, a job Rosie happily delegated, and the birds would be placed in the scullery freezer until Monday morning.

The farm derived its income from the sale of dressed chickens, a multitude of fresh-laid eggs, chicks for raising as layers, and layers for households whose families wanted to keep chickens solely for the purpose of bringing their own 'home-grown' eggs to their tables. There was also an income from raising lambs for the market, since they had a flock of sheep which grazed their two large fields, and were served yearly by a hired ram.

When their intensive Saturday work was over, they would have Sunday free. Hortense and Joe, Bible-readers, would go to church. Not to their immediate local one, which was High Anglican, but to the Congregational Church in Caterham Valley. There, the atmosphere of reverence was less formal and the ornamentation simple. Matthew would drive them there and pick them up when the service was over. It was no more than a ten-minute journey.

The work of continuous plucking was hot,

and lately Rosie had begun to wonder if this and other aspects of chicken farming were really what she wanted for the rest of her life. Coincidentally, a month ago, she and Matthew had received an offer for their holding from Sprowles, big in the poultry-farm industry. They had turned it down. However, she had brought the subject up again last week, and Matthew had suggested they could give the offer serious consideration, if that was what she would like. Rosie said she was at least prepared for a discussion, but asked what they would do if they sold. You could join the family firm, said Matthew, and I could run a set-up for the repair of cars. He was a top-class mechanical engineer with the highest qualifications. Rosie said well, then, they must think seriously about selling. The matter was on her mind now.

When the floor of the shed was beginning to look as if it was covered by a downy quilt, they heard a car enter the forecourt fronting the farmhouse.

'A customer?' said Matt.

'For a sackful of feathers?' said Rosie.

'Miz Chapman, ma'am, there ain't no-one gonna rid us of all these here in one sack,' said Hortense.

'The contractors will collect on Tuesday,' said Matt.

'By then, boss, us'll be standing knee-high

215

in them,' said Joe.

A female voice reached their ears through the open door of the shed.

'Anyone home?'

'In here,' called Matt.

'Oh, goody.' The next moment Maureen appeared. 'Crikey,' she said, as she saw the multitude of feathers, a large crate containing freshly executed chickens, and a long steel-topped table on which rested an extensive heap of naked fowls. 'Crikey,' she said again.

Rosie looked at the girl in the doorway, recognized her and said, 'Maureen? Well, you're a surprise. Have you come to help? Step in, then, take a seat and start plucking.'

'Me?' said Maureen.

'It's fowl work,' said Matt, his pun blatant, 'but we need an extra hand.'

'Oh, go on, Mr Chapman,' smiled Maureen. She had met Rosie's husband at Boots's special party. 'I wouldn't know where to start.' She eyed the West Indians with curiosity.

'Maureen, meet Hortense and Joe, our happy labour force,' said Rosie, wondering exactly why Cassie's daughter was here.

'Oh, hello,' said Maureen. West Indian immigrants weren't unknown to her. There were quite a few around Walworth and Camberwell. And Brixton.

'Pleasure,' beamed Hortense, fingers

working rapidly on the feathers of a large, plump chicken.

'Sho' is a pleasure,' grinned Joe.

Matt, noticing how pretty Maureen looked in her blue frock and attractive hairdo, said, 'I don't think she's dressed for plucking chickens, Rosie.'

'Oh, put one of those aprons on, Maureen,' said Rosie, indicating several hanging on pegs. There was a teasing light in her blue eyes, since she was sure Maureen's reason for calling had nothing to do with helping to pluck chickens.

'Mrs Chapman,' said Maureen, not backward about coming forward, 'I hope you don't mind, but I've come to have me photograph taken.'

'Well, you look sweet enough,' said Rosie, 'but we don't do photography, we raise chickens and lambs.'

'No, I mean I've come with me photographer,' said Maureen, 'he's going to take photos of me for the *Daily Mirror*, and we thought–'

'Pardon?' said Rosie, a wayward feather lightly resting on her corn-coloured hair.

'Yes, honest,' said Maureen, 'and he wants to do them in the country, like here, and we thought you might let us go in your fields and do them there. He said getting chased off by farmers somewhere is what we don't want. He talks like that. Would you mind if

217

we did the photos by one of your gates?'

'I wouldn't mind myself,' said Matt, 'and I'm sure Rosie wouldn't. And I don't think the sheep would object. Did you say the photos are for the *Daily Mirror*?'

'Yes, they print pin-ups,' said Maureen.

'Pin-ups?' said Rosie, and laughed.

'What might they be, Miz Chapman?' asked Hortense.

'Saucy,' said Rosie.

'Oh, my,' said Hortense.

'Mr Anderson – that's me photographer – says he'll pose me as the girl next door,' smiled Maureen, not a bit self-conscious about all this.

Matt coughed, and a couple of floating feathers wavered and drifted slowly down to settle on the mass.

'The girl next door?' he said.

'Come to, Matt,' said Rosie, 'you've heard that phrase, haven't you?'

'So I have,' said Matt, 'and if I remember right, there was a girl next door to my family in my young days. There was a Dorset saying about her. Let's see, how did it go? "Down by Dorset land they tell, were a girl called Esmerelda, all round and fat she were, so her parents went and selled her."'

Maureen shrieked. Hortense giggled and Joe grinned all over. Rosie laughed.

'Matt, that's one of your worst,' she said.

'True, enough,' said Matt.

218

'True as the man in the moon,' said Rosie.

'Can I get Mr Anderson to meet you?' asked Maureen.

'Yes, let's have a look at the chap,' said Matt.

Maureen turned and called.

'Come on, Mr Anderson, come and meet me mum and dad's friends.'

Amos appeared. Over his right shoulder was a long leather strap, depending from which was his black leather bag containing his equipment. On his face was his friendly smile, which slightly slipped when he saw the feather-encrusted floor and four people, including two West Indians, all plucking chickens in mechanical fashion despite their interest in their visitors.

'Good afternoon,' said Amos, 'a fine day, eh? So sorry to interrupt you. I'm Amos Anderson, Camberwell Green photographer.'

'Welcome,' smiled Rosie, highly tickled.

'That's Mrs Rosie Chapman, and that's Mr Chapman,' said Maureen.

'Hello,' said Amos.

'And that's Joe and Hortense, their helpers,' said Maureen.

'Hi,' said Amos.

'Oh, and where are your son and daughter, Mrs Chapman, that I met at your dad's special birthday party?' asked Maureen.

'They disappeared into the wilds as soon

as they suspected they might be dragged into this shed,' smiled Rosie.

'Kids, they know what they don't want, eh?' said Amos.

'Mr and Mrs Chapman said we can do the photos in their fields,' enthused Maureen, 'so come on, let's get started. Oh, thanks ever so much,' she said to Rosie, 'we didn't want to get to a place and have farmers' dogs chasing us off. See you all later.'

And with a saucy whisk of her flared dress, she disappeared, along with Amos.

Rosie looked at Matt.

'A pin-up for the *Daily Mirror*?' she said.

'Ought to be worth a look,' said Matt.

'Stay where you are,' said Rosie.

'That young lady, ain't she mighty pretty?' said Hortense, chicken feathers flying.

Matt, fishing one more dead fowl out of the crate, thought well, a lot prettier than this bird. Which thought made him dwell on Rosie's inclination to sell up. Well, perhaps they'd had their time as poultry farmers. His old affinity with the repair and maintenance of cars surfaced. He glanced at Rosie.

'Yes, Matt?' she said.

'There's more to life than feathers,' said Matt.

Rosie got the message, but only said, 'There are a few around today, old thing.'

It wouldn't do to discuss selling the farm in front of Hortense and Joe, their devoted and happy workers. In the event that they did decide to talk to Sprowles, they would want to make sure the prospective new owners kept the contented West Indians in their jobs.

Amos and Maureen passed the large wired enclosure protecting the commodious henhouse and a mass of fluffy yellow chicks, which were chirruping as they foraged in the earth for tiny insects. Out in the field, scores of fat Rhode Island Red fowls were darting, pecking and scratching in search of worms amid the dry summer grass.

'Well, look at all these,' said Maureen, 'there's hundreds.'

'Hundreds is good for your friends,' said Amos, 'one a fortnight is enough for me.'

'Well, if you ate one a day,' giggled Maureen, 'you'd grow more feathers than in that shed.'

'See, there's a gate,' said Amos.

Maureen saw it, at the far end of the long, wide field. Chickens squawked and scampered as she and Amos advanced, she with the eager step of a girl opting for a glamorous career. Perhaps she might even become a famous fashion model, like those whose photos were always in the papers, and in exclusive and glossy magazines such as *Vogue*.

Reaching the gate, they saw it opened onto a farm lane. But quiet was reigning, the lovely country quiet of the Surrey Hills. Woldingham itself was well above sea level, and much to Amos's professional satisfaction there was a natural breeze, a breeze already plucking at the skirt of Maureen's dress.

He unzipped his bag, took out his camera, already loaded, and his light meter. In the bag was a good supply of extra film. He stood back from the gate and measured the light reflected from Maureen and her dress.

'Stand there, Maureen, that's it, against the gate – no, wait, give us your handbag,' he said. 'Handbags we don't want. They're not what we call photogenic, unless you're modelling one for a manufacturer's mail-order catalogue.'

Maureen passed him her handbag, and he placed it down at the foot of the gatepost. She put her back lightly against the gate, and fluffed at her hair a little. Amos, quite sure her make-up needed no retouching, told her to put the heel of her right shoe on the bottom bar. She did so, and with her hands resting against a bar, her pose became natural.

'Is this all right, Mr Anderson?'

'That is all right definite,' said Amos. His camera, slung around his neck by a thin strap, came up in his hands, and he opened up the viewfinder. 'My life, all right definite is good, and, well, well, so is the breeze, eh?'

It was co-operating as if under instruction, lifting Maureen's blue dress and white lacy slip. Sheer nylons gleamed in the soft light.

'Oh, me dress,' she said.

'No dress is what we don't want, though, eh?' smiled Amos, studying the picture in his viewfinder. 'Skittish dress we do – my, that's very good – great – hold it now – keep that smile – great.'

Click went the camera, catching the smile of a 'girl next door', along with her breeze-blown dress and her nyloned legs.

The outdoor session had begun, the conditions perfect, especially the soft light governed by high white clouds.

Disinterested chickens clucked about, fluffy chicks hopped and twittered, and in the adjacent field sheep and lambs peacefully grazed, apart from the moments when wandering lambs went baa-ing in search of their mothers.

In the shed, feathers floated and fell, with Rosie and Matt, and Hortense and Joe, working towards the bliss of refreshing teatime.

Chapter Twenty

'Well, I'm damned,' said Major Gorringe, retired. No-one asked him what he was damned about. He was up in his roomy loft, eye to his telescope that was mounted on a

223

tripod in front of the window. He frequently liked to let his magnified gaze sweep the countryside. It came from a habitual sweeping of enemy lines with his field glasses during his years of campaigning on the North-West Frontier throughout the Twenties and Thirties. It rarely failed to help him spot an unfriendly native blighter or two. These days, his telescope helped him to spot civilian blighters, such as itinerant gypsies heading for the open spaces around Woldingham. Not that he objected to gypsies, only to having them camp next door to him, more or less. The proximity of gypsies and their pots and kettles sent Mildred, his wife, diving for the shelter of a trench. That is, the space under the marital bed. Funny woman, Mildred, but it was his duty to protect her. Eye still glued to the telescope, he muttered, 'Can't believe my blasted eyes. Giving the place a bad name. Have to do something about it.'

Down he went, gathered up his hat and stick from the hallstand, and called to Mildred that he was going to take half an hour's walk.

'Well, no longer,' replied Mildred from the living room, 'I'll be making tea by then.'

'Right.' The major decided not to give the reason for his outing. It would shock Mildred and probably send her to the phone to call the police.

Out he went, marching briskly. He was a bluff old soldier, but a bit choleric in the way of his kind. Didn't think much of women in trousers and that tin-can rock 'n' roll music, or any music except the stirring stuff of a military band.

As he marched, legs still active, despite being over sixty, he kept a firm grip on his walking stick.

'Great – just the job – head to the left a bit – that's it – I like it, don't I?'

Click went the camera for the umpteenth time. Amos was in the lane now, Maureen perched on the outside of the gate of the adjacent field, that which was dotted with the grazing sheep and their frisky lambs. Maureen, seated sideways, had her right leg drawn up, her left leg down, but curved at the knees. Her dress and slip were the playthings of the breeze, constantly lifting and fluttering to reveal her shining stockings and the glimpse of a saucy white suspender or two.

'How we doing, Amos?' she asked happily.

'Well, I like it, didn't I say so?' said Amos, just as happy as his sitter. He was taking his time to pose her for each shot. 'What do we want, eh? The pretty girl next door, and don't we have it? Now, put your hand to your forehead, shade your eyes and look at the aeroplane.'

'What aeroplane?' asked Maureen.

'We've got imagination, haven't we?' said Amos.

'Oh, you mean pretend there's one,' said Maureen, and shaded her eyes and looked upwards. The breeze gusted, lifting her dress and slip high.

'Hey, you there! By George, damned if I saw anything more disgusting in the shadiest bazaars of Bombay.' Major Gorringe bore down on Amos, walking stick at the ready.

Maureen let out a startled squeak, and Amos backed off from the portly, red-faced figure in tweeds.

'What's up, what's wrong?' he asked.

'Wrong? Wrong?' Major Gorringe waved his stick as if signalling a charge. 'Damned if you aren't photographing this wench in her underclothes. Never saw the like in all my born days.'

'Here, d'you mind?' said Maureen, down from the gate. 'I'm fully dressed, I am.'

'Much good that's been doing you,' said the outraged old buffer. 'Sitting on these gates, showing your drawers–'

'Here, leave off,' said Maureen, indignant but blushing rosy red, like any nice girl next door in the face of embarrassing accusations. 'Amos, give him a talking-to.'

'Kind sir,' said Amos, protecting his camera by clasping it close to his chest, 'I assure you, I'm photographing only pretty poses for the–' He thought, he took in the tweeds and the stout walking stick. 'For *The Times*.'

'Eh? What?'

'*The Times*,' said Amos, 'a most respectable newspaper, isn't it?'

'Damned if I believe that,' growled Major Gorringe, certain the editor wouldn't accept photographs of a young wench showing her legs and unmentionables. 'I'll have you know these fields are private property, so be off with you or I'll call the police.'

'Excuse me,' said Maureen, still indignant but now unblushing, 'we've got permission to be here from the owners, and we're not in the fields, anyway.'

'Damn my ears, what a minx,' said Major Gorringe, 'I'll see about that.'

All four chicken-pluckers were now around a garden table outside the farmhouse kitchen. They were drinking welcome tea. A large, cosy-covered pot stood on the table, and so did a plate containing what was left of an icing-topped lemon cake. The mild sharpness of the lemon was enough to take away the taste of chicken-feather dust. The day-long job of plucking was over, and a host of birds to be dressed now awaited Hortense and Joe.

'Hello, hello,' said Rosie, 'I think we've got another visitor.'

All heads turned. Halfway up from the gate was Major Gorringe. The old boy lived half a mile away, but had become a good neighbour and friend, if a bit eccentric at times. Striding purposefully, causing chickens to flutter in panic from his path, he eventually arrived at the table.

'Hello, Major, what brings you to our teapot?' smiled Matt.

'Afternoon, Matt, afternoon, Rosie,' said the major, and nodded, not unkindly, at Hortense and Joe, whom he regarded as well-behaved natives from the West Indies. 'Afternoon,' he said.

'Afternoon, Majah, sir,' said Joe.

'I say, look here, Rosie,' said the major, 'I'm damned if you don't have the enemy at your gates.'

'Enemy?' said Rosie.

'Some dubious photographic johnny taking pictures of a young Piccadilly tart,' growled the major. 'Seen 'em with my own eyes.'

'Did you say a Piccadilly tart?' asked Matt, hiding a grin.

'That's her,' said Major Gorringe, whisky-red face mottled. Well, it wasn't every day that Woldingham was invaded by a dose of pornography. 'Showing her legs like billy-o. And more. Mildred won't like it. Never shown any of her legs all her life. Out of respect for herself, y'know. Fine woman in her time. Won her spurs nursing the wounded in the hospital at Poona. Gone off a bit lately, but still a fine woman.'

'And still a fine figure in the saddle, I daresay,' said Matt.

'Would be, Matt, would be,' said the major, 'but we don't run to a stable and oats these days. Mildred's limbs not what they were, y'know, and she's off oats herself. Prefers a kipper. Where was I? Oh, yes, this photographic wallah and his Piccadilly hussy. Giving your place a bad name, y'know. Thought I ought to warn you what they're up to.'

'Oh, I think the photographer's quite respectable, Major, and the young lady isn't from Piccadilly,' said Rosie.

'Somewhere like that, I shouldn't wonder,' growled the major. 'The fellow had the nerve to tell me he was photographing her for *The Times*.'

'*The Times?*' said Rosie.

'Cartload of rhubarb, I fancy,' snorted the major. 'The only decent legs I've ever seen in *The Times* belonged to Lord Kitchener and his nag. Fine selection of limbs all round. I was a cadet at the time.'

'Oh, well,' said Matt, 'I get the impression one newspaper's much like another these days.'

'Not *The Times*,' said the major, firmly enough to be credited with sticking to his guns. 'Look here, Matt, the minx told me they had your permission to be here. Can't believe that.'

'It's true,' said Rosie. 'Well, the young

lady's not unknown to us. Her mother's an old friend.'

'And very respectable,' said Matt.

'Well, blast my boots, could have sworn she was a bit much,' said the major.

'I'm sure the photographs won't be in the least offensive,' said Rosie.

'Skirt blowing in the wind, y'know, Rosie,' rumbled the major. 'Still, I daresay I can take your word.'

'Have a cup of tea, do,' said Rosie.

'Kind of you, Rosie,' said the major, 'but Mildred will be putting the old campaign kettle on any moment, and if I'm not back in time she'll probably phone Constable Harris and tell him to go looking for me. Gets a bit rattled if I'm not there when she's filling the pot. Must be off. Good day to you, Rosie, good day to you, Matt. Apologies for intruding, but the situation looked a bit critical to me. One can never be sure how or when the enemy will strike. And damned peculiar camouflage they use these days.' He nodded at Hortense and Joe. 'Good day.'

'Goodbye, sir,' beamed Hortense who, like Joe, hadn't the foggiest idea of why Major Gorringe had been so purple.

Off he went, portly but fit, this time using the front gate, turning into the road to stride briskly homewards in the hope of reaching Mildred before the kettle boiled.

'Well,' said Rosie, and laughed.

'Skirt blowing in the wind,' said Matt.

'One man's eye-catcher is another man's horror story?' suggested Rosie.

'Miz Chapman,' said Hortense, 'me and Joe, we best start dressing them ole chickens.'

'Well, thank you, Hortense,' said Rosie, and the West Indian couple made their way through the kitchen to the scullery, where crates of plucked birds awaited two pairs of quick and efficient hands.

Outside, Matt said, 'Here they come.'

Amos and Maureen were entering the field, Amos closing the gate behind him. Maureen waved.

'Here we are!' she sang. 'We're finished.'

'Hope not,' murmured Matt, 'we don't want them expiring on the premises. It'll look as if the major fatally winged them, and we'll have to phone Constable Harris and let him know who's the main suspect.'

'Mildred won't like that,' said Rosie.

'No problem,' said Matt, 'I think we can count on the walking wounded to reach this pot of tea. That'll cure them.'

He and Rosie sat there, resting and waiting. Finally, Amos and Maureen arrived. Amos looked as affable as ever. Maureen looked sparkling.

'Oh, my stars,' she said, 'did a stout bloke come up and complain about us?'

'Only Major Gorringe,' said Rosie.

'Oh, that's his name, is it?' said Maureen.

'What a funny bloke, his face was all red and his eyes popping.'

'Oh, yes, regarding his eyes,' said Rosie, 'he went on about a skirt blowing in the wind.'

'Well, true, true,' said Amos, 'except dress, not skirt. And blowing in the wind we wanted.'

'Sit down,' said Rosie. She lifted the tea cosy and felt the pot. It was still hot. 'Have some tea and a slice of lemon cake. Matt?'

'Right,' said Matt, coming to his feet. He went into the kitchen to fetch two more cups and saucers, and two tea plates.

'Oh, ever so kind of you, Mrs Chapman,' said Maureen, and she and Amos seated themselves. Out came Matt with the extra china, and he reseated himself. Maureen said she and Amos had done some terrific photographs, although they'd been a bit upset by that funny old bloke, Major Gorringe, who hadn't been at all nice, and all over nothing, really. Rosie, pouring the tea, said the gentleman, actually quite kind and neighbourly, wasn't exactly on the same wavelength as younger people. In fact, said Rosie, he thought ladies' legs should remain unseen, and had just declared that his wife's had been covered all her life.

'Oh, no, go on,' said Maureen, 'you're joking. Even me granddad, who was born when Queen Victoria was still alive, isn't as old-fashioned as that. He says if a girl's got good legs, who's going to complain? Crikey, fancy that funny old geezer having a funny wife. Oh, thanks ever so.' She received her cup of tea and a slice of cake with a glow of happiness. Amos received his with a delighted smile, and a few typical words.

'Tea and cake are good, eh?' he said.

'Any time,' said Matt. 'By the way, I hope you'll send us a couple of the photographs.'

Amos said that reminded him of a lamb. Rosie asked if he meant Maureen. Amos said Maureen was young and pretty, but not a lamb, and that the one he was talking about had come right up to the gate to have a good look at his camera. So, of course, he took a photograph of it. He would send a print.

'I think my husband had Maureen in mind,' smiled Rosie. 'He sees our lambs every day, but not a dress blowing in the wind.'

Amos shouted with laughter. Maureen giggled.

'Now that is funny, Mrs Chapman,' said Amos, 'and real funny we like. So, I'll send you some prints of Maureen, then, eh?'

'Or a copy of the relevant issue of the *Daily Mirror*,' said Matt.

At that point, his son and daughter, Giles and Emily, put in an appearance. Giles was just over fourteen, Emily just under thirteen. Both were lively, Emily owning the fair hair of her mother, and Giles owning an untidy mop and a ruddy complexion that made Rosie see him as the son of his Dorset-born father.

'So there you are, scamps,' she said. 'I'm delighted you remembered this is where you live.'

'Has all the plucking been done?' asked Giles, looking ready to disappear again if the answer was delivered in the negative.

'All done,' said Matt, 'but you and Emily can help Hortense and Joe with dressing the birds, if you feel you must.'

'Ugh,' said Emily. She'd grown up on the farm and knew all about the life being down to earth, but she still nearly puked at the idea of dragging the innards from dead chickens. 'I don't want anything to do with that disgusting job.'

'Well, you can both meet our visitors,' said Rosie. 'That's Maureen, Cassie Brown's daughter, and that's Mr Anderson, a photographer.'

'What does he photograph?' asked Giles.

'Lambs,' said Matt.

'Pooh,' said Emily, and reached in between her father and Amos to grab the last piece of cake. Rosie gave her a look. Emily had been named after Boots's first wife, Rosie's adoptive mother, but lately she had developed tendencies that were uncomfortably remindful of Rosie's natural mother, a woman utterly shallow, vain and selfish, who had vanished into her own artificial world many years ago. These tendencies weren't known to Matt, but they were to Rosie. Matt, however, had had reason lately to speak to his daughter about her manners.

Maureen interceded.

'Mrs Chapman, thanks ever so much for your kindness,' she said, 'but me and Mr Anderson had best be on our way now.'

'Yes, thank you for everything,' said Amos. 'Kindness we all like, don't we?'

Rosie smiled. There was something endearing about the photographer and his way with words.

'You've both been a happy diversion,' she said. 'And an unusual event in the life of Major Gorringe,' said Matt.

Amos laughed. Then he and Maureen said goodbye and left. Emily and Giles followed them and watched them get into Amos's car.

'We've got a better car than that,' said Emily, 'and a van as well.'

'Lucky you,' said Maureen.

'You shouldn't say things like that,' said Giles to his sister. He waved as the car moved off.

Away went the photographer and the up-to-date version of the girl next door.

Chapter Twenty-One

Wilhelm and Leila were among the many people in the East Street market of Walworth. Michal and Judith were there too, shopping. Leila had actually said yes when Judith invited her and Wilhelm to join them on the excursion.

'I think it will be OK for us to go out once more,' she said to Wilhelm.

'Sure, I'd like to,' said Wilhelm.

'Wear the hat,' said Leila.

Michal said he'd drive them in the car, so that only the people in the market would see them. He didn't think either the police or any other representatives of the law would be there looking for Wilhelm. He doubted, in fact, if any serious search was now going on, except in America.

The afternoon was advancing, but the market crowds were as thick as usual. Not until about seven on a Saturday would they begin to thin. While Judith and Michal shopped, Wilhelm and Leila followed at a short distance, interesting themselves in what the cockney stallholders were offering.

'In Israel,' whispered Leila, 'the stalls would be laden with melons, oranges, lemons and other fruit.'

'I'll look forward to that,' said Wilhelm, hat pulled well down.

'Also,' whispered Leila, 'I am being pushed and having elbows jabbed into my ribs.'

'It would surprise me if you didn't find something to complain about,' said Wilhelm. 'I feel good myself at being out of the house, and mixing with all these cheerful people.'

The people did seem cheerful, the hustle and bustle good-natured and an everyday part of the atmosphere.

Unexpectedly, Leila said, 'Oh, I am sorry. You are right, it is good to be out. In the house it is always waiting, waiting.'

'I guess we both feel that,' said Wilhelm, although he remembered she had said she was used to waiting, and that it didn't worry her.

There was a sudden disturbance ahead. They saw Judith and Michal turn from a stall to watch a market bobby dealing with two men who, very much less than cheerful, had come to blows. People backed off to give the bobby room to handle the situation, which he did with commendable speed. Separating the contestants, he advised them to get lost or he'd run them in. Off the blokes went, their going a disappointment to spectators who had hoped to see a stand-up bawling and hollering fight.

The bobby came on, strolling through the

crowds. Wilhelm and Leila tensed, for the uniformed policeman seemed to be casting his eyes all ways. They'd had a previous encounter with a constable, an uncomfortable one.

'He's looking for someone,' breathed Wilhelm. 'Take my arm, talk to me and walk on,' whispered Leila.

Wilhelm curled his arm around hers, talked quietly to her about American films, and made a slow way with her through the immediate crowd. The market bobby looked at them. But his glance was casual and he passed them by. Leila's arm pressed Wilhelm's to signal all was well.

'It's going to be like this all the way to–' He checked from mentioning Israel. There were always ears. 'To our home,' he said.

'We shall get there, my friend, believe me,' said Leila, pressing his arm again.

Holy Elijah, thought Wilhelm, she's softening.

The shopping over eventually, Michal drove them home, with Judith asking if they felt better for the outing.

'I sure do myself,' said Wilhelm.

'Yes, so do I,' said Leila. Then, 'Thank you.'

When they reached the house in Camberwell Grove, she immediately wondered if she had made a mistake in absenting herself. Her prime contact, Stargazer, might have phoned, since his call could come through any time.

Oh, well, if he had phoned and received no response, he would phone again later.

Half an hour later, a sound disturbed them, not of the phone ringing, but of the front door knocker being smartly used. Rap, rap.

Michal answered the summons. A slim, dark-featured man in a casual check shirt and blue jeans, and carrying a suitcase, transferred himself adroitly from the doorstep to the passage. Michal, recognizing him, closed the door.

'Shalom,' he said.

'Hello, Michal,' said Stargazer in easy English, 'how are the caged birds?'

'Flapping,' said Michal.

'Of course. Well, it's been tough for both of them, but they'll be taking wing tomorrow.'

'Tomorrow's the day?' said Michal, visibly relieved.

'I'll be picking them up at eleven thirty in the morning. Where are they?'

'In the kitchen,' said Michal. 'Enjoying a cup of tea, and another of Judith's honey cakes.'

Stargazer smiled, and his dark face became pleasant.

'You and your tea,' he said. 'I have been in London two years and have drowned in tea several times over. But I'll eat a slice of honey cake with you, and perhaps some coffee instead of tea.'

'You're welcome.' Michal led the way to the kitchen, where Judith, Leila and Wilhelm were seated at the table, keeping company with a teapot and the cake.

Leila, quick to recognize the visitor, said, 'So there you are.'

'So here I am,' said Stargazer, placing his suitcase on the floor. 'Greetings, Judith.'

'Hello,' said Judith, who did not know the man as well as Michal did. But she did know he was an agent for Mossad, and would be responsible for seeing Leila and Wilhelm safely out of the country.

He touched Leila's shoulder in a comradely gesture, and shook hands with Wilhelm. While Michal put the coffee percolator to work, the visitor apologized for the long wait, which was due, he said, to the time taken to process documentation. He was not a man who apologized very often. A Palestine-born Jew, he was as hard as steel, and, like others of his kind, had not welcomed immigrant survivors of the extermination camps with open arms. Again like others, he had actually expressed contempt for all European Jews who had allowed themselves to be herded into concentration camps without resisting, had discovered the truth of such places and still

240

not fought for their lives. The only Jews who had fought were those of the Warsaw ghetto. They alone merited commendation, as did Wilhelm Kleibert for his deed in New York.

He came to the point of his visit. All documents were ready, along with plane tickets. The tickets were for a return flight, a precaution against the possibility that one-way tickets might arouse curiosity in the wrong quarter. He would, he said, be driving Leila and Wilhelm to London Airport tomorrow morning to catch their flight to Nice. They were to be ready by eleven thirty.

'I'm relieved to hear this,' said Judith. 'In fact, I'm sure Michal and I are delighted for our friends.'

'I'm frankly delighted for myself,' said Wilhelm.

'I can only say this development is not before time,' said Leila, 'but the apologies are accepted.'

'Jolly decent of you, dear girl,' said Stargazer, taking off an upper-class English type to perfection. Then, briskly, he told Leila and Wilhelm that he had the new passports, that he'd been in touch with Anderson, and would see him at six for the purpose of fixing the photographs. Leila and Wilhelm were to stay where they were and not move out of the house until he picked them up tomorrow.

'Coffee,' said Michal, interrupting on a

hospitable note.

'Thanks,' said Stargazer, taking the mug. The coffee was black and strong. Michal knew the man liked it that way, but he smiled as he watched him help himself to liberal spoonfuls of sugar.

Mossad's agents, Indian Moon and Stargazer, glanced at each other. Stargazer looked relaxed, Indian Moon looked impatient.

'There's more?' she said.

'The question of what each of you will wear.'

'So I should hope,' said Leila. 'If Wilhelm is to travel to Nice as a fashion representative, and myself as his secretary, we should not look like tourists.'

'Agreed,' said Stargazer, and advised them that Wilhelm would wear a Savile Row suit, and Leila a stylish suit with a purloined Worth label. These were in his suitcase, and could be tried on while he was with the photographer.

'Have I heard of Savile Row?' asked Wilhelm.

'Savile Row makes the finest tailored suits in the world,' said Michal.

'Will mine fit me?' said Wilhelm.

Stargazer said it would, that he had supplied the tailors with all the necessary measurements.

'Wilhelm, you'll be the smartest and best-looking young man at the airport,' said Judith.

'If that means he will attract attention, I shan't like it,' said Leila.

'Oh, only from ladies,' smiled Judith. 'Especially young impressionable ladies.'

Conversation developed, but although there was an air of relief that the waiting was now over, there was also an underlying tension. That would exist until Leila and Wilhelm were actually on the plane at take-off.

'They are two good people,' said Amos Anderson. He had stuck the photographs to the passports, one identifying the holder as Charles Philimore, fashion representative of London, the second belonging to Amy Hargreaves, secretary, also of London. He pressed the metal stamp to emboss the passports, a forged embossment. 'Wilhelm especially is a fine young man, eh?'

'He is,' said Stargazer. 'My friend, thank you for everything. If we need you again, I'll let you know.'

'Of course,' said Amos. But not too often, he hoped. Business was good, business was legal, and legal was always very good. And in a day or so he would be ready to send to the *Daily Mirror* photographs of a discovery of his, the perfect girl next door.

Stargazer departed into the twilight of the September evening, and Amos was then able to close his studio and go home to his homely and affectionate wife. It had been a busy day. In Israel, he would have had a quiet day, for there he would not have been allowed to open on the Sabbath. Orthodoxy was paramount.

A little after eight that evening, Rosie and Matthew were taking advantage of the soft air of balmy dusk to spend more time at the garden table, Matt with a glass of beer to hand, Rosie with a glass of chilled white wine. Giles and Emily were watching television, and Hortense and Joe, their long and hard day over, were having their own kind of supper in the annexe.

'Penny for your thoughts, Rosie,' said Matt.

'You're welcome,' said Rosie. 'I'm thinking we should come to a definite decision about whether or not to sell up.'

Matt said they'd been good friends to chickens and sheep for some years now, but that he personally would be happy to say goodbye to them, and to the darned old foxes and their shrieking vixens. Rosie leaned and patted his knee.

'What's that for?' he asked, a smile breaking out.

'It's for thinking as I do,' said Rosie. 'We've money in the bank, and can look forward to what the sale of this freehold farm will fetch.

244

Matt old dear, after spending so much time today living in a shedful of feathers, I think I'd like a complete change.'

'Snap,' said Matt.

'You're really sure?' said Rosie. 'After all, you're a country boy at heart.'

'So's Jonathan,' said Matt, 'but he and Emma opted for a change from chickens, which suited Emma.' Jonathan and Emma had been their poultry-farm partners for several years. 'And this country boy never quarrelled with running a garage before the war.'

'And you'd like to do that again?' said Rosie.

'This time, mainly a car-repair set-up,' said Matt.

'I know we've already discussed being definite,' said Rosie, 'but let's make a decision before the weekend's out.'

'How about if I tell you now that I'd like us to talk to Sprowles on Monday with a view to selling before the summer's gone?' said Matt. 'We'd ask for Hortense and Joe to be considered, and for time to find a house.'

'Of all things, old sport, it would be careless to quit the farmhouse before we've a roof over our heads,' said Rosie.

'Take it from me, Rosie, we'll not make that mistake,' said Matt. 'We'll go looking, for a house first, and once we're in, I can go after finding a place in which to set up a car-repair workshop.' He smiled again. 'We won't, I fancy, look for a house down in Dorset.'

'Denmark Hill or Dulwich,' said Rosie, as the dusk turned into night and the stars came out. A fox barked and a vixen responded in her yowling fashion. 'D'you mind?'

'Foxes?'

'No, silly, moving nearer the family.'

'Where you go, Rosie, I'll never be far behind.'

'How sweet. There'll be no problems with Giles and Emily. Giles is a country boy himself, but his ideas don't run to chickens.'

'Giles is after building bridges,' said Matt. 'He'll end up as an architect and engineer.'

'He gets that from you,' said Rosie. 'As for Emily, she's already well off chickens.'

'Can't blame her,' said Matt, 'the world of the young is far more exciting for girls than in our time.'

'In my time as a teenager,' said Rosie, 'the world gave me everything I ever wanted.'

'I know,' said Matt, finishing his beer by the light coming from the kitchen window.

'Except you, Matt.'

'Except me, Rosie?'

'Happily, old dear, your arrival was only deferred.'

'My years with you, Rosie, have been the best.'

The clouds that had rolled away to uncover

the stars rolled back again, but Rosie and Matt still sat there, quite content. They had made an important decision together and in complete accord, and that was something to make them feel affectionately close.

At eleven, Wilhelm slipped into bed. He doubted he would sleep. Excitement was running through his mind. He thought how much he and Leila owed to Judith and Michal, the nicest of people and the kindest of hosts.

The Savile Row suit, a charcoal grey of the finest worsted, had fitted him perfectly, just as the stylish suit of honey-brown had made Leila look uncommonly graceful.

Tomorrow, London Airport and the plane to Nice.

Wilhelm lay thinking.

The bedroom door opened quietly, and was closed almost without a sound. A pale figure moved in the darkness.

'Wilhelm?' Leila whispered his name.

'Leila?'

She was beside his bed then, and wearing nothing.

'Would you still like to find out if you're a man?'

'Holy Moses, are you offering?'

'That is why I am here.'

The whispers floated.

'My God.'

'Move over, Wilhelm.'

He shifted. She lifted sheet and blanket, and slipped in beside him. He turned to her. She kissed him and put her body close to his.

It was three in the morning when she returned to her own room, her parting comment another whisper.

'You did not need to prove you're a man. You are a man, and I'm glad for you.'

Wilhelm was sound asleep ten minutes later, mind and body content.

Chapter Twenty-Two

Sunday morning.

Breakfast time for the Brown family.

'Well,' said young Lewis, going to work on his egg and bacon, 'where's the photos, then?'

'Photos?' said Freddy, dressed in trousers, shirt and braces. He would only put a tie and jacket on if Cassie wanted them to go to church. 'Who's he talking to?'

'Me, I should think,' said Maureen, wearing a pink Sunday dress.

'Yes, come on,' said Lewis, 'where's the photos?'

'Up in the sky,' said Maureen.

'But weren't they taken yesterday?' asked Lewis.

'Yes, but you don't suppose Mr Anderson developed them on our way home in the car, do you?' said Maureen.

'If he did,' said Cassie, her looks and her summery dress knocking a few years off her age, 'he's a magician.'

'He'll do them tomorrow,' said Maureen, 'and I'm going to pop into his studio when I leave work and let him show them to me.'

'Bring 'em home,' said Lewis, 'Grandpa wants to see them.'

'I don't recollect asking,' said the Gaffer, comfortable in an old open-necked shirt and even older trousers, the latter held in place by a leather belt originating with the First World War. He never threw anything away. Cassie had to do it for him, and in her time she'd disposed of some relics which Freddy said must have dated from the Battle of Waterloo. Cassie said some of them must have been in the battle. 'Did I ask?' The Gaffer put the question to Freddy.

'No, Lewis did,' said Freddy.

'We're all interested,' said Cassie.

'What photos are they?' asked the Gaffer.

'Come on, Grandpa, they're of Maureen as a pin-up,' said Lewis. 'At least, that's what she said. Here, Mum, suppose she's been telling porkies and they're only photos of

249

country birds?'

'Lewis lovey,' said Cassie, 'stop teasing.'

'Be a laugh, that would, if our Maureen brought home pictures of a skylark,' said Lewis. 'Well, she said they were up in the sky.'

'What a looney,' said Maureen. 'D'you think we went up in a balloon, then?'

'Maureen love, I hope you thanked Rosie properly for being so nice to you and Mr Anderson,' said Cassie.

'Mum, I told you I did when I got back yesterday,' said Maureen.

'Well, I do think some young people today don't have a lot of good manners,' said Cassie. 'Mind, you and Lewis aren't like that, thank goodness, but I just wanted to make sure.'

'Did somebody say something about a pin-up?' asked the Gaffer, coming to.

'Only about twenty times since Maureen first told us she was going to be one,' said Freddy.

'Clara Bow,' murmured the Gaffer.

'Ur?' said Lewis.

'Who's she?' asked Maureen.

'Hollywood film star,' said Freddy, 'and your grandpa's favourite pin-up.'

'Never heard of her,' said Maureen.

'Nor me,' said Lewis, 'and I don't consider meself ignorant.'

'Just big-headed, that's all,' said Maureen.

'Saucy sexpot, Clara Bow,' said the Gaffer

reminiscently. 'Fine pair of limbs and all.'

'Of course, she's getting on a bit now,' said Cassie, 'she must be nearly fifty.'

'Or sixty,' said Freddy.

'Poor old thing,' said Lewis, 'no wonder I never heard of her. Mind, I have heard of Queen Victoria.'

'Choke him, someone,' said Maureen.

'Who's coming to church this morning?' asked Cassie.

'I didn't hear that,' said the Gaffer.

'I'm meeting Mary Donoghue,' said Maureen.

'I'm meeting me mates Gordon and Barry,' said Lewis.

Cassie looked at Freddy.

'I'm putting a jacket and tie on,' said Freddy.

Halfway through the morning, Tim and Felicity were in their vegetable plot at the top end of their garden. They were harvesting the fat pods of green peas, Tim by sight and quick hands, Felicity by feel and touch. Jennifer was visiting a friend and her hamster, and Maggie was in the kitchen, preparing potatoes for roasting with a joint of beef. Meat supplies were improving rapidly, and so was the economy.

Felicity was lightly singing, having reached the last lines of a nursery rhyme.

'...the maid was in the garden, hanging

out the clothes, when down came a black-bird and pecked off her nose.'

'Dangerous,' said Tim, thinking how resilient she was, and brightly in tune with both the song and the sunny morning. Her recent moment of clear vision had really lifted her. 'Think about our own blackbirds,' he said. 'Cover your nose up.'

'Would you love me without one?' asked Felicity, snapping off a very fat pod and dropping it into her trug, her arm through the handle.

'Of course,' said Tim, 'I'd go as far in my devotion as to buy you a false one.'

Felicity laughed and straightened up. The movement – she supposed it was that – brought about one more blow from life's spiteful hand. It delivered into her head a piercing shaft of intense pain that almost felled her. She gasped and staggered. The trug slipped down her arm and dropped, spilling green pods. Tim, bending to the row of garden peas, came up and leapt at her, winding his arms around her. She gasped again, her face white, and sagged. He held her.

'Oh, my God, my head,' she moaned.

'Felicity? Puss?'

Felicity clung for long moments, then quivered, lifted her face, and rested her chin on his shoulder.

'I can't believe this,' she said, 'it's gone.'

'What has? Another vision?'

'No, a blinding head pain,' she said wonderingly. 'It came and it went. Tim, I think I need a drink.'

'A brandy,' said Tim. 'Come on, let's get you to a garden chair. I'll sit you down and fetch you the brandy.'

The brandy taken, she was herself a little later, but saying if her head was going to be frequently subjected to that kind of punishment, she'd opt for a blackbird pecking it off, ears, nose and all.

'And that's a fact, Tim,' she said.

'I'll tell you what I think,' said Tim. 'I think it's something to do with your eyes. Isn't an eye affliction responsible for headaches in some people, a good many people?'

'Such as strain caused by myopia?' said Felicity 'Well, I haven't got myopia, Tim, far from it.'

'But you've got an affliction,' said Tim.

'Don't we both know it?' said Felicity, grimacing. 'Is the sun shining?'

'Yep,' said Tim.

'OK, then,' said Felicity, 'I'm going to sit here and wait optimistically for a sight of it, while you go and finish picking peas. I'm pretty sure Maggie will be ready to shuck them in ten minutes. Oh, let me have a bowlful out here. I can do that many myself.'

'Right,' said Tim, 'let's both be optimistic

about you and the sun saying hello to each other.'

But he was sad rather than optimistic. It could be that the strain of all the damned ups and downs she'd suffered was responsible for punishing her head.

A woman like Felicity, equal to all that had been demanded of her during the rough and tumble of her time with 4 Commando in Troon, and every damn thing that blindness still demanded of her, was well overdue for a kind gesture from the presently bloody-minded gremlins.

It occurred to him on his way back to the vegetable plot that the assassin of Dr Rokovsky still hadn't been caught, not according to any news broadcasts. Although everything touching on the daylight execution in New York, including the arrest and then the escape of the suspect, was no longer a feature of the news, he was sure that recapture of the young Jewish man would make headlines again. On the other hand, if he had reached the safety of Israel, it was unlikely to be publicized by that State.

But if he wasn't there, where was he? Still hiding up somewhere in America? The United States, a huge land mass, could offer a thousand and more hideaways to any number of people on the run from the law. Until the trial of Wilhelm Kleibert took place in New York, Tim supposed for the umpteenth time that evidence showing Rokovsky to have been an SS doctor would not be made public. Certainly, no British court would allow its disclosure, on the legal grounds that it could prejudice a jury.

Tim resumed picking peas.

Felicity relaxed.

'Who the hell–?' Michal curbed his tongue. But the knock on the front door did make him suspicious about who was calling. He and Judith weren't expecting anyone, not until half eleven, when they were sure Stargazer would arrive on the dot.

Judith glanced at him, then at Leila and Wilhelm. They were all having morning coffee in the kitchen.

'Who is at your door?' asked Leila, tensing.

'No idea,' said Michal, but he did know representatives of the law in the UK did knock on doors on the Christian Sabbath when critical and immediate action was necessary. 'But vanish – and Judith, get rid of their coffee cups. And Wilhelm, get your luggage out of sight.'

The knock was repeated. Speedily, Leila and Wilhelm vanished, not upstairs but in the backyard, the small garden. They took their luggage with them.

While Judith put two coffee cups out of sight, Michal took himself to the front door, braced himself, and opened it.

'Vell, vhat a fine morning, Michal, ain't it?' said his stepfather, Eli Greenberg.

'Hey, Pop,' said Michal, 'what are you doing here?'

'Calling, ain't I, and don't call me Pop. It ain't respectful.'

'I'm still asking why you're calling,' said Michal.

'Vhy, can't I come round like a caring father to see you, my son, and Judith that's vith child?' said Mr Greenberg, surprisingly impressive in a fine navy blue suit and a black homburg. Mrs Greenberg insisted on presentable attire for the synagogue on Saturdays, and out of courtesy to Gentile customs on Sundays.

Eli stepped in. Michal, perforce, stood aside. He guessed why his stepfather had come. To take a look at the visitors, and to sum up if they were hard-nosed people of a kibbutz, and accordingly troublesome. Old Eli accepted most people in a kibbutz were honest and hardworking, but suspected there were always some who became too much like the men of the Stern terrorist organization, responsible for the murder of British soldiers and civilians in the late 1940s.

'Would you like a cup of coffee, old one?' suggested Michal, leading the way to the kitchen.

Mr Greenberg said he hadn't come to stay

awhile, he had only called while passing, but would be pleased to meet the visitors. Michal said they were out at the moment. Which they were. Well, out of the house, at least. But he didn't say where. Judith, seated at the kitchen table, sipping coffee, looked up at the entrance of her stepfather-in-law.

'Why, how nice, you dear man,' she said, coming to her feet, 'such a pleasant surprise. Will you have some coffee?'

'Vell, that's kind of you, ain't it?' said Mr Greenberg. 'But no. Judith, are you in good health?'

'My health is excellent, my spirits high, my expectations happy,' said Judith.

'A blessing, Judith, a blessing,' said Eli with warmth. 'But I regret not being able to meet your visitors. Michal tells me they're out.'

Judith said yes, and that she'd no idea when they would be back. Perhaps not until dinner was on the table. Eli said being out when they might have been in was a disappointment, which he would have to put up with.

'Never mind,' smiled Judith, 'here am I, and here is Michal, and we aren't a disappointment, are we?'

'Vhy, how could you be?' said Eli. 'All is fine vith these friends?'

'Old one,' said Michal, 'stop worrying.'

'I should sometimes?' said Eli. 'I should. Vell, I von't stay, no. Shalom, Judith.'

257

'Shalom, good Father,' said Judith, and Michal saw the old man out.

When he rejoined Judith, he said, 'He's suspicious.'

'And why is he suspicious?' asked Judith.

'He thinks our friends are of the wrong kind, and a worry to me. He thinks he can spot that worry every time I arrive at the yard.'

'The dear man is no fool,' said Judith, 'and it's as well Leila and Wilhelm made themselves scarce, for I'm sure your mother's husband has an eye sharp enough to confirm his suspicions.'

'You think he'd recognize our young man?' said Michal.

'I wouldn't bet on a blank,' said Judith.

'The point is,' said Michal, 'would he tell us to get rid of them or would he be sympathetic?'

'Sympathetic,' said Judith, 'but I think he'd still tell us we're making trouble for ourselves. My life, Michal, I'll be happy to see them go, as long as it means a safe journey to Israel for Wilhelm, such a good young man.'

'Well, they'll be on their way in less than an hour,' said Michal.

'For which I'll be thankful,' said Judith. 'Our home will be our own again. That prospect fills me with bliss.'

'Bless you,' smiled Michal. 'Our friends can come back in now.'

258

Chapter Twenty-Three

London Airport.

Among the passengers checking in for the flight to Nice were a well-dressed man with a neat, pointed black beard, and a shapely young woman in a very fashionable suit and a soft, trilby-style hat. He had a suitcase and a briefcase. She had a suitcase and a large handbag. He appeared absorbed in himself. She appeared interested in the people shuffling slowly forward in front of her. She was, however, almost certain she could smell security men at her back. Not that she suspected they were on the lookout for a fugitive from America. No, not that. If they were in this departure hall, it would be in connection with the cold war. The cold war was hotting up, Soviet Russia and the West fanatically suspicious of each other.

All the same, eyes might focus on Wilhelm.

Reaching the check-in for BOAC inter-national flights, Wilhelm placed the luggage on the platform and Leila handed over tickets and passports. The woman on the desk, having weighed and labelled the luggage, showed a smile as she glanced at Mr Philimore and Miss Hargreaves, and checked their passports and the tickets. She returned the passports, handed Leila the boarding cards that contained confirmation of their booked seat numbers, and wished them a good flight.

They made their way to the departure lounge, found a seat and sat down to wait for the flight to be called. Stargazer, who had been watching them from a distance, slipped away to find a viewing platform.

It was hot. At least, Wilhelm felt hot. He took off his hat and used a handkerchief to lightly dab his forehead.

'Are you nervous?' murmured Leila.

'Sure I am,' murmured Wilhelm, 'aren't you?'

'A little.'

'I guess by now I ought to be used to this kind of thing, but it still gets under my skin.'

'Go and buy a fashion magazine at the news-stand.'

'I think you should do that. By the way, is this the right time and place to tell you you have a very fine body?'

'It's something to talk about, I suppose, but it would look better if we were discussing fashion photographs in some magazine or other.'

'You'd be better at buying the right kind than I would.'

'I am not interested in fashion.'

'You should be, you look cute in that suit.'

'Cute? Cute? Wilhelm, that is like telling me I am a dressed-up china doll.'

'So sorry,' Wilhelm smiled. 'Kind of stylish, then.'

'I am not concerned with being stylish.' Leila looked around. The departure lounge was not exactly impressive. Along with the departure hall and other buildings, it was due to be replaced by a structure far more imposing. Air travel was increasing week by week. Leila could not see any obvious security men or women, but then, such people could always look innocuous.

Suddenly, their flight was called. She came alive. So did Wilhelm. Passengers rose from their seats and began to make their way to the boarding gate.

'Let's go,' said Wilhelm, dabbing lightly at his forehead again.

'Don't rush,' said Leila, and they steeled themselves to follow other passengers.

They began their walk.

A man sped after them. He called.

'Sir? Excuse me, sir.'

Leila froze. So did Wilhelm. They turned.

'Yes?' Wilhelm, who had escaped hunters for many long months, spoke the word out of a dry throat.

'You left your hat behind.' And the man handed over Wilhelm's homburg.

'Thanks,' said Wilhelm, recovering like an old hand at this kind of thing. 'I guess I'll leave my head behind one day.'

'We all do that kind of thing at airports,' said the stranger, and went smiling back to his seat.

Leila and Wilhelm went on, Wilhelm wearing the homburg. Both were conscious of feeling vulnerable.

'We are both idiots,' whispered Leila fiercely, 'one of us should have remembered your silly hat. And you were supposed to say very little here. Your American accent does not belong to an Englishman born in London.'

'I couldn't say nothing. Get the boarding cards ready.'

'Ah, now you are giving me orders?'

'That'll be the day,' said Wilhelm, and grinned.

Leila's firm lips twitched.

Not long after all that, Stargazer watched them traversing the tarmac along with other passengers heading for the standing plane. He watched them board, and he waited until the plane took off. Its engines powered it swiftly upwards into the canopy of blue sky and white clouds. It disappeared.

He left the viewing platform then, a slight smile on his dark face.

In the afternoon, Sammy answered the ringing phone.

'Hello?'

'Philip here, Uncle Sammy,' said pilot officer Philip Harrison. 'Is Phoebe there?'

'Hold on,' said Sammy, 'I'll call her.' He turned. 'Phoebe, phone.'

'Coming, Daddy.'

Sammy turned back to the phone and said, 'Are you locked up, Philip?'

'Not in the sin bin, simply confined to quarters, all leave stopped,' said Philip. Phoebe arrived, and Sammy passed the phone to her.

'Philip's on the line, pet,' he said.

'Well, bless me, not before time,' said Phoebe, now nineteen and attractive enough to compete with Maureen and any other girl who had ideas about decorating glamour magazines. But Phoebe's ideas didn't follow that course. Her environment was one of happy family life, especially that of her adoptive parents, and the aunts and uncles. Her mum and dad were so funny together, Uncle Boots and Aunt Polly so engaging. Then there was Aunt Lizzy taking such good care of Uncle Ned, as well as Uncle Tommy and Aunt Vi who had given a home to Aunt Vi's ageing mother. So Phoebe's ideas pointed her at a happy family life, as long as her chosen mate didn't order her about. Grandma Finch had once said out loud that husbands liked to be lords and masters, and it was up to their wives to keep them in their ordered place, which was to be protective and providing, and not to get above themselves.

'Hello, you there, Phoebe,' said Philip, cousin to her but not by blood.

'Oh, it's you,' said Phoebe, 'and not before time.'

'Might I inform you I phoned only a couple of days ago?' said Philip.

'Did you?' said Phoebe. 'Well, it seems ages to me. Where are you, at home?'

'Unfortunately, no,' said Philip, 'I'm in a phone booth and still inside the barbed wire.'

'Well, I don't think much of that,' said Phoebe. 'Anyone would think there was a war on, and you were surrounded by a Russian army with snow all over their tanks.'

The cold war atmosphere was responsible for that kind of remark.

'The squadron's still on standby,' said Philip.

'What for?' asked Phoebe.

'Don't ask me,' said Philip, 'ask our Prime Minister. Listen, I've had a rush of blood.'

'Oh, dearie me,' said Phoebe, 'is it hurting?'

'No sauce, cheeky,' said Philip. 'Phoebe, you're a lovely girl, even if you do answer me back, and I had this rush of blood on account of thinking you might run off with some fast-working Italian count.'

'Oh, flattered, I'm sure,' said Phoebe.

'So I want you to promise you won't,' said Philip.

'Give me a good reason,' said Phoebe.

'Marry me next year, say in the mad sunshine of summer,' said Philip, heading towards twenty-one, which he considered made him eligible as a husband for a young lady six months short of twenty. He'd spent quite some time thinking this over.

'Beg your pardon?' said Phoebe, little quivers running around her spine.

'Daisy, Daisy, give me your answer, do,' said Philip.

'Philip, you want to marry me?'

'Not half.' Philip had to put another sixpence in the call-box slot before Phoebe could respond.

'Philip?'

'I'm still here.'

'Philip, I have to ask you, will you promise to love, honour and obey me?'

'Will I what?' said Philip.

'Well,' said Phoebe through mounting quivers, 'you're an RAF officer, and you've probably got ideas of lording it.'

'Listen,' said Philip, 'any bloke who could lord it over you would have to be a walking marvel, you cheeky pussycat.' That was his favourite appellation for the bright, perky star of his Aunt Susie's household.

'Crikey, what impertinence,' said Phoebe.

But her quivers were overcoming her in shockingly weakening fashion. 'Would you mind telling me exactly why you want to marry me?'

'It's eternal love,' said Philip. 'At least, that's what it feels like.'

'Philip, you love me?'

'Like a lunatic.'

'Oh, I feel off my head myself,' said Phoebe, swamped by blissful vibrations. 'Yes, then.'

'Yes?'

'Yes.'

'Next June, say?'

'Lovely,' said Phoebe.

'Wear something nice,' said Philip.

'Like a wedding gown?' said Phoebe.

'Brilliant,' said Philip. 'Must ring off now, there's an impatient bloke knocking on the door. So long, darling pussycat, see you sometime, I hope, and when I do we'll go buy a ring.'

'My, all this is so sudden, but goodbye, Philip love,' said Phoebe. Putting the phone down, she danced her way into the garden, where Susie was cutting roses for the house, and Sammy, shirt-sleeved, pulling the mower from the shed. 'Mum! Dad! What d'you think?'

'That the roses are lovely this year,' said Susie.

'Oh, blow that,' said Phoebe, 'think about

next June.'

'What about next June?' asked Sammy.

In breathless fashion, which was only to be expected, Phoebe let them know Philip had proposed, she'd accepted, and the wedding was going to be next June. Susie looked at Sammy, Sammy looked at Susie, and they smiled. Then Susie hugged flushed Phoebe, and Sammy said although he didn't want to lose her, it would be his highly personal pleasure and privilege to give her away in due course to Annabelle and Nick's favourite son.

'Daddy, he's their only son,' said Phoebe.

'Is he?' said Sammy. 'So he is. Well, I thought there was a reason why he's favourite. And he's a good lad.'

'Wake up, Daddy, he's a man now,' said Phoebe.

'All right, me pet,' said Sammy, 'give us a kiss to celebrate he'll be old enough next June to marry you.'

Phoebe gave him one, smack on his cheek.

'Oh, you're a lovely old dad,' she said.

'I'll make a pot of tea,' said Susie, happy for her adopted daughter, although not wanting to lose her any more than Sammy did. Phoebe was the last of their children at home. Daniel, Bess, Jimmy and Paula were all married and living their own lives. Only Phoebe, so bright and affectionate, was left. And next June would see her gone. Susie felt touched. 'Yes, let's all have some tea,' she said.

Phoebe smiled. That was how all the families reacted to news, good or bad. Let's have some tea. Would she and Philip be saying that in time to come?

Probably.

Well, even though times and attitudes were now fast-changing, she didn't think any Adams would let go of every little custom or habit that had been handed down by Grandma Finch.

The extraordinary happened. The afternoon was hot, and Felicity, who disliked feeling the least bit sticky, was about to take a refreshing shower before Maggie served Sunday tea. Entering the bathroom, she reached for the waterproof curtain that closed off the shower. She groped, found its edge and pulled. The curtain ran back on its rail, and the scales fell from her eyes. As clearly as could be, she saw the white-tiled shower, its soakaway, and the chrome tap that delivered a mixture of hot and cold water. She stared at that which until now she had only known by touch. Exultation flooded her. She turned, and the bathroom itself, walled with flower-patterned tiles lightly tinted with the palest blue, enchanted her eyes. The bath gleamed and huge white towels, fluffy, hung from chrome rails.

Felicity wanted to shout with excitement.

She felt like a young girl might at seeing winged fairies emerging from a bank of daffodils. A dream come true.

She drank in the scene, then, in her birthday suit, she ran into the bedroom, to the window, and there she saw the world outside sharp and clear, as once before. The houses, the hedges, the road and the trees. The vision stayed, and she knew now, she was certain, that a blinding headache was the forerunner of sight. She was also certain the vision would fade, but this time perhaps not for quite a while. She crossed to her wardrobe, the wardrobe she could see, slid open a door and reached for her light summer dressing gown. Even a blind woman who was actually enjoying vision should not rush down to show herself naked to her husband, daughter and maid, however exultant she was.

She slipped into the dressing gown and tied the satin sash. Clear sight was staying with her, staying, but she had an instinctive feeling it was going to desert her again, and that the opening and closing was natural in the process of healing. Nevertheless, hope that vision would last long enough for her to see Jennifer encouraged her as she left the bedroom. However, when she reached the top of the stairs, and was about to descend, her instinct proved all too right. Blankness once more cut her off from her visual world.

She sighed, her lips twitched in a wry smile, and she simply sat down. But eureka, the happening had lasted for long minutes again, and she was certain, utterly certain, that clear vision would repeat itself for lengthier periods until life turned about and delivered a miracle instead of a blow.

Tim, appearing in the hall, looked up to see her sitting in her dressing gown at the top of the stairs.

'Felicity?'

'Come up and sit with me, old soldier, I've something exciting to tell you,' she said.

Although blind as a bat again, she was smiling.

Chapter Twenty-Four

Monday, and Londoners trudged back to work with their umbrellas up after a sunny weekend. Soft September rain was falling over the south-east of England, but it was still as wet as any other kind of rain. Cockneys on late-season holiday in Margate put on their macs and left their boarding houses to seek shelter in arcades and gift shops.

On the second floor of a government building in Whitehall, a semi-bald gentleman who made up for the lack of hair on his head by sporting a bushy moustache, spoke to a colleague with a handsome thatch.

'So what's the answer, Toby?'

'A lemon.'

'That's no bloody help.'

'Nor is the fact that he was recognized by a German army nurse. A West German court might query any other kind of witness, but not one of its wartime nurses. That, of course, is if he's extradited.'

'Out of order, you know that. Can this German woman be bought off?'

'I feel doubtful about that, sir.'

'Well, one thing's for certain, she can't be told the facts.'

'I suppose we could consider an arrangement that would allow for her and her family to enjoy a month in the South of France, all expenses paid, in the hope that by the end of it she'll have forgotten our man.'

'Now look here, Toby,' said the senior figure, 'I had a foul weekend, and on top of that I've got a lousy Monday morning feeling, so stop making funnies. Get our man out of the country, tell him to take a holiday.'

'He'll have to give Moscow a good reason for his absence from London. He's presently passing information on developments in respect of the Suez crisis. Incorrect developments, of course.'

Which was a reminder that the man in question was a double agent. Double agents

271

abounded on both sides of the Iron Curtain. The UK had suffered, and was still suffering, from the activities of British-born double agents, men who had become closet Communists while students at Cambridge University. Not all these men had been uncovered.

'It's his job to find good reasons whenever required to,' said bushy moustache. 'Try to get him away within a couple of weeks.'

'And what do we advise our Foreign Office friend to tell the German woman who recognized him?'

'Nothing.'

'Nothing?'

'For the time being.' Bushy moustache paused to consider the matter. 'That is, not until our man is out of the UK and out of sight.'

'Somers will phone again if he doesn't hear from us. He has to give some answer to the lady. She is, apparently, determined to be a – um – nuisance.'

'If and when Somers does phone again, tell him Professor Knox is being investigated.'

'Somers is no unimportant clerk.'

'He's a nuisance himself.'

Anneliese, waiting for something to happen, phoned Polly to ask if Boots had made any progress in respect of the man she had identified as a war criminal. Polly, recognizing a woman utterly set on bringing the man to justice, said not to worry, since she knew Boots wasn't likely to let her down. Anneliese said she was having bad dreams about the ex-SS swine, one of Himmler's fiends out of hell. Polly told her to go to bed on a glass of hot milk and dark rum, then all her dreams would be gentle lullabies.

'That is a joke?' said Anneliese.

'No, a cure recommended by Boots for heads that lie uneasily on a pillow,' said Polly.

Anneliese said she regarded Boots as a man of many good graces. Polly said if she told him that, he'd think Anneliese was a little feverish. Anneliese said she wasn't at all feverish, only sure that Boots would help her to put that ex-SS murderer away.

That induced Polly to phone Boots at his office.

'Now look here, old love, sorry to interrupt your busy business life and all that,' she said, 'but Anneliese has been on the line asking to know exactly what's happening about the frightful bounder calling himself Professor Knox.'

'Good question,' said Boots.

'Find out, there's a sweetie,' said Polly, 'and by the way, Anneliese thinks you a man of many good graces.'

'Well, I won't argue with such a delightful

273

woman,' said Boots, 'I'll accept the compliment.'

'You don't think she's exaggerating?' said Polly.

'If she is,' said Boots, 'I'll give my good graces a polishing. As for Professor Knox, I'll do some prodding.'

'Good old warhorse,' said Polly.

Boots put a call through to the Foreign Office.

The switchboard operator, sounding polite but starchy, wished to know if his business with Mr Somers was official. Official and urgent, said Boots, and Mr Somers will tell you so.

He was connected.

'I'm told a gentleman by the name of Mr Robert Adams wishes to speak to me,' said Bobby.

'Correct,' said Boots, 'while allowing for the fact that I query gentleman. Bobby, old lad, what's being done about putting the handcuffs on Professor Knox?'

'I'm glad you asked,' said Bobby, 'because I'd like to know myself.'

'Your contact hasn't been in touch?'

'My contact's failing me, Boots. That's to say no, I haven't heard from him. I'll phone him and pull rank. I'm nobody's office boy.'

'Leave it with you, Bobby. Will you ring me back?'

'Promise. You're nobody's office boy, either.'

Bobby made the call. Over the line, his contact in Intelligence greeted him like an old friend, much as if they'd been at Eton together, and went on to ask about the health of his children, the interests of his wife, and next year's holiday destination of himself and his family. Monte Carlo? Bobby smelled procrastination. He had not been taken on by the wartime SOE (French) for being simple-minded, or by the Foreign Office by reason of who his parents were.

So, in effect, he requested his contact to cut the cackle and let him know what was being done about this Professor Knox character.

'Ah.'

'Yes?'

'Professor Knox, you said?'

'Come clean, Toby.'

'Half a tick, old chap. Oh, yes, that fellow. Of course, yes. He's being investigated. I'll let you know how it turns out.'

'You'd better, or the lady with the information on him will probably knock on the front door of Scotland Yard. You could put a clamp on Scotland Yard, but not on the lady, believe me.'

'Now you know, old man, that–'

'No go, Toby. I know you're doing me a favour, but hurry up the investigation.

Nobody wants the lady to go to Scotland Yard, or worse, to phone the *Daily Express*.'

'The *Express*? Good God, are you trying to spoil my lunch?'

'I'm just hoping you'll get a move on,' said Bobby.

'I'll do my best, naturally.'

'Good. Regards to your wife, your mother and father, and your grandparents. And have a happy Christmas.'

Thus spoke the live-wire assistant of Mr Humphrey Travers, high-up official of the Foreign Office.

Bobby made the promised return call to Boots, and told him he'd put a firework under his contact and would set light to it if nothing happened by Wednesday. Boots said he was much obliged.

'Anything for you, old soldier,' said Bobby.

Boots rang Anneliese that evening to inform her that something was definitely being done about the credentials of Professor Knox. Anneliese said she hoped so, very much, since the actions of Germans of that kind were particularly shameful to her, a German woman. Memories of such men and their atrocities were like staring at chapters of a revolting book.

Boots advised her not to wear a hair shirt so close and so often, since she herself had done nothing to deserve it. You've made a new life, you've a family and you have many friends, so make the most of all that and put the war behind you, he said.

'I would still like to see that man convicted and hanged,' she said.

'Keep hoping,' said Boots, who, for all his tolerance of fools and even some villains, had no quality of mercy for Himmler's SS. He had too many sickening memories of all that he had seen at the Belsen concentration camp. He remembered now his day with Polly and his stepfather at the Nuremberg trial of the leading Nazis, including Goering, a man of cunning, graft, greed and wit, a flabby creature entirely unremorseful. It had been a day of exposed infamy.

Boots's one regret was that Hitler himself had escaped having to face up to his prosecutors and a disbelieving world. He had sent millions of his own soldiers to their deaths, but a coward himself at the end, he committed suicide. Boots frankly hoped he was living in hell.

Although the war had been over for eleven years, so much of it was still fresh in the minds of many people worldwide.

The latest family news that Phoebe had become engaged to Philip had travelled all over the grapevine. It was received with the usual enthusiasm by Chinese Lady and her extensive clan, to whom every new marriage meant a natural broadening of family ties. Down in the family's old haunts of Walworth, there were one or two people who, whenever the Adamses were mentioned, would say, 'Oh, that lot breed like rabbits, yer know.'

Chinese Lady did have second thoughts, reminding Sir Edwin that Phoebe and Philip were cousins, and wasn't it against the law for cousins to marry? Sir Edwin, as soothing as ever, said not in this case, for there were no blood ties. Phoebe, he said, was an adopted member of the family. So Chinese Lady said well, if you say so, then I'm sure it'll be all right and proper, and they're such a nice young couple.

There was also Lizzy, very much like her mother in her regard for what was proper. She had the same kind of second thoughts, which Ned tried to put at rest by emulating Sir Edwin. He assured Lizzy there was nothing in the way of preventing the marriage unless Philip jilted Phoebe, or vice versa.

'Jilted? Jilted?' said Lizzy, horror-struck. 'That's never happened to anyone in the family, it's only what rich and selfish people get up to, the kind that play fast and loose with other people's feelings.'

'There you are, then, Eliza old girl,' said Ned, 'it won't happen. Phoebe wouldn't touch fast and loose with, a bargepole, and nor would Philip.' Philip was their grandson, born of their eldest daughter Annabelle and son-in-law Nick.

'Well, that's a relief,' said Lizzy, giving her husband a comforting pat. He still suffered heart trouble, and she kept a constant eye on his movements, for overexertion did him no good at all.

Lizzy did not know it, but Philip's squadron had just received orders that meant an immediate departure to the Middle East. Philip just had time to scribble a hasty letter to Phoebe.

It was the last week of school holidays for the twins. Polly reminded them that on Thursday they were due to have their photographs taken.

'Did you say so before?' asked James, still tanned from his time in Cornwall.

'I did,' said Polly.

'Is it compulsory?'

'It is.'

'Let's see,' said Gemma, 'what's it for?'

'Monkeys,' said Polly, 'you both know very well it's for Grandmama Simms.'

'Oh, well in that case,' said James.

'We'll co-operate,' said Gemma. 'Did you say which day, Mum?'

'I did. Thursday, at two thirty.'

'Oh, I think I can manage that,' said Gemma.

'And I'll do my best,' said James.

'You will indeed,' said Polly.

'Especially as it's for Grandma Simms,' said James.

'How very magnanimous,' said Polly, 'we are overwhelmed.'

'We?' said Gemma.

'Speaking as queen of this castle,' said Polly, 'we are obliged to both of you for your promised co-operation. However, any backsliders will be beheaded. Is that understood?'

James and Gemma looked at each other, and Gemma addressed her elegant mother.

'Quite understood, Your Majesty. Crikey, aren't you posh?'

Chapter Twenty-Five

Maureen, leaving her work at the end of the day, hurried to the Green and to Mr Anderson's studio. He was there, in his office, having just finished photographing an old couple about to celebrate their golden wedding.

'Ah, Maureen, a good mood I'm in, such a happy old couple I photographed a little while ago,' he said, his smile almost a beam.

'Smashing,' said Maureen. She added teasingly, 'Happy old couples are good, Amos?'

'Delightful, aren't they?' said Amos. 'Now, you want to see your photographs?'

'Oh, not half,' said Maureen.

Amos had them on his desk, a number of contact sheets and several blow-ups.

'Come round,' he said, and she moved to his side of the desk to inspect the black and white blow-ups with him, one at a time.

'Wow,' she said. There she was, sitting on the gate, smiling, her dress and slip breeze-lifted, nyloned legs shining, stocking-tops peeping with a glimpse of lacy suspender and thigh. She liked herself very much in the pose. It showed she did have really good legs, and that her hairdo was perfect.

'Feminine, eh?' said Amos, as they inspected others, each one just a little different, but always a playful image of what a happy breeze could do to the flared skirt of a dress. 'And feminine we want, don't we, for the girl next door?'

'Feminine?' said Maureen, thrilled at the array of blow-ups in front of her eyes.

'That's it,' said Amos, 'shy but charming.'

'Shy?' said Maureen, who had never had to struggle with that handicap.

'Sure,' said Amos. 'See how you smile in that one? That is the shy smile of the girl next door.'

'Crikey, no wonder, look at me legs,' said Maureen, although she couldn't remember any moment of shyness. 'Here, Amos, I've just realized, they're all the wrong way round. I was always sitting facing right, where the

281

breeze was coming from. But you've got me facing left.'

Amos said that he'd done the blow-ups from reversed negatives, so that they showed her as she would see herself in a mirror, which pleased the eye of some sitters, especially pin-up girls. See, he said, if we had had a large mirror there, you would have seen yourself as you usually do in one.

'So, how do you like that, Maureen?' he said.

'Smashing,' said Maureen. 'Amos, d'you think they're really good, good enough to get published?'

'Charming, aren't they?' smiled Amos. 'With a touch of the unexpected.'

Maureen asked what the unexpected was. Amos said the playful breeze. Girls next door didn't sit on a gate with the deliberate intention of showing their legs. A breeze that lifted their skirts was most unexpected, and, of course, embarrassing. Pin-up fans will like that, he said.

'So are you going to send some to the *Daily Mirror?*' asked Maureen, eager for fame.

'That is what we want, don't we?' said Amos.

'You bet,' said Maureen, and looked at the contact sheets, five of them, and each consisting of twelve shots. 'Crikey,' she said, 'all these.'

'It's to make sure we get a selection of very

282

good ones,' said Amos. 'In fashion, many famous photographers will take sixty shots of a model in order to get the perfect one.'

'Is that what they're famous for, taking sixty photos just to get the best one?' asked Maureen, thinking that one day a fashion photographer might take sixty of her in a Paris-designed creation.

'They're famous for producing the perfect one, which is what they want, don't they?' smiled Amos. 'See, these contact sheets show I've taken sixty of you, all but one of a lamb. So all these blow-ups are of the best, eh?'

'Oh, I do like them,' said Maureen. 'Could I have some to take home and show me family?'

'Of course,' said Amos. 'Take six, the ones you like the most, and keep them. I'll put them in an envelope for you, and I'll be in touch.'

'About what the *Daily Mirror* says?'

'Keep your fingers crossed,' said Amos, pleased with the results, pleased with himself, and pleased with his versions of a girl next door.

Maureen, of course, was just as pleased when she left with the envelope and six shots.

Cassie, Freddy and Lewis all crowded round to look at the depictions of Maureen as the shy girl next door sitting on a gate and showing her legs. Shy according to Mr

283

Anderson, said Maureen.

'Well, my goodness,' said Cassie.

'They don't look like you, Cassie, when you were next door to someone,' said Freddy.

'I can't see anything shy,' said Lewis, 'just Maureen's legs, and I've been seeing them all me life.'

'The *Mirror* readers haven't,' said Freddy, whose experiences of hard life and jungle warfare were too broadening for him to play the heavy and disapproving father. If Maureen was set on a glamour-girl career, why not? There was more money in that than as one more insurance copy typist.

'I must say they're ever such good photos,' said Cassie, 'but look what that breeze is doing to her dress, Freddy.'

'Legs ahoy,' grinned Freddy.

In came Cassie's good old dad, the Gaffer.

'Supper ready?' he said.

'In a minute, Dad,' said Cassie, 'we're just looking at Maureen's photos.'

'Her pin-up ones,' said Lewis, a bit tickled by his sister's ambitions.

'Eh? What?' said the Gaffer, and pushed his head in to take a look. 'Well, strike me pink, it's Clara Bow, ain't it?'

'It's your granddaughter,' said Freddy.

'Yes, me, Grandpa,' said Maureen, 'don't you think they're kind of fab.'

'Fat?' said the Gaffer.

'Fabulous,' said Lewis.

'Blow me,' said the Gaffer, 'if that's our young Maureen, someone had better pull her skirt back in place.'

'But, Grandpa, they're what's called leg shots,' said Maureen.

'That and a bit more,' said the Gaffer, 'so don't let Mrs Hobday see 'em.'

Mrs Hobday was a neighbour, a buxom body with a heart as large as her bosom. She was also a retailer of gossip and little titbits of scandal. One could say she carried them from door to door without putting a strain on her weight.

'She's a good old girl,' said Freddy.

'I don't recollect ever seeing her legs,' mused Lewis.

'Well, sit her on a gate and watch the wind blow,' said Freddy.

The Gaffer chortled, Cassie prepared to put supper on the table, and Maureen replaced her photographs in the envelope. She glanced at her dad.

Freddy gave her a good-luck wink.

It's nice having a broad-minded mum and dad, thought Maureen. If Jane Elkins, one of her friends, ever showed her legs in a magazine or a newspaper, her mum, for a start, would probably order her out of house and home, and her dad, to finish with, would probably chuck her suitcase and her favourite records after her.

That made Maureen think of all the lively

young people and their parents she'd met at the sixtieth birthday party of the man they called Uncle Boots. None of the girls there were ordered out of the house for dancing like crazy to the rock 'n' roll records. It had been a riot of fun and laughter. Maureen fell a bit for one young man called Jimmy Adams, but what a let-down when she found he was married to the girl he was dancing with most of the time. A girl by the name of Clare.

Oh, well, there were lots of nice blokes all over, and some rich ones up West.

Phoebe received the short letter from Philip the following morning and waved it about at the breakfast table.

'Would you believe it?' she said.

'Well, I can see it, Phoebe love,' said Susie, 'but I don't know what's in it.'

'That Philip,' said Phoebe witheringly, 'one day asking me to marry him, and next day, good as, telling me he's off to see the world, like some ancient mariner.'

'He's bought a boat?' said Sammy.

'Daddy, be your age,' said Phoebe, in temporary neglect of her breakfast cereal, 'he's a fighter pilot, not a sailor.'

'Well, you said – no, never mind.' Sammy hid a grin. 'What's the problem?'

'His squadron's going abroad,' said Phoebe.

'It happens, pet,' said Sammy. 'But he'll be back.'

'Yes, but when?' Phoebe attacked her cereal half-heartedly. 'I could be a lonely maiden stuck at her spinning wheel for goodness knows how long. Mum, that's not funny.'

Susie was laughing. 'And I don't know why you're grinning like a Cheshire cat, Daddy.'

'It's lonely maidens,' said Sammy.

'And spinning wheels,' said Susie.

'It's still not funny,' said Phoebe, frowning. 'I mean, just when we've got engaged, that's not a bit funny. Suppose he's not back by next June? I'll be there, waiting at the church with no bridegroom. I'll look like a leftover dummy.'

'Of course he'll be back by then, Phoebe love,' said Susie.

'RAF units often have to go overseas for exercises, but not for very long,' said Sammy. Neither he nor Susie had the Suez crisis on their minds. It was something the Prime Minister talked about in Parliament, but Susie hadn't been interested in any Prime Minster since the retirement of Winston Churchill. And Sammy only read, or paid attention to, news items about the economy and anything that related to business prospects. Or on how his favourite sporting teams were doing. 'We've still got a bit of an Empire, y'know, pet.'

Phoebe's smile was a little weak.

'Oh, well, it's something I'll have to get used to, Philip being moved about,' she said. 'And I wouldn't want him to leave the RAF until his time's up. Without being a bit goofy, I must say he looks as sexy in his uniform as Kenneth More.' Kenneth More was a rising screen and stage star who had made a name for himself in the hilarious film *Genevieve*.

Susie smiled. To the younger generation of girls, any bloke who had real man appeal was called sexy. In her day, the word had been swell for a bloke, or stunning for a girl.

'Sexy, yes,' she said. 'Sammy, were you ever called sexy when you were young and walking in the park in your best Sunday suit?'

'No, I was only addressed in regard to me generous inclination to treat a girl to tea and a bun,' said Sammy, 'which made some 'orrible holes in the trousers of me best suit, I can tell you. Anyway, glad to see you cheering up, Phoebe. Don't forget you and your mum can organize some regular shopping visits to our branches. That'll keep you perky.'

'Shopping for what?' asked Phoebe, still thinking of, not being able to talk to Philip on the phone for quite a while.

'For your bottom drawer,' smiled Susie. 'I think that's what your dad meant.'

'And not forgetting you'll get a handsome family discount,' said Sammy.

Phoebe's bright spirits took over.

288

'OK, Mum, let's do that now and again,' she said, 'I don't think I really want to sit around with some old spinning wheel.'

Rosie took time off to go to Camberwell and have lunch with Boots at his usual pub. She'd arranged it with him over the phone.

When Boots arrived at the pub from his office, Rosie was already there, seated at what she knew was his favourite corner table. She was dressed in a cream-coloured lightweight jacket and matching skirt, with a snowy-white shirt-blouse and a loose navy blue cravat. Her little round hat, also navy blue, had an upturned brim. Apart from her healthy outdoor complexion, few people would have thought her a farmer's wife up from the country. Boots, who had never lost his special feelings for his adopted daughter, thought her delightful.

He leaned, kissed her cheek and said, 'Well met, poppet, are you early or am I late?'

'I'm early,' said Rosie. 'Oh, I've ordered an old ale for you and a glass of wine for myself. And a ham salad for both of us. How's that for a start?'

'Perfect,' said Boots, placing himself beside her on the cosy, padded bench seat. 'As usual, you look a walking wonder, and your hat's a little gem. How are you, Rosie?'

'How am I?' Rosie smiled. 'All the better for seeing you, old darling.'

'If that's the case, am I to assume there's something wrong at the farm, then?' asked Boots, hoping nothing unhappy was touching her life.

'Something wrong? No, not at all,' said Rosie, 'I made a mistake if I gave that impression. Simply, old dear, I do like seeing you.'

'I'm touched,' said Boots.

'You're welcome,' said Rosie.

Joe, the everlasting barman, brought the drinks then, together with a smile for his most regular customer.

'Thanks, Joe,' said Boots.

'Pleasure, Mr Adams, salads coming up,' said Joe, and returned to his white, marble-topped counter, as old as the pub itself, and unlikely to be replaced by something modern from a plastics factory.

'So what did you want to talk to me about, Rosie?' asked Boots.

'The future,' said Rosie, sipping white wine and taking in the old-world atmosphere of this ornamental saloon bar, which had remained unaltered for many a year.

'Whose future?' asked Boots, and took a welcome swallow of his beer.

'Mine and Matt's' said Rosie.

'What exactly does that mean?' asked Boots, always interested in the shifts and turns of Rosie's life.

Rosie waited until the salad and condiments arrived, then went into detail about the proposed sale of the farm. 'Alas that I have to confess Matt and I have lived with chickens long enough,' she said. Boots smiled. Rosie could say 'alas' without sounding melodramatic. His French daughter Eloise could say something as humdrum as 'Oh, dear,' and sound as if the house was about to catch fire. Eloise was always excitable, Rosie usually in control of herself and events. The differences between them were entirely diverting. At least, he thought so.

'Carry on,' he said.

Rosie went on to say as long as Sprowles, the firm interested in acquiring the farm, agreed to keep Hortense and Joe on, she and Matt would negotiate the sale. Matt would like to run a car-repair workshop, and she herself felt she might be useful to a thriving business firm willing to take on an old lady of forty-one. Boots said some, old ladies of forty-one didn't look their age. Some firms, in fact, would take on some old ladies for their looks alone.

'Leaving aside all the flannel,' said Rosie, enjoying her salad, 'what kind of firms do you. have in mind?'

'Your kind,' said Boots.

'My kind?' said Rosie.

'That is, where would you prefer to point yourself, young lady?' said Boots.

'Young lady?' Rosie laughed. 'That's stretching it a bit, isn't it?'

291

'Not from a man of my age,' said Boots.

Rosie smiled.

'Tell me,' she said, 'how well is the family firm doing at the moment?'

Boots looked at her. Rosie returned his look. Eyes met eyes, smile met smile. Rosie's cards were patently on the table. Boots was not going to quarrel with that. Far from it.

'I think we've got a classic situation here,' he said. 'Two minds with but a single thought. Very classic.'

'So?' said Rosie.

'Come into the business,' said Boots.

'Is that a serious invitation, or a kind gesture?' asked Rosie.

'Charity might begin at home, poppet, but not between you and me,' said Boots. 'I'm serious, believe me. Come into the business.'

'Well, that I'd like, very much, especially if Matt and I could find a home nicely south of Camberwell,' said Rosie, 'but I have to be serious too about your invitation. I'd need to be taken on for what I could contribute, and not because I'm family. You might like this hat I'm wearing, but I'm not going to be just a hat around the offices.'

Boots assured her that even a bowler hat wouldn't be acceptable, unless it had brains in full working order. Sammy was against paying wages to empty noddles. Further, said Boots, the firm was doing exceptionally well, and he and Rachel were so loaded with work at times that he was convinced they'd need an assistant any moment, a position that wouldn't mean merely answering the phone or sharpening pencils.

Rosie said she counted that as glad news, but in the event, could she possibly come in on a part-time basis, from nine until three, while Emily and Giles were still at school? She didn't believe, she said, that children should come home to an empty house. Boots remembered his own schooldays, and those of his sister and brothers. Chinese Lady had always been there on their arrival home, and so had a warm glowing fire in the days of winter. So had a cup of hot tea and a slice of cake. It was that kind of simple principle that built up the strength of a family.

'That won't be a problem, Rosie, we'll settle for part-time,' he said.

'Aren't you a lovely bloke?' said Rosie.

'Lovely's coming it a bit,' said Boots, 'I'll settle for obliging.'

'And I'll settle the lunch bill,' said Rosie.

'Out of order,' said Boots.

'Not on this occasion,' said Rosie. 'It was at my suggestion, and I was here first.'

'Still out of order,' said Boots. 'How's Matt, and how are Emily and Giles?'

'Matt's as fit as a gypsy's fiddle, and is going to talk to Sprowles again sometime today,' said Rosie, 'and Emily and Giles are like your two, they're growing up and having a lot to say for themselves.'

'I see.' Boots smiled. 'Much the same as all the other young people in the family. Much the same as Sammy was in his teens.' He mused. 'And as your grandma will certainly tell you, as I was.'

Rosie laughed. Other patrons looked. Older coves thought back to the days when they'd have put on their best suits and braces for so attractive a woman, and worn a carnation in one of their buttonholes.

'It's my belief, Boots,' she said, 'that when you and I are really old, South London will be populated by Grandma's descendants, and all of them making themselves heard.'

'There's already an extra family in prospect,' said Boots. 'Phoebe's marrying Philip.'

'So I heard,' said Rosie, 'from Annabelle. Well, Phoebe's sweet and, according to Emily, Philip is definitely very sexy.'

They said goodbye outside the pub a little later, Boots asking Rosie to keep in touch concerning events, and Rosie assuring him she would.

'So long, then, poppet.'

Rosie laughed again. Passengers on a bus beginning its climb up Denmark Hill glanced at her, and wondered, no doubt, why she was so amused.

'I think I'm the only forty-one-year-old poppet in the Western world,' she said. She kissed Boots, asked him to give her love to

Polly, then left to walk to the parked family car. She turned when she reached it, and waved a gloved hand. Boots reciprocated, watched her slide into the car, and waited until she drove away. He then crossed the road to the offices, thinking that of all his nearest and dearest, Rosie was with those at the top, as she had always been.

Chapter Twenty-Six

On her way home, Rosie stopped to call in on Grandma and Grandpa Finch. Chinese Lady, opening the door to her, showed one of her rare smiles.

'Rosie love, what a nice surprise,' she said in frank pleasure. Chinese Lady had a very special affection for Rosie who, as a girl of five, neglected and abandoned by her shallow mother, had endeared herself to Boots and Emily, and to the whole family.

'I was passing and couldn't resist dropping in, Grandma,' said Rosie, kissing her. 'How are you, and how's Grandpa?'

'Oh, we're fine,' said Chinese Lady, closing the door. The spacious hall of the large, three-storeyed house on Red Post Hill was imposing with its oak-panelled walls and polished parquet flooring. The house was worth far more than it had cost Edwin when he purchased it during the Twenties.

'Edwin's in the garden, reading a book about Napoleon, but I don't know why. Wasn't he a blessed warmonger, like that man Hitler?'

'Not quite like Hitler,' smiled Rosie, 'although they had one thing in common. They were both corporals in their younger days.'

'A pity both of them weren't done away with at the time,' said Chinese Lady in one of her moments of death-to-the-ungodly. 'Well, come and say hello to Edwin, Rosie, and if you've got time, I'll put the kettle on.'

'Sweet of you, Grandma, but I've only just finished having lunch with Boots,' said Rosie, 'and that included two glasses of wine. But I've time to sit in the garden with you and Grandpa for a while, then I must get home.'

They went through to the garden. Sir Edwin, relaxing comfortably in a deckchair on the patio, looked up as the ladies emerged from the kitchen. He put his book down and came to his feet, and Rosie thought that even at eighty-three he was still a distinguished man. A little thinner, perhaps, a little more lined, but his silvery hair was suffering no loss, and his colour was really quite good. If any man knew how to grow old gracefully, Sir Edwin did. Such a wonderful couple, he and Grandma, and so devoted. Each was of the old school. But then, so are Boots, Lizzy,

Tommy and Sammy. And so am I.

'Rosie, such a pleasure to see you,' said Sir Edwin, wearing an old-fashioned striped blazer, white shirt, blue tie, and dark blue trousers. The blazer was inimitably English. Perhaps it represented its wearer's affection for England and English customs and traditions. Boots was still the only member of the family to know his stepfather had been born a German. 'My dear Rosie,' smiled Sir Edwin, 'you look quite delightful.' He kissed her.

'Thank you, Grandpa,' said Rosie, 'and you look wonderful. You both do.'

'My, how kind,' said Chinese Lady. 'Mind, I suppose I'll feel my age one day, but I don't feel it yet. Sit down, Rosie love, and you can give us all your family's news.'

They all seated themselves, the day warm and bright, although rain was forecast for tomorrow. Rosie spoke of the decision she and Matthew had made in respect of selling their farm. Chinese Lady said she was never more surprised, but of course Rosie and Matthew would know what they were doing. Mind, she said, Rosie and Matthew were the only ones she knew who had gone in for bringing up chickens. She'd had a tame rabbit herself when she was young, which she kept in a hutch in the backyard, and when it died her dad lifted up one of the paving stones so's they could dig a grave for it and give it a proper burial, which they did. She used a kitchen skewer to scratch 'RIP' on the paving stone.

'Very touching, Maisie,' smiled Sir Edwin.

'But of course, a rabbit's not the same as chickens,' said Chinese Lady.

'Nor does it have feathers,' said Rosie.

'Rosie, my dear, when you sell up,' said Sir Edwin, 'what comes next for you and Matthew?'

'Matt wants to go back to poking about in cars, to running a repairing workshop,' said Rosie, 'and I'm going to take on a part-time job for the family firm. It has to be part-time while Emily and Giles are still at school.'

'You're going to work for Boots and Sammy?' said Chinese Lady.

'Boots assured me I had talents that Sammy would welcome,' said Rosie. 'I'm happy to believe him. So there you are, as soon as the farm has been sold, and we've found a new home, I'll be ready to enter the firm. I'm delighted.'

'You're going to do some house-hunting?' said Sir Edwin.

'We must,' said Rosie.

'Where?' asked Chinese Lady, who always interested herself in the location of family members. She had a quaint idea that related families ought to be within walking distance of each other, or at least only a bus ride away. It was almost a grief to her that Bess,

Sammy's eldest daughter, had settled down in Kent with her American husband, Jeremy Passmore, and that Alice, Tommy's daughter, was living in Bristol with husband Fergus MacAllister. To Chinese Lady, these places were almost like foreign parts. To many other families, the farther away they were from certain relatives, the better they liked it. Australia was a good place for some. But Chinese Lady, of course, was Victorian in her clanish outlook. 'Where, Rosie?'

'Somewhere around here,' said Rosie.

Chinese Lady looked happily at Edwin.

'Rosie,' he said, 'it's not for us to help you decide, that's for you and Matthew alone. But it so happens there's a rather handsome house some way up from us. We know the owners, the Clayburns. They're moving to Guildford in late October, and will be putting their house up for sale any moment now.'

'Really?' said Rosie, quick to give it thought. The location was splendid, the hill and the immediate area exclusively residential, roads and avenues tree-lined. The prospect of an early acquisition might save her and Matt from weeks of looking for something suitable and well located. 'It's a fine family house, Grandpa?'

'If you have time right now, Rosie,' said Sir Edwin, 'why not take a little walk there with me? I always think the exterior of a house is the first thing a purchaser should find pleasing. Certainly pleasing enough to invite a full inspection of the interior. If you like the look of the place, Rosie, I'll speak to Mr Clayburn this evening, and ask him if he'll show you over before he puts it up for sale.'

'I've time to take a look,' said Rosie, not in the least averse to the prospect of living near her grandparents. 'And I'd like to, very much.'

'Let's all do the little walk,' said Chinese Lady.

Which they did, once she had put her hat on. Never, from the time when she first began to wear hats, had she been seen out of doors without one. It simply wasn't proper.

It was a measured, seven-minute walk up the hill for Chinese Lady and Sir Edwin, and from the gate Rosie took a long look at the frontage of the house, built of warm, russet-coloured brick and red tiles, the tiles mossy. There were two storeys and a loft, or attic, with an attractive eyebrow window. A porch led to the oak door, which was central, and the windows of the ground and first floors were latticed, giving the house an old-world charm. It was fully detached, and a garage had been built to the right of the property.

'Grandpa, I'm impressed,' said Rosie. 'I like it enough to want to look it over with Matthew.'

'You're really interested, Rosie?' said Sir Edwin.

'Seriously so,' said Rosie. 'I'll talk to Matthew.'

'Then I'll have a word with Mr Clayburn,' said Sir Edwin. 'He may be delighted with the prospect of finding a buyer before putting the sale in the hands of an estate agent.'

'Well, won't that be nice for everyone?' said Chinese Lady, more than happy at the possibility of having Rosie and her family close by.

'We'll see how things work out, Grandma,' said Rosie. 'Now, I really must get home.'

Chinese Lady and Sir Edwin walked back with her to their own house, Rosie noting that her grandmother was still upright, her grandfather still quite able. She said goodbye to them at their gate, then entered her car and drove away, a gloved hand gesturing in farewell out of the open window.

'Such a nice girl,' murmured Chinese Lady.

'Girl, Maisie?'

'Well, you know what I mean, Edwin.'

'I know,' said Sir Edwin. It meant that the matriarch of the Adams clan never allowed herself to accept that certain members of the family had grown up.

'It's as well you never knew her wretched mother, a woman that never gave her own child any love, and thought only about herself,' said Chinese Lady, still standing at their front gate with her husband. 'I couldn't hardly believe it when Boots told me she'd gone off and left Rosie, and the child only five. Even Boots – well, you know how airy-fairy he is about people and their faults – even Boots hated her for that.'

'I think, Maisie, that when Rosie's mother abandoned her, it was perhaps the best thing that could have happened,' said Sir Edwin. 'It gave Boots and Emily the chance to adopt her and care for her.'

'Well, I'm glad to hear you say so, Edwin,' said Chinese Lady. 'Let's go in now, and I'll make us a pot of tea. You'd like a nice cup of tea, wouldn't you?'

'Maisie, you are the most civilized woman on earth,' said Sir Edwin.

At that moment, a dizzy spell took hold of him, and suddenly his legs seemed about to lose control. He faltered a little as he followed Chinese Lady into the house. Saying he had a letter to write, he managed to slip into his study off the hall. Chinese Lady, going straight through to the kitchen and her kettle, said she'd call him when she was ready to pour the tea.

In the study, Sir Edwin sank gratefully into his desk chair. He was dizzy indeed, and his legs felt as if they did not belong to him. With his body slumped, he asked himself a question. The uphill walk, although taken slowly, was that responsible? Yes, probably, that and my age, he thought, amid the giddy sensations afflicting mind and limbs.

He sat there, applying himself sensibly to a

302

complete relaxing of his body and faculties. His elbows on his desk, his face resting in his hands, thoughts intruded. If his time was up, he could not complain. His life had been long and adventurous. He had known Imperial Germany at the height of its glittering martial pomp, Berlin alive with colour, uniforms and military bands, its Kaiser a figure of self-important majesty. His years in espionage for the German Secret Service, more especially the years spent as an agent in England, had had a profound effect on him. Eventually the time had come when, disillusioned with the Kaiser and his warlike generals, and their conduct of the First World War, he had defected to England to serve the country he had come to admire and care for.

Since then, he had known the happiness of his marriage to Maisie and his acquisition of a ready-made family, a family entirely remarkable. He admired no man more than Boots, a cherished friend who had kept his every secret.

No, he could not complain.

His mind, clearer, acknowledged that fact.

'Edwin?' Maisie was calling. 'I'm just going to pour tea.'

He straightened his body. Magically, it was no longer threatening to fail him. The dizzy spell had gone from head and limbs. In quite exultant relief, he came to his feet, and all morbid thoughts and maudlin reflections made their exit. He smiled. Perhaps he had a little more time left, after all.

'Coming, Maisie.'

Old Mrs Blake of Walworth had been a friend and neighbour to Chinese Lady for years before and after the First World War. She was over eighty now, and so was her husband, who had once driven one of London's horse-drawn coal carts.

Mr Blake was having a little nap in an armchair at this moment, while his old lady entertained an unexpected visitor, a woman in her sixties who had dressed herself up in an attempt to look younger.

'Well, me memory ain't what it was,' said Mrs Blake, after ten minutes of chatting with the visitor, 'and I don't have much recollection of you, but I'm beginning to get a sort of vague idea you did live close to Mrs Adams and her family.'

'Oh, I was a real friend to them, dearie,' said the visitor, 'but I ain't seen much of them since I had to go away due to me circumstances at the time. You sure you don't know where I can find some of them?'

'I could ask around,' said Mrs Blake, whose memory really was failing her. Otherwise, she'd have remembered a lot more about her visitor. 'Yes, I could do that for you. There's still some neighbours that might know.'

'Well, ain't you kind?' said the dressed-up

304

woman. 'Um, I suppose you couldn't give me a bed for a couple of nights, could yer, ducky? Only I'm right down on me luck, me old man having passed on a year ago.'

Mrs Blake, born like many Walworth people to be neighbourly and hospitable, especially to those suffering a hard time, said, 'Oh, we can find you a bed all right, just for a couple of nights, except I hope you won't ask me to make up the bed for you in the mornings.'

'Well, I might be down on me luck, dearie, but I know me natural obligations.'

'Well, you're welcome, then, and while you're here, I can do me asking around,' said old Mrs Blake.

'I must say that's real kind of you, and I won't be no trouble.' The visitor emitted a little laugh. It sounded a bit cracked. 'I'm past me high-kicking days. Well, I was on the stage for a bit, yer know.'

'My, you must tell me about it,' said Mrs Blake, scenting some interesting titbits of a saucy nature. She might be over eighty, but her hearing, unlike her memory, wasn't failing, and she was still game for taking in a fund of such titbits.

She listened to some while her old man napped on.

Bobby received word from his contact in Intelligence that Professor Knox had slipped them. Bobby expressed his disgust forcefully, and the telephone line, shocked at having to transmit such undiplomatic language, almost fell apart. Certainly, for a brief moment, it blurred a word or two. However, British Intelligence, represented by Toby, took in Bobby's earful, and responded by suggesting that that kind of language was a bit off, old man. Bobby said the Foreign Office would send a note of protest to the Home Office at such unbelievable incompetence.

'Look, do we want a hornets' nest flying about, old chap?' said Toby.

'Find the bugger,' said Bobby.

'I say, what's happening to the Foreign Office? Oasis of calm, usually. None of us can touch you fellows for good manners. Usually.'

Bobby said his good manners were taking a holiday, and wouldn't get back until Professor Knox was limited in his movements by an old-fashioned ball and chain.

'Find him.'

'Look here, old fellow, I must point out–'

'That you don't take orders from the Foreign Office? I know all that, so don't bother. Who let go of Knox's collar?'

'Ah, yes. Well, as I understand it, he was in urgent need of his bathroom, and while we were letting him relieve himself, he climbed out of the window and disappeared.'

Bobby couldn't believe he was being given

a chestnut as old and as hoary as that. Something was going on, something that didn't add up.

'I've a feeling you're giving me fairy stories,' he said, 'and I stopped listening to those on the day I found out Daddy Christmas didn't come down our chimney.'

'Oh, my dear old mater put me wise to that not long after I was out of my cradle. Very practical woman, you know, and no-nonsense stuff. Sorry about naughty Knox, but we'll do what we can to find him.'

'I'll be sending a uniformed messenger round between now and tomorrow morning,' said Bobby. 'With a shotgun.'

'I like your sense of humour, old chap.'

'You won't like it when the German lady arrives on the doorstep of the *Express*,' said Bobby, and hung up.

Curse it, he thought. The Foreign Office, of course, was officially supposed to stay in its own backyard. But it could still exert influence. In a case like this, however, only with the approval of the Foreign Minister himself. And that important bloke was presently locked in daily with the Prime Minister while they discussed the Suez crisis. The possible uncovering of a German war criminal was of minor importance, anyway. Thousands had been uncovered since the end of the war, and one more would be of no great interest.

So what should Boots tell Anneliese now?

Chapter Twenty-Seven

Rosie, arriving back home, was greeted by the news from Matt that he'd had a long phone conversation with Sprowles, and that agreement had been reached, including the company's willingness to retain the present workers, namely Hortense and Joe. Sprowles would be writing to confirm everything, including the purchase price of £7,500, two thousand more than Matt and Rosie had originally paid for the freehold of land and farmhouse. Matt had told the kids, who hadn't been in the least upset. Both seemed to feel that chickens and sheep didn't rate as much as the teenage world that was going on outside a chicken run. They were into this rock 'n' roll gig.

'Gig?' said Rosie.

'That was the word Emily used,' said Matt.

'I think teenagers are inventing a new language,' said Rosie. 'Matt, what about Hortense and Joe, did you tell them?'

Matt said yes. The prospect of working for new employers had laid them back on their heels for a moment, he said, but they liked it here, they liked the work and their only regret would be in having to say goodbye.

Rosie said she would hate it if the idea had made them miserable. We must, she said, give them a large handshake, say fifty pounds each. Matt agreed. His mind was pleasantly fixed on his new venture, a car-repairs workshop, which would do away with those nights when lambing time brought him out of bed at two in the morning to deal with foxes prowling in search of the helpless new-born. Sprowles would sell off the sheep and increase the chicken yield.

'How did your lunch with Boots go, Rosie?'

'Happily,' said Rosie, and told him that the lovely old warrior had offered her a job with the family firm on a part-time basis. Matt asked if she was really keen to commit herself to a job outside the home. Rosie said yes, she couldn't stomach the idea of having nothing to do after years of so much mental and physical activity on the farm. House-work would only take up a small part of her time. Then she informed Matt she'd called on Grandma and Grandpa Finch on her way home, and described the house they had looked at on Red Post Hill.

'A whizz,' said Matt.

'Whizz?' said Rosie.

'Meaning great, according to what Emily and Giles will probably say,' said Matt.

Rosie laughed.

'Well, I suppose we ought to learn their

language,' she said, 'or we'll get left behind in this new world.'

'If Grandpa Finch can help us not to get left behind in the house-hunting race,' said Matt, 'that'll be something to celebrate.'

'Is there an old Dorset saying for that?' smiled Rosie.

'There be an old Dorset saying for everything,' said Matt. 'In this case, "Down by Dorset land a man needs much more than strawberry jam, for his family housing calls for a roof and four good walls." Durn my shirt tails, Rosie, how about that?'

'Corny, but acceptable,' said Rosie, 'and hang onto your shirt tails.'

Boots was talking to Sammy, and Sammy was listening with both ears.

'It's definite, Rosie and Matt are selling up?' he said, interest sparking.

'Definite,' said Boots, 'and as soon as they're settled elsewhere, Rosie will be joining the firm as assistant to Rachel and myself, and Matt will be after a place he can convert into a car-repair workshop. So now, Sammy, what does the property company own in the way of an undeveloped site?'

'For sale to Matt? Hold on.' Sammy phoned through to the property office. 'That you, Daniel? Good, come and see me, will you, you and Tim?'

The joint managers of the property

310

company presented themselves to Sammy and Boots, and were asked about undeveloped sites. Was there one that could be sold to Matt and turned into a garage and workshop? Tim said there was, in Peckham High Street, and accordingly well worth considering. But Matt was still bringing up lambs and chickens, wasn't he?

'Not for much longer,' said Boots, and explained in detail.

'Well, shoot my hat off,' said Daniel, 'our Rosie joining the firm, and Matt going back to pulling cars to bits? I'm chuffed.'

With an eye to business, Tim said the company would like a quick decision, since various contractors were interested in the Peckham site, and he and Daniel had been playing one off against the other in order to get the best offer.

'What's your best offer so far?' asked Boots.

'Good question,' said Sammy.

'Five thousand,' said Tim.

'And what did we pay for it?' asked Boots.

'Two thou, two hundred, two years ago,' said Daniel.

'Congratulations,' said Boots, dry humour uppermost. He looked at Sammy. Sammy nodded. 'Offer it to Matt for three, Tim.'

'Seriously?' said Tim.

'Matt's family,' said Sammy.

Daniel said, 'Might I remind you elderly gents that Tim and I are entitled by terms of our contract to receive twenty per cent of all profits on all site sales? Ten per cent each?'

'Ignoring your saucy reference to elderly gents, which your grandma wouldn't like,' said Sammy, 'Matt's still family.' He looked at Boots, and it was Boots's turn to nod. 'Keep fifty per cent of the profit, which, if me mental equipment is still working, means two hundred quid apiece.'

'That's welcome talk,' said Tim.

'Well, you're family too, you and Daniel,' said Sammy.

Matt received a phone call later from Tim, who asked if it was true he was after a site for a garage and workshop. Matt said yes. So Tim told him a site in Peckham High Street was available. Would he like to come and look at it? The property company could offer it to him for three thousand.

'Damn me,' said Matt, 'three thousand? I thought I'd have to fork out far more than that for the right kind of site. It's not a postage stamp, is it?'

'We only buy postage stamps for sticking on envelopes,' said Tim. 'Call here as soon as you can, and I'll take you to see the site.'

'Tomorrow morning, say about ten?' suggested Matt.

'You're on,' said Tim.

'Who's responsible for this offer?' asked Matt.

'The family,' said Tim.

Boots, having been advised by Bobby that Intelligence had lost Professor Knox, phoned Anneliese during the evening. It was her husband Harry who answered the call.

'Hello there, Boots,' he said in amiable greeting. Harry was so easy-going that he was a pushover for his precocious daughter, Cindy. 'Let me guess, are you going to tell me something satisfying about the Professor Knox character? Anneliese is bathing Harry junior at the moment, as you can probably hear?' Their infant son was thirteen months old and lusty-lunged.

'Give mother and junior my regards,' said Boots. 'As far as Professor Knox is concerned, however, the blighter's slipped the investigation, apparently.'

'That'll please Anneliese, I don't think,' said Harry, and they talked about his German wife's certainty that Professor Knox was an SS war criminal who had escaped the Allies.

There was a young German Jew, thought Boots, just as certain, it seemed, that the ophthalmic surgeon he had shot dead in New York had been a fiendish SS doctor at Auschwitz. Wilhelm Kleibert had also slipped away. From American police custody. Incredible that Polly was sure she had seen him at the photographer's studio.

'Tell Anneliese that I don't intend to leave it at that, Harry,' said Boots, which meant that Bobby was going to continue worrying his contact, since he thought something fishy was going on in the murky bowels of a certain government building.

'I'll tell her,' said Harry. 'Thanks for calling. Regards to Polly and the twins. So long now.'

'Before you hang up,' said Boots, 'how's your new thriller coming along?'

'Painfully,' said Harry.

'I've heard that some authors go through fire and water with every novel they write,' said Boots.

'Oh, they're the soul-searching kind, I imagine,' said Harry.

'And what does that mean?' asked Boots.

'That they suffer agony if they find they've split an infinitive,' said Harry. 'I split several on every page, and hope no-one will notice.'

'They passed me by in your first thriller,' said Boots.

'What a pal,' said Harry.

Subsequently, when passing Boots's message to Anneliese, Harry rather expected her to lose her cool. She could remain cool under all kinds of circumstances, but never when reminded of what Hitler, Himmler and their infamous SS battalions had done to Germany. On this occasion, however, her calmness prevailed.

'He won't escape,' she said.

'Knox won't?' said Harry.

'The man who calls himself that,' said Anneliese.

'Why are you so sure?' asked Harry.

'Instinct,' said Anneliese.

'Hold onto that, then,' said Harry, 'I think it's called feminine intuition, and I'm told it's highly reliable.'

Wednesday.

Mr Humphrey Travers of the Foreign Office regarded his chief assistant thoughtfully. Bobby was used to that look. Old Humph was never lost for thought.

'Ah, Somers my dear fellow.'

'I'm in the soup?' said Bobby.

'Good heavens, perish the idea. I merely wanted to point out that that extraordinary young man – um, Wilhelm Kleibert – need no longer worry us or the Home Secretary, if the latest rumour is true.'

'What rumour, sir?'

'That Kleibert is now in Israel.'

'He's made it?' said Bobby.

'It's only a rumour, of course,' said old Humph.

'There's been nothing in the press,' said Bobby.

'It's possible that *The Times* will ask questions, but I'm sure the Israeli government will deny the rumour.'

'Which could mean it's true,' said Bobby.

'We shall accept the denial,' said Mr Travers.

'Best thing,' said Bobby.

'Quite, quite.'

In Tel Aviv, Wilhelm was being fussed, congratulated and honoured, all on the quiet. There were promises of a new identity and a well-paid position with an organization devoted to the uncovering and hunting down of Nazi war criminals.

In her apartment, Leila was in confrontation with Zeke Freyer, her lover.

'You're telling me it's over between us?' he said.

'I'm telling you exactly that,' said Leila.

He protested vigorously and argued heatedly. The crunch came when he asked her if there was someone else.

'Come on, is there?'

'Of course. Someone who wishes to marry me.'

'But you're not the marrying kind.'

'True. But it's what he wishes, and I've said yes.'

'The hell you have. Who is it?'

'Wilhelm.'

'Wilhelm? Wilhelm who?'

'Kleibert. Goodbye, Zeke.'

Chapter Twenty-Eight

The following day, in the time-honoured fashion, Rosie and Matt killed two birds with one stone. Together, in company with Tim, they saw the Peckham site, found its potential excellent and its location, in the heart of busy, bustling Peckham, all that Matt could have hoped for. He clinched the deal with Tim, and at the offices he and Rosie left a dozen freshly-dressed chickens for the family.

In the afternoon they looked over the house on Red Post Hill, its owner, Mr Clayburn, giving them a guided tour. The place was in perfect order, apart from some rear window frames that needed replacing, and the garden was large and well kept. Rosie and Matt accepted Mr Clayburn's asking price, thus avoiding any timewasting, which suited Mr Clayburn very well.

'Once a week,' said Mrs Hilary Shoesmith, 'my depression lifts delightfully.'

'And what would you say was the reason?' asked Professor Knox, fluent, well-spoken, soothingly professional, and sheltered under the umbrella of MI5. Any suggestion that he had slipped some kind of investigation was someone's porkie. But porkies did fly about when it was necessary to protect a useful double agent.

'The reason? Why, you must know it's my weekly consultation with you,' said Mrs Shoe-smith, a lady in her mid-thirties. She was extremely attractive, but also neurotic, and in Professor Knox she had found a psychiatrist very much to her liking, so sympathetic, so understanding, so uplifting. And so handsome. He never suggested at any time that her troubles were of her own making, as her previous consultant had. 'Doctor, I so look forward to my appointments with you.'

'I'm here, dear lady, to do all I can for every patient,' said Professor Knox, regarding her with a soothing smile. The couch he provided for his patients was a sofa with red plush upholstery and restful head cushions. Mrs Shoesmith lay there, expression dreamy, body relaxed inside a silk dressing gown. She always insisted on undressing down to her lingerie, since the removal of her outer garments, she said, removed her troublesome inhibitions and freed her mind. Professor Knox, careful of his ethics, insisted in turn that she wear a dressing gown. Which she did. On this occasion, the gown had parted to reveal a glimpse of her nyloned legs.

'You do wonders for me,' she murmured.

'It's satisfying to know these consultations lift your depression,' he said. 'Does it return

318

as soon as you get back to your home? You have said it does. Does it still?'

'Unfortunately, yes,' she said. 'Every room in my home resembles four walls that always seem to be closing in on me.'

'As a child, did your parents ever put you into a dark cupboard as a punishment for being naughty, perhaps?' His voice was a vibrant baritone untouched by any accent, although he had been born in Bavaria. He was a natural linguist. He spoke Russian, Hungarian, and French, as well as English and his own tongue.

'My parents adored me and gave me everything I ever wanted as a child.' The patient's voice was murmurous and silky, rather like that of a woman imagining herself in the arms of a lover. 'So I never had cause to be naughty.'

'You suffered nothing in your childhood or at college that caused fits of angry resentment or deep depression?'

'Nothing, dear doctor.'

He passed the unwanted endearment by. As for his doctorate qualifications, these were represented by a splendid forgery. His practice of psychiatry was an amusement to him, as well as a cover.

'You've told me that your periods of depression began two years ago,' he said. 'And that this condition became permanent six months ago, when it began to affect your marriage. Is that still the case?'

'It's hardly a marriage any longer,' she murmured.

'Why?' What a silly woman she was, deluding herself into believing she was suffering depression when her state was only boredom.

'I no longer enjoy making love,' she said. A pause, a turn of the head, and an inviting smile. 'Except I know I would with you.'

'Madam, you must know I don't want to hear that kind of response.'

'But I'm sure it would help me.'

'It would destroy my practice,' he said, 'and you know that too.' He looked at his watch. 'The hour is up, and this is the right moment to end it, I feel.'

He stood up. Mrs Shoesmith's smile was still inviting.

'The same time next week?' she said. Her consultations were always from three to four in the afternoon, and the last of the day for Professor Knox. His hours were from ten to four, with an hour's break for lunch. He had other work to perform, the kind that had nothing to do with analysing the minds of confused men and bored women.

'Unfortunately, I can make no appointments for a little while,' he said, 'I'm taking a holiday.'

She made a face.

Outside, a well-dressed, broad-shouldered man was speaking to the receptionist.

'Is my wife, Mrs Shoesmith, with Professor Knox at the moment?'

'Yes, sir,' said the receptionist, an entirely innocent party.

'Right.'

'No, sir, wait, you can't go in.'

But Mr Shoesmith wrenched at the handle of the door to the consulting room. He flung the door open, and burst in. He saw his wife on the sofa, her right leg slipping from her dressing gown, foot on the floor, her hand extended in a gesture. Professor Knox, leaning, was about to take her hand and help her to her feet, as far as he would go in physical contact with any patient.

'Bitch!' Mr Shoesmith shouted the word at his startled wife. 'So this is your lousy love nest, is it?' Then he shouted at Professor Knox in the usual way of cuckolded husbands. 'You filthy swine!' He hurled himself at the psychiatrist, and struck him a violent blow in the chest. Professor Knox fell backwards, and his head made crushing contact with the white-painted metal radiator. The central heating system was off, the radiator cool, but still as hard and rigid as steel could be. The violent contact of the back of Professor Knox's head with the radiator smashed his skull, and red blood spattered the white paint. The victim slumped and lay lifeless.

The man had not been killed because of being a war criminal or a double agent working for Communist East Germany and Britain, but for what Mr Shoesmith thought him to be, his wife's lover. Which he was not. And death, though violent, had been accidental, for Mr Shoesmith had only sought to beat him up.

Mrs Shoesmith screamed and fainted.

Mr Shoesmith stared down at the body, at the seeping blood, his eyes transfixed, his face white.

There was another scream. This time from the receptionist, who then rushed to the phone on her desk and called the police.

Only High Omnipotence knew what the gods of mercy thought, but perhaps they considered the death, albeit by accident, of ex-Colonel Tomas Neumann of the Waffen SS, alias Professor Knox of Mayfair, not entirely undeserved.

From the West End police station, a sergeant and a constable were on the spot in quick time. Mr and Mrs Shoesmith and the lady receptionist were in paralysed shock, Professor Knox indisputably a corpse. The police constable phoned for an ambulance, and he also contacted the dead man's doctor, while the sergeant asked necessary questions. The receptionist answered stammeringly, Mrs Shoesmith answered faintly, and Mr Shoesmith answered like a man standing stricken at the gates of hell.

Mrs Shoesmith and the receptionist were able to confirm death had been caused by the victim's head smashing against the radiator, and its blood-spattered paint was further evidence of this. Nevertheless, the police sergeant said he would have to report the matter to the CID.

When the doctor arrived, the ambulance crew were examining the dead man. The doctor took over. Mrs Shoesmith, fully dressed by now, was huddled on the couch in a distraught condition. Mr Shoesmith was still on his feet, but looked only a ghost of his usual self. The police sergeant and constable were waiting for the arrival of CID colleagues.

A man, casually attired in an open-necked brown shirt and camel-coloured slacks, entered the house and walked into reception. The receptionist was there, seated, elbows on her desk, face in her hands.

'Excuse me,' he said.

She looked up, her eyes bleary with lingering shock and tiredness.

With an effort, she said, 'The consulting room is closed.'

'Well, yes, it usually is at this time of the day, I know,' said the caller, 'but is Professor Knox available? I need to see him.'

The receptionist struggled to overcome emotion.

'I'm afraid – I'm afraid that isn't possible. Are you a friend or–'

'An acquaintance.' The man saw the open door to the consulting room, and his ears picked up the sound of voices. 'Is Professor Knox entertaining?'

'Oh, God, I wish he was,' said the receptionist, and broke down. The man, kind and persuasive, elicited stumbling information from her. His manner, matching his clothes, changed. The receptionist's head sank eventually, and she buried her face in her hands again.

The police constable, coming out of the consulting room, found her sobbing. No-one else was there. She was quite alone.

The time at that stage was close to five thirty. Government departments in Whitehall were disgorging Civil servants. However, some people were still at their desks.

The following morning, when Bobby picked his daily paper off the mat, his eye was caught by a short report at the bottom of the front page. It concerned the death of a well-known London psychiatrist, one Professor Knox. He had been attacked in his consultancy by the husband of one of his women patients, had fallen heavily and suffered a fatal skull fracture. The police were investigating the tragic incident.

'Jesus,' breathed Bobby.

'Breakfast, Daddy, breakfast,' sang Estelle from the kitchen.

Well, thought stunned Bobby, one bloke who won't be enjoying cornflakes and toast is Professor Knox.

He kept quiet about this dramatic news over breakfast. It wasn't something to be talked about in front of his children. When Helene saw him to the door on his way out to the station, he spoke a few words to her.

'Look at the front page of our *Telegraph*.'

'Why?' asked Helene.

'That bloke, Professor Knox, has had a nasty accident. He's dead.'

'Dead?'

'He is, according to that report.'

'Well, I'm not going to weep for him,' said Helene. 'I shall tell Anneliese, and I'm sure she won't weep, either.'

Bobby grimaced, kissed her, and departed.

'So we've lost him,' said the senior man, the one with the bushy moustache.

'By an unfortunate accident,' said his deputy, the man called Toby.

'If you'd managed to get him out of the country, that accident would have been avoided.'

'He was making arrangements to go. He'd cancelled all his appointments for a month.'

'It's a stinker, Toby, a stinker. You've spoken to Scotland Yard?'

Toby said yes, he had, last evening. He was still at his desk when in came the man who

325

had spoken to a shocked receptionist. From him he had received the news of Knox's unfortunate demise. Scotland Yard had said it looked like death by accident, but there'd be complications if the coroner's inquest returned a verdict of manslaughter. Bushy moustache said bloody hell, a criminal court case could leave all kinds of dirty washing hanging on the line. The press would start ferreting. The last thing the department wanted to be made public was even a hint that a German war criminal had been turned into a double agent by the UK for the benefit of the UK.

'The Home Office would slap a restriction order on the press, sir,' said Toby.

'But, possibly, not until some damned rag printed an opener. For God's sake, Toby, do something to ensure the accident to our man is played down by the Yard.'

'I also perform miracles in my spare time,' said Toby, 'and we'll need one if the inquest does return a verdict of manslaughter.'

'You're going to turn my fishing weekend into one in which the fish won't bite,' said bushy moustache. 'What about the nuisance from the Foreign office?'

'He's nothing to worry about now, nor has the German lady. If they've read their morning papers, they'll know Knox is dead.'

'Pity. Very useful agent. However, his death gets the Foreign Office chap off our back.'

All the same, Toby received a phone call from Bobby half an hour later. Bobby wanted to know if the press report was definitely true, or a put-up job manufactured for some reason entirely dubious.

Toby assured him that dubious really was out of order, old chap, and that it could be arranged for him to inspect the body, in company with the German lady, if that was what she would like. The body was in the freezer, and would remain there until the inquest was over. And the police were satisfied that death was accidental, that the husband of the woman patient only intended to give Knox a bloody nose.

'So you see, my dear fellow, everything straightforward and above board, although very unfortunate for Professor Knox.'

'Tell me,' said Bobby, 'how did he come to be at his practice?'

'Mmm?'

'You informed me he'd slipped your investigation and was probably out of the country.'

'Ah. Yes. Yes. It seems he slipped back under our noses for some reason or another. We'd called off our bloodhounds at the time.'

'Now tell me the one about Goldilocks and the Three Bears,' said Bobby.

'Of course, even though he's now a stiff, we'll probably continue our investigations into his background. By the way, my dear chap, heard from your old pal Guy Burgess lately?'

Bobby ground his teeth. Burgess, now in Moscow, had worked for the Foreign Office. He'd favoured Communist Russia since his time as a student at Cambridge University. During his years at the Foreign Office, he had supplied Moscow with a feast of valuable information. When he realized British Intelligence was beginning to investigate him, he fled to Moscow with another of his ilk, another Cambridge man, Donald Maclean.

Cambridge was still blushing, and so was the Foreign Office.

Bobby, irked but unblushing, said, 'Next time we have lunch together, you old bugger, I'll think of something painful to shove up your waistcoat.'

'Yes, let's have fun, mmm? Oh, give my regards to the German lady. She's a splendid woman, I'm sure.'

Chapter Twenty-Nine

Boots had called on Anneliese on his way to work.

'You've seen your morning paper?' he said.

'Harry saw it first,' said Anneliese. 'It

astonished him, and yes, myself too. But, Boots, our very good friend, I'm sure that to please me you didn't actually hire the patient's husband as a hit man, did you? That is right, a hit man? Harry says so.'

Boots, standing with her in the hall, laughed. She liked the sound. Men such as Harry and Boots had an infectious baritone vibration to their spontaneous laughter.

'A hit man? I think not, Anneliese.' Boots sobered. 'That poor devil seems to have been the victim of unhappy circumstances. I doubt if he meant to kill Knox. The police are investigating it as accidental death.'

'Well, dear Boots,' said Anneliese, 'I wish him well, and I wish the dead man a long stay in hell with Himmler. In any case, somehow or other, I feel you waved a magic wand.'

'I also dance with fairies,' said Boots. 'Whatever, you can now put Knox right out of your mind, and live your life with your family. Oh, by the way, you're all invited to my mother's eightieth birthday knees-up next Saturday week. Sunday is the actual day, but the family's organizing the event to begin at six on Saturday evening, and we'll toast her the moment her old Westminster chimes mantlepiece clock strikes the last note of midnight.'

'Boots, how lovely, we'll all be delighted to be there.' Anneliese sparkled with pleasure. 'But a knees-up? What is a knees-up?'

329

'You'll find out,' said Boots, and departed smiling.

Rosie, invited by Mr and Mrs Clayburn to inspect the house again, did so. She wanted to take note of exactly what kind of new furniture was necessary, and what items of her existing furniture would fit in.

On her return to Woldingham in the late afternoon, Matt emerged from the farm-house kitchen as soon as she alighted from the car.

'Matt, I've a list of–'

'I think you'll have to keep it for later,' said Matt. He grimaced. 'There's a woman here who says she's your mother.'

'What?'

'I hope to God she's not,' said Matt. He knew all about Rosie's life, from her lonely and desolate childhood through her years of happiness as the adopted daughter of Boots and his first wife, Emily. In the farmhouse now, gulping tea, was a woman old, painted and raddled, a creature who had said that, as Rosie's natural mother, she'd come to live with her. He gave Rosie an outline.

Rosie might have come out with some-thing totally at odds with her civilized self. Instead, she spoke quite calmly, if firmly.

'She's not my mother. My mother, Mrs Emily Adams, is dead.'

That denial of her natural mother was not

the first. She had made it before, on other occasions. Right from the day when Boots and Emily took her in and later adopted her, she had seen them alone as her true parents. She had loved them from the beginning, particularly Boots, to whom she genuinely felt she belonged as if born of him. Although she eventually discovered her natural father, Charles Armitage, was an entirely likeable man, he remained secondary to Boots. His indiscreet dalliance with a flighty young woman called Milly Pearce had occurred in the heady atmosphere of August 1914. It resulted in Rosie's birth, unknown to the father at the time.

Charles Armitage was eventually killed during the Western Desert Campaign of the Second World War, and Rosie, who had come to care for him, was genuinely saddened by his loss, and emotionally touched to find he had left her the sum of twenty-five thousand pounds to ensure she never wanted.

The woman of her childhood, Milly Pearce, she had put out of her mind years and years ago.

Heavens, was she really here, in the farmhouse?

'Who's that, who's there? Is it you, Rosie?' The questions came from the kitchen, the voice both whining and ingratiating, and its owner appeared at the open kitchen door.

Rosie could not believe her eyes.

331

The woman wore a bright pink dress, a dress fashioned for the young, not the old. And old she was, her face rouged and powdered, her mouth a lipsticked slash, her hair bleached to a brittle blonde. If ever old mutton had been dressed up in the hope of looking like lamb, this was an example of hope impossible.

Peering curious eyes took in the picture of Rosie, neither painted nor bleached. Her complexion was nature's handiwork, her hair a natural corn-coloured gold.

Matt, repelled by the visitor, said, 'I asked you to wait in the living room.'

'Now don't be like that,' said the old hag. 'I need a bit of comforting now I'm down on me luck, don't I?' The eyes peered again at Rosie. 'Here, who's that? She ain't me daughter, is she? Come on, where's me little girl, where's me Rosie?'

Hortense was feeding meal to the chickens, Joe transferring the sheep from one field to the other. Both had seen the strange woman, and both were keeping their distance. Giles and Emily were out with friends, making the most of their last holiday week before returning to school.

The visitor was staring, staring at the well-dressed woman standing by the car. Rosie hadn't moved. But she spoke then.

'I'm Rosie, Mrs Rosie Chapman. Who are you?'

'Well, my, ain't you fancy, Rosie, and all grown-up? You look like you've done well for yourself. I'm your mother, come to pay you a visit.'

'You are not my mother.' Rosie was still quite calm. 'I've just reminded my husband that my mother, sadly, is dead.'

'No, I ain't Rosie love, I'm standing right here.' Mutton hopelessly dressed up as lamb essayed a wheedling smile. It parted the red slash. 'I know I'm not as young as I was, but I'm your mum all right, so come and give us a kiss.'

Rosie felt utter distaste. She was very much like Boots in her ability to ride life's unpleasanter moments, and to tolerate misfits, but there was nothing about this particular misfit she could accept. There was no love, no affection, no caring.

'I'm sorry, but I recognize only one woman as my mother, and that isn't you,' she said.

'My, Rosie, ain't you proud and haughty?' The pink dress shimmered on the thin body. 'Mind, it does me eyes good to see how well me daughter's done for herself. It's always hurt me that I wasn't able to bring you up meself, owing to me hard-up circumstances, and it near broke me heart when I had to give you up to be adopted, didn't it? But I told meself it was best for you, didn't I?'

Matt's grimace had become permanent. He felt too helpless to intervene. This

333

confrontation had to be decided by Rosie.

Rosie had only a dim recollection of what her mother had looked like. Her memory recalled a vague figure of oppression, a woman forever finding fault, a woman who obviously wished her child had never been born. She regarded her now as an apparition both repellent and totally unwelcome. She asked a question, quietly but witheringly.

'Tell me,' she said, 'how much were you paid for your sacrifice?'

Boots and Emily had handed over several hundred pounds before this woman would agree to sign the adoption papers. Rosie had found that out from Grandma Finch.

'Now don't be hurtful, Rosie,' the crone whined. Matt looked on in disgust. He knew what this must be doing to Rosie, and his one instinct was to bundle the old bitch off the premises with money to pay her fare back to where she had come from. Rosie owed her nothing, nothing at all, but the cost of the fare would be willingly forthcoming. What was the woman saying now? Again that she was down on her luck, that she only had her widow's pension. Yes, her husband'd passed on last year. Rosie remembered him, didn't she, Mr Rainbould, Mr Clarence Rainbould?

Rosie said she had no recollection whatever of the gentleman. Boots could have told her that Clarence Rainbould had been a second-rate conjuror and magician, but Rosie had never asked questions about either her natural mother or the man she married in the hope of going on the stage herself.

'No, I don't recollect him in any way.'

'My, don't you talk nice and educated, Rosie? I can see that letting you be adopted was best for you, even if it did grieve me something painful. You can give your old mum board and lodging for a while, can't you? And a bit of money for odds and ends, can't you, dearie?'

'Absolutely not.' Rosie was still in control of herself. 'You must understand that I mean it when I say I don't regard you as my mother, which is entirely your own fault. How did you find my address?'

'Rosie love, I wish you wouldn't keep saying I ain't your mum. As to finding where you lived, well, old Mrs Blake and some neighbours down the street helped me. My, she's gone to seed a bit. Me; I've always tried to keep meself looking smart, specially when I was doing stage work with me husband. I've had a hard life, Rosie. It was always a struggle for me and Mr Rainbould, but I always kept hoping that one day we'd be comfortably off so's I could bring you back and give you the kind of life I always wanted to but couldn't afford.'

'I'm sure,' said Rosie, gently sarcastic. She sighed. What was she supposed to do? Strangely, as the voice of self-pity whined on, she felt the onset of pity herself. Perhaps this woman had had a hard life, perhaps her attempt to make herself look younger than she was pointed to a struggle for self-preservation. All the same, what could be done about such a wreck?

Matt did intervene at that point, thinking correctly that Rosie would like to talk to him. He addressed the tarted-up woman.

'Would you like a drink?'

That hit the jackpot. An eager smile opened up the red slash and cut the rouged face in half. False teeth gleamed.

'Well, I would, mister, I ain't touched a drop for a week and more. Mind, I'm not one of your soaks, I just like a small glass now and again. Would you have some gin handy?'

'Come inside,' said Matt. He glanced at Rosie, indicating she was to stay where she was. Then he took the painted widow through to the living room. He reappeared a few minutes later. 'She's settled with a glass and the bottle, Rosie. So now, what's on your mind?'

'What to do for her,' said Rosie, 'and I think I'd like to phone Boots. He knows far more about her than I do or you do, believe me. Would you mind if I spoke to him?'

Matt knew she was asking him to accept that her adoptive father was the best one to consult.

'Go ahead, Rosie darling, use the extension phone in the shed.'

'Thank you, Matt.'

Not long after that, Boots took a phone call in his office.

'Rosie, that's you?'

'Yes, Daddy darling.' That was Rosie as a girl, as a woman. 'Can you spare a few minutes?'

'I can always spare unlimited time for you, poppet.'

'I badly need your advice,' said Rosie, and went on to tell him her natural mother had turned up, looking for board and lodging at the farmhouse. Boots, stunned for a moment, came to.

'God Almighty,' he said.

'You'd say a lot more than that if you could see her,' said Rosie. 'She's well past her best, if there ever was a best, but, dear man, how can I simply send her away? On the other hand, how can I let her stay? I shudder at the effect it would have on Giles and Emily.'

'Give me a moment to think,' said Boots.

'Take all the time you want,' said Rosie, 'but this really is a cry for help.'

There was an interval of silence at the other end of the line before Boots spoke again.

Then he said, 'There's one thing that counts in her favour, Rosie, the fact that she gave birth to you. Whatever she was herself, she gave birth to a child of sweetness and light, for which I personally will be forever grateful.'

Rosie, gulping like a child, said huskily, 'Are you trying to make me cry?'

'No, poppet, only suggesting you and I, and Matt, owe her something, after all.'

'Don't tell me you think Matt and I should give her a home with us.'

'Perish that hideous thought,' said Boots. He suggested there was one way out, to give her twenty pounds now and to begin with, and then make arrangements with her bank to pay her thirty pounds a month on her assurance that she would find herself lodgings and stay there. The arrangement would stop the moment she attempted to foist herself on Matt and Rosie. That might sound hard, but it was no more than reasonable, and if he was any judge of her character, the thought of an allowance of thirty pounds a month would make her jump through hoops to get at it.

'Oh, you lovely man,' breathed Rosie, 'she would get that on top of her widow's pension. Thank you, darling; for being what you are.'

'And what am I?' asked Boots, his smile in his voice.

'My dear and caring father. Don't you know even now that you were born for me, and I was born for you?'

There was another little silence before

Boots said, 'I only know I love you, poppet, that I always have and always will. What more could I ask of life? Rosie, you and Matt have heavy expenses to meet in the immediate future, and if it would help for me to take on the payments to–'

'Nothing doing, old sport,' said Rosie, still a little husky, 'the interest I get from the property company for my investment will easily take care of that.'

'Quite sure?'

'Yes, you old darling, and what would you like for a Christmas present?'

'Well, since you ask, a Christmas card and a bottle of fine old malt whisky. By the way, if Matt has a bottle of gin to spare, tell him to give that to the old lady, along with the twenty pounds, and I'll guarantee she'll toddle off as happy as a Billingsgate fish porter heading for a pub.'

'Aren't you a clever old soldier?'

'That's your imagination, poppet. Phone me again if you need to. Regards to Matt, love to the kids.'

'Goodbye, Daddy love, and a thousand thanks.'

Chapter Thirty

Parental advice had been taken, with Matt's approval, and the deed was done.

Mrs Milly Rainbould, carrying a suitcase containing her worldly goods and a wrapped bottle of gin, and with twenty pounds stuffed eagerly into her handbag, boarded a train at Woldingham railway station, it would take her to London Bridge, and drop her close to the pubs and lodgings of Southwark.

Matt, who had driven her to the station, stood on the platform, determined to see the train depart, and her with it.

The train began to move, its old but still gleaming engine puffing smoke. The compartment window jerked down. A face appeared, and in the fading afternoon light its paintwork looked as if it needed repairing. The red slash opened.

'Here, dearie, tell me darling Rosie I'll be all right now, and give her a kiss for me.'

'Look after that gin,' said Matt.

The face moved back a little as the train pulled out, but there were still more words to come.

'Oh, I will, ducky, it's me consolation. Ta-ta.'

The face disappeared. The train gathered speed. Matt watched until it was out of sight, then he walked back to his car and drove himself home. Giles and Emily had just returned from their outing, and Rosie was asking Emily to mind her manners. The girl was grabbing at fruit buns made by Hortense.

Matt little knew Rosie's suspicions of her daughter's tendency to take after the raddled old bag had suddenly hardened.

'Everything fine, Matt?' she asked, thankful that her good-tempered husband had hastened the departure of the woman before the boy and girl returned.

'Fine, Rosie, fine,' said Matt. He saw her relief. 'So's this piece of old Dorset doggerel. "Down by Dorset land they say, old folks come and often stay, best then to do more'n pray, by sending such folks on their way."'

'Passable,' smiled Rosie.

'But what's it mean, Dad?' asked Giles.

'Nothing much,' said Matt.

'Why'd you say it, then?' asked Emily.

'Because I'm a Dorset man,' said Matt. 'Here come Hortense and Joe, so let's put the kettle on for a cup of tea, shall we?'

'I'll do it, Dad,' said Giles.

Later, when he and Rosie were comfortably alone, Matt said he'd seen the old biddy off for certain, since he didn't think she'd jump

341

off the train in case it damaged the bottle of gin.

'I still feel upset that she turned up,' said Rosie.

'I'm not surprised,' said Matt. 'I tell you, Rosie, it beats me all ends up that a woman like her ever managed to give birth to you. I'm giving thanks to Boots for adopting you, and for working out how to deal with the woman. He couldn't bring himself to call her Rosie's mother, any more than Rosie had ever been able to regard her as such. 'First-class solution, burn my braces.'

'You really didn't mind my talking to him?' said Rosie.

Matt came up from his armchair, moved close, bent and kissed her.

'I've never minded anything you've ever done, Rosie, and you know, don't you, how much you've always meant to me? There's no other Dorset man ever been as lucky as I've been.'

Rosie smiled.

'Is there an old Dorset saying for that too?'

'Surely,' said Matt. "Down among the Dorset men, there's women sweet and tall, but for him, the luckiest, there's one the best of all."'

'You're forgetting something,' said Rosie.

'Am I?'

'Yes. You're forgetting I'm the luckiest. I'm closely related to the two best men ever born. My husband and my adoptive father.'

Matt kissed her again. Like Boots, and like Rosie herself, he saw how marriage could develop into cherished companionship.

It was that which Chinese Lady was enjoying with Sir Edwin in the twilight of their lives.

The photographs of the twins had been taken by Amos Anderson without his studio having trembled and tumbled by reason of their unbounded energy. Indeed, neither he nor Polly had found it necessary to curb them. They were astonishingly co-operative. Well, the fact of the matter was the chosen portrait was for Grandma Simms, a lady of charm and generosity. The twins could always rely on super birthday and Christmas presents, together with postal orders of munificent value. It was not the gifts alone, however, it was the affection they had for their maternal grandmother that made them behave perfectly during the sitting.

Polly, having chosen the shot she and her stepmother liked best, called on Amos to collect the finished item. He had fixed it into the frame she had also chosen. The whole thing was frightfully expensive, although not as far as Polly was concerned. She liked it far too much even to think about the cost. There they were, the twins, seated back to back, heads turned to face the camera. Gemma was dreamy-eyed, James showing the lightest of smiles, these expressions induced by Amos during the sitting, the head and shoulders portrait perfect.

'Lovely, Mr Anderson, lovely,' said Polly, 'but can these two angels really be the imps I encounter at home?'

'Imps we like, Mrs Adams, don't we?' said Amos. 'And, Mrs Adams, will you accept from me two whole plate prints of the one I took of you with your twins?'

He had persuaded Polly to pose with Gemma and James for the last shot on the roll of film. Polly did resist persuasion initially, for she was no longer enamoured of herself as a subject for anyone's camera. She was sure she would come out looking her age and, horrors, even worse. Polly was not growing old gracefully, but very reluctantly. Perhaps there were times when she thought Boots's eyes might wander to a younger woman, although she rarely doubted his fidelity. He was, and always had been, his Victorian mother's son.

However, she gave in to persuasion, which came not only from Mr Anderson, but from Gemma and James too. So just the one shot was taken, and there it was of herself and the twins. She had thought their youth would emphasize her decline, but wonder of wonders, there was no frightful comparison, no crow's feet, no lines and no neck wrinkles. Not that she yet had any of the latter, although she was sure they would arrive one day. No, everything was so smooth and complimentary that she looked years younger than she was.

'Mr Anderson, how did you get such an effect?' she asked, delighted not only by her own image, but by those of the twins too.

'Mrs Adams, by reason of my sitters, didn't I?' said Amos, keeping to himself, of course, that he had delicately touched up both prints by deft and artistic use of an airbrush. Such a fine woman, a true lady, deserved a little help. 'You would accept them as a gift from me?'

'I'd be delighted,' said Polly, 'but will pay for you to frame them, as you have with the twins' portrait.'

'Well, well, then we shall both be delighted, won't we?' said Amos. 'If you have time to spare, I'll frame them now.'

'Thank you,' said Polly, 'one for my husband and one for my mother.'

'A moment, then, while I get the frames,' said Amos, and disappeared.

Polly, seated at his desk, which was heaped with all kinds of photographic paraphernalia, noticed a photograph beside his hat, under which was his phone. It took her attention, and she could not resist turning it.

A picture of a girl sitting on a gate, her dress fluttering, her nyloned legs showing,

345

came to her eyes. Deliciously saucy, and yes, she actually knew the girl. Cassie and Freddy Brown's daughter Maureen. Polly, no prude, smiled to herself. She turned the photograph back round.

Amos reappeared, with the frames. He sat down, dismantled the frames and inserted the photographs. He showed the finished results to Polly.

'Perfect,' she said. 'Thank you so much, Mr Anderson. Now, how much do I owe you altogether?'

Amos quoted the cost, informing her there was a discount of twenty per cent on the two frames she had just ordered. The amount was still high, but Polly said she considered he had more than earned his charges and wrote him a cheque there and then.

'Sometimes, Mrs Adams,' he smiled, 'sometimes my work, which is always a pleasure, is more so, isn't it?'

'And sometimes a customer is more than satisfied,' said Polly. 'Mr Anderson, do forgive me, but I couldn't help noticing that photograph of a girl on a gate. You see, I know her. She's the daughter of old friends of my husband.'

Amos positively beamed.

'Maureen Brown? Well, well, a small world, isn't it?' he said. 'I photographed her for the *Daily Mirror* or other newspapers or magazines as a girl next door–'

346

'Excuse me?' said Polly.

'Yes, don't you see?' Amos showed her the print. 'Shy, but appealing, isn't she?'

'Shy?' Polly laughed. 'Young Maureen?'

'I'm hoping she'll come to represent the country's girl next door, which we both would like,' said Amos, his smile containing a twinkle.

'I'm fascinated,' said Polly.

'Happily,' said Amos, 'I've just received a letter from *Weekend*, a Saturday paper, to which I sent shots similar to this one. I've just heard from them to say one will be published next Saturday. I must now let Maureen know.'

'Will you do me a favour?' asked Polly. 'Will you let me tell her first? Then I'll ask her to phone you.'

'You'd like to do that, Mrs Adams?'

'Mr Anderson, it would tickle me.'

'Ah, being tickled we all like, don't we?' beamed Amos. 'Yes, tell her, I don't mind in the least, and ask her to come and see me tomorrow morning, will you?'

'Promise,' said Polly.

Amos wrapped up the three framed photographs, gave them to her and saw her out.

'Goodbye, Mrs Adams, and perhaps I'll have the pleasure of seeing you again sometime, eh?'

'I'm sure,' smiled Polly, and left.

There are people and people in this world,

thought Amos, there are people like the SS savages, and people like Wilhelm Kleibert and Mrs Adams, for whom we should be grateful to God.

'Polly?' Boots, home from the office, was looking at a framed portrait photograph of his wife and children, a quite enchanting work of art. He had already seen the portrait of the twins, and expressed unreserved approval. 'Polly, it's a delightful portrait of you and the kids. It's for me?'

'For you alone, ducky, for your study,' said Polly. 'I want you to have it on your desk to give you a daily reminder not to forget.'

'Not to forget what?'

'Why, you old sweetie, that we belong to you, what else?'

'Are you all going away, then, say to darkest Africa?'

'I've been to Africa. I went there before the war. To get you out of my system. God, I can still remember I was no sooner there than I was desperate to get back. No, old love, I give you that photograph in the hope you like it, very much.'

'Love it,' said Boots, 'it's a beaut, especially of you.'

'Yes, don't I look good?' said Polly triumphantly. 'Mr Anderson has worked a miracle, of course. Could he, I wonder, feed five thousand starving Chinese with five fishes?'

'He could, if he could also walk on water,' said Boots.

'Listen, dear man, I've something that will tickle you.'

'Is it something I've been on close terms with during our marriage?'

'Whatever do you mean?' said Polly.

'Is it something else, then?' asked Boots.

'Very much something else,' said Polly.

Boots spent the next several minutes being tickled, Polly insisting on telling him about the saucy photograph of Freddy and Cassie's daughter Maureen, how Amos Anderson intended to promote her as the UK's girl next door and had received word from *Weekend* that it would publish one of the shots next Saturday.

'Freddy's family,' said Boots, 'which means this is the end of all that Chinese Lady holds dear. Someone will have to tell Edwin to keep that paper out of her way. Do we take it?'

'No, but we could order it,' said Polly.

'Do that,' said Boots. He laughed, Polly laughed. At which point the twins showed up. Invariably, when one appeared, the other was never far behind.

'What's funny?' asked Gemma.

'Jokes, usually,' said Boots.

'Darlings,' said Polly, 'here's your framed portrait all ready to be given to Grandma.'

'Oh, let's see,' said Gemma, and she and James studied the finished work of photographic art. 'Crikey, is this us?'

She and James exchanged ribald comments, but decided the portrait was just about good enough for their maternal grandmother.

Flossie called.

'Supper's ready, Mrs Adams.'

This meant it wasn't until later that Boots was able to talk to Polly about his phone conversation with Rosie.

Polly listened with intense interest. She knew how Rosie had come to be adopted, but had never known the natural mother, never met her, and had never heard Rosie speak about her. Boots's solution to the problem of how to get rid of the woman struck her as expensive but salutary.

'I'm proud of you, old fruit,' she said. 'Rosie and Matt have more than enough to do in selling up, moving home and beginning new lives. You've saved them taking on a cross as heavy as Mrs Thingamajig.'

'Mrs Milly Rainbould,' said Boots.

'That's as much of a thingamajig as anything else I can think of,' said Polly. 'Would you like a shot of Scotch, old warrior?'

'Haven't I had one?'

'Not yet. Allow me.'

'Polly?'

'Well, lover?'

'You're a poppet.'

Chapter Thirty-One

'Hello?' said young Lewis Brown.

'To whom do I have the pleasure of speaking?'

'Me,' said Lewis.

'Billy Butlin?' Billy Butlin was the originator of imaginative holiday camps.

'Crikey, me Billy Butlin? No, I'm Lewis Brown.'

'Good evening, Lewis, I'm Mrs Polly Adams.'

'Oh, Aunt Polly? I'm honoured.'

'I'm sure. Is your sister at home?'

'She will be when I tell her it's you – hold on a tick. Maureen! Aunt Polly on the phone!'

Maureen arrived at the phone.

'Aunt Polly?'

'Hello there, Maureen. I've news for you.'

'No, really? What news?'

Polly told the girl about Mr Anderson and *Weekend*, the light-hearted Saturday paper. Maureen went over the top, and a little shriek of delight pinged into Polly's ear.

'Crikey, that's great! He really said that? I'm really going to be in *Weekend* next Saturday?'

'So Mr Anderson said. As the nation's shy girl next door.'

'Shy? Isn't he funny? He asked me if I could blush a bit, and I said how could he photograph a blush, and he said he could make me look as if I was. Crikey, am I excited, it could be the start of me life in glamour.'

'I wish you luck,' said Polly. 'Oh, Mr Anderson would like you to call on him tomorrow morning.'

'Oh, I'll go and see him in me lunch hour. Thanks ever so much, Aunt Polly, for letting me know.'

'Not at all,' said Polly, 'I'm tickled.'

'Well, blowed if that ain't a reg'lar knock-out,' said the Gaffer.

'Our Maureen in that weekly paper,' said Cassie.

'Clara Bow and all,' mused the Gaffer, comfortable with a half-pint of his favourite wallop. 'Saucy minx, she was, tent pegs up to her bum.'

'Now, Dad,' said Cassie.

'How much will the paper be paying you, Maureen?' asked Freddy.

'Oh, they pay Mr Anderson, and he gives me twenty per cent,' said Maureen, still flushed with excitement.

'Well, that ain't right, is it?' said Lewis. 'I mean, it's not his legs, is it? And who'd want to see his, anyway?'

'But he's the photographer, they're his copyright on account of him being professional and posing me to me best advantage,' said Maureen. 'And I've already had three pounds.'

'Anyway, how much will he get?' asked Freddy.

'I don't know yet, do I?' said Maureen. 'I expect he'll tell me when I see him tomorrow lunchtime.'

'I ain't seen a picture of Clara Bow since I don't know how long,' said the Gaffer, raising his glass and wetting his whistle. 'Nor her legs.'

'Just as well, Gaffer,' said Freddy, 'she might have varicose veins by now.'

'Reg'lar sexpot, she was,' said the Gaffer.

'Dad,' said Maureen, 'on the day *Weekend* comes out with me photo in it, can you order lots of copies to be delivered?'

'If your dad doesn't, I will,' said Cassie.

'I'll take one to school,' said Lewis, his summer holiday now at an end.

'Dad, stop him doing that,' said Maureen, 'I don't want any pimply kids goggling at me photo.'

'Lewis,' said Cassie, 'you're not to let any of them boys do any goggling, d'you hear?'

'What about the ones like me that don't have pimples,' said Lewis, 'is it all right for them to goggle?'

'Dad, hit him,' said Maureen.

'I've done a bit of goggling in my time,' said the Gaffer, 'at pictures of Clara Bow. Called the "It" girl, she was. Reg'lar tease. Now what've we got? I asks yer.'

'Girl next door, that's what we've got,' grinned Freddy.

'I've just thought,' said Cassie.

'Let's hear it, Mum,' said Lewis.

'I just hope all this won't make us notorious,' said Cassie.

'Clara Bow,' mused the Gaffer, 'I tell yer, tent pegs all the way up to her bum.'

Maureen saw Amos during her lunch hour the following day. Having phoned *Weekend*, he was able to confirm next Saturday was the big day, that the paper would pay twenty guineas, and would be sending a reporter to interview her this evening.

'Crikey,' breathed the glowing girl next door, 'fame and fortune all at one go.'

'A fortune we'd like, eh?' said Amos. 'Well, you'll get four guineas out of the fee. And we'll take some more pin-ups before the weather gets cold, won't we?'

'Not half,' said Maureen.

The meeting of the directors of Adams Fashions with the senior directors of Coates took place on Monday afternoon, at Coates's head office in Kensington.

Accompanying Rachel, Sammy and Boots

was their chief auditor, Isaiah Binney. Isaiah, friend as well as auditor, was fifty-six and a widower. He was one of several eligible gentlemen who had hopes of marrying Rachel, but Rachel had no thoughts of marrying again. She was too content with her life as it was, added to which she looked after her benign and revered father, now over eighty and a widower himself for many years.

Isaiah was frankly flabbergasted that his respected clients, prompted by Boots, intended, if necessary, to quote two hundred thousand as their asking price.

'My friends–'

'No buts, Izzy,' said Sammy.

'Boots–'

'No buts, Izzy,' said Boots.

'Rachel, I implore you–'

'No buts, Isaiah,' said Rachel. 'In us, you see the three musketeers, and you shall be our d'Artagnan.'

'Heaven preserve me,' groaned Isaiah, 'I could never ride a horse.'

However, he figuratively mounted a fine charger when presenting the accounts to Coates, whose managing director chaired the meeting. All three senior directors were commendably friendly and forthcoming, and their hospitality included a tea tray laden with cakes and biscuits, teapot, coffee pot, cream and milk. Sammy willingly accepted a generous slice of fruit cake, while Isaiah rode into the fray with a formidable array of balance sheets going back to 1950. Reaching the end of his presentation, he paused and waited for a response. The chairman looked at Boots.

'And your estimated turnover for the current year, Mr Adams?' he said.

Boots addressed Isaiah.

'Mr Binney?'

'Double the year '54–'55,' declared Isaiah with professional confidence.

'Is that a guess or a certainty?' asked the chairman of the meeting.

'A promise,' said Isaiah, 'I have the balance sheet for the first six months of the current year.' He issued copies to everyone present. The Coates directors devoured the figures and compared them with last year's.

They whispered among themselves.

'Well, Mrs Goodman and gentlemen,' said the chairman, 'we know a great deal about Adams Fashions, gained over our years of trading with you, and we feel we know something about your future potential. For lock, stock and barrel, we are willing to offer £50,000.' So saying, he sat back in happy anticipation of a delighted response. Or at least a welcome one.

'Ah,' said Isaiah, alias d'Artagnan, feeling his steed beginning to collapse under him.

'It's with you, Mr Adams,' said the chairman.

'Ah, yes,' said Boots, 'generous but conservative.'

'How conservative?' said the slightly surprised chairman, looking at Sammy this time.

'Well,' said Sammy, 'not liberal, if you get me.'

'Not quite,' said the chairman. 'Do you have a figure?' This was asked of Isaiah, who had a figure but felt it was too heavy for his weakening horse. 'Mr Binney?'

'My clients,' said d'Artagnan, 'do have something in mind that doesn't – um – quite agree with yours.'

Rachel spoke up.

'We thought we would begin the financial negotiations at a hundred thousand,' she said.

'A hundred thousand?' Backs stiffened.

'To see how favourably you regarded it.'

'Favourably? Is a hundred thousand the figure your auditor has in mind?'

D'Artagnan fell off his charger. That is, he sighed, slumped and looked appealingly at Boots.

'What I think we'd like to do at this stage,' said Boots, 'is to go away, give ourselves time to consider your offer and whether a compromise can be reached. Then we'll come back to you. As it is, we've enjoyed this meeting, and your hospitality, never forgetting how much we've appreciated all these years

of trading with Coates. Thank you, gentlemen.'

D'Artagnan sighed again, this time with
relief, and everyone shook hands.

Isaiah departed in his own car, and Boots
drove Rachel and Sammy back to Camberwell.

'Well, what do we all think?' asked Rachel.

'It's going well,' said Sammy, 'we've laid
the ground on which we can pull out
gracious and no hard feelings.'

'I think they'll meet our figure of a
hundred thousand,' said Boots.

'That's when we come up with two
hundred thousand?' said Rachel.

'No need,' said Boots. 'That's when we
quote a refusal to sell by our shareholders.'

'So what was two hundred thousand all
about?' asked Sammy.

'To see how we ourselves regarded a figure
as high as that,' said Boots, weaving into the
busy stream of traffic leading to Waterloo
Bridge. Eleven years from the end of the war
meant an increasing number of cars on the
roads and streets of London and elsewhere.
'And we agreed no amount of money would
persuade us to let go of your own particular
baby, Sammy old lad.'

'I'm appreciative of that reminder, Boots
old cock,' said Sammy. 'Which reminds me
of something else.'

'What, Sammy?' asked Rachel.

'I hardly touched my slice of fruit cake,' said Sammy, 'but forget about going back for it, Boots.'

The Riley car quivered with laughter as the three musketeers entered the north side of Waterloo Bridge. Which was another reminder, that of Wellington giving Napoleon his last runaround.

That evening, by arrangement, a lady reporter from *Weekend* called on Maureen to interview her, to find out what kind of personality she had, what her interests, recreations and ambitions were, and what her background was like. The inferences drawn in that order were bright, varied, typically teenage, unlimited (as long as they put her into a glamour world), and cheerfully cockney.

The interview, conducted in private and in the nicest possible way, made Maureen feel she was famous already.

Afterwards, Freddy treated the lady to a gin and tonic, which she downed in a flash. Cassie accepted a sherry, Lewis a Coca-Cola, Maureen a daring port and lemon, the Gaffer half of old ale. Oh, and the lady reporter had another gin and tonic, and went home feeling her job that evening had been well done.

On Saturday morning the paperboy delivered a shipping order of ten copies of

Weekend to the house in Wansey Street, and at breakfast in the cosy kitchen, everyone had a copy. Cereals were neglected, and pages rustled about as they were opened up.

'Crikey!' gasped Lewis.

'I can't believe it,' said Cassie.

'I can, it's in black and white,' said Tommy.

''Swelp me,' said the Gaffer, 'is that our Maureen?'

'Yes, it's me, Grandad, don't I look famous?' said Maureen, delighted.

Famous was in the form of a fluttering dress and lace-hemmed slip, nyloned legs and an inch or so of bare thigh.

And a headline, 'WALWORTH'S GIRL NEXT DOOR', followed by a write-up, which ended with an implication that the readers would see more of her.

'Hold up,' growled the Gaffer, 'what's more of her if this ain't enough? Freddy, you ain't going to let her show more of herself, are yer?'

'Don't worry, Gaffer,' said Freddy, crunching toast, rereading the write-up and gulping hot tea, 'we'll put her in trousers.'

'Here, Dad, give over,' said Maureen, 'I'm not going to do glamour poses wearing trousers.'

'Just a sweater and knickers, I suppose,' said Lewis.

'Hit him, someone,' said Maureen.

'Now, Lewis love,' said Cassie, 'you

360

shouldn't be teasing Maureen on her big day.'

'But, Mum' said Lewis, 'if Dad puts her in trousers, and she takes them off–'

'Suit of armour, more like,' said the Gaffer, 'she won't get that off in a hurry.'

'Talking of a hurry, I'd better go and open up the store,' said Freddy.

'And I'd better get off to meet a mate,' said Lewis.

'I don't think I'll bother to go to work on Monday,' said Maureen.

'Yes, you will,' said Freddy.

'But, Dad, now I'm into fame and fortune, I don't need any boring job,' protested Maureen.

'Don't count your chickens,' said Freddy, 'go to your work on Monday, me girl.'

'Yes, you'd best go, Maureen love,' said Cassie.

'Here,' said the Gaffer, rustling through his copy of *Weekend*, 'ain't there any pictures of Clara Bow?'

Polly had ordered a copy of the paper. She and Boots discovered the published photograph of Maureen before the twins came down to breakfast. Polly was tickled all over again, Boots vastly amused.

'Saucy,' he said.

'Sexy,' said Polly, 'in a sweet kind of way. What d'you think of the blurb?'

'Promising,' said Boots.

'That it'll invite enquiries from model agencies?'

'What's a model agency?'

'That question doesn't fool me,' said Polly, 'you're not quite an old Victorian yet. And why are you looking at me like that?'

'I'm wondering,' said Boots, 'if next time Mr Anderson photographs Maureen, you shouldn't join her as the Dulwich girl next door. You're still the proud owner of a fine pair of legs and some flashy nylons.'

When the twins came down to the dining room only seconds later, they found their newly dignified mother belabouring their distinguished dad with a ringed table napkin. They gawped.

Flossie put a stop to it with her singing voice. 'Breakfast coming up, Mrs Adams.'

A letter addressed to the managing director arrived at Coates's head office during the third week in September. It was couched in the most tactful terms, regretfully advising him that at a shareholders' meeting, the board had accepted a vote to retain full ownership of Adams Fashions Ltd. It was hoped that this would not affect the trading relationship that Adams Fashions had enjoyed with Coates over many years.

Chapter Thirty-Two

On the evening of the third Saturday in September, Chinese Lady was chief guest of honour at the party given to celebrate her eightieth birthday at the handsome home of Boots and Polly. Earlier in the week, she had phoned Boots to implore him not to have any loud music. She wouldn't mind, she said, if Lizzy played some nice tunes on the piano. Lizzy could play quite nice, she said. So Boots told her he'd ask Lizzy to play the kind of songs he knew she liked. Yes, like 'Roses of Picardy', said Chinese Lady. All right, old lady, will do, said Boots. Don't call me old lady, said his mother, and what's 'will do' mean? It means I'll ask Lizzy to play that song and others like it, said Boots. Well, you ought to say so, said Chinese Lady. Still, you've grown up quite respectable, she added, so I'm not actually complaining.

Polly had also done some imploring of her husband as long as a month ago.

'Listen, old sport, make the celebrations joint,' she said. 'I honestly don't want my age to be the sole reason for any ragtime high jinks. I know I'll be sixty, but I want to avoid it being made too obvious. Combine

363

your mother's eightieth with my sixtieth. After all, my birthday arrives only a few days after hers. Naturally, she must be the bright star of the evening, and I'll be happy to glow dimly in something dowdy.'

'Dowdy?' said Boots, raising the proverbial eyebrow.

'Well, not too dowdy,' said Polly. 'Arrange a combined celebration, will you, dear man?'

Boot said he understood, and would arrange it just as she wished. He'd let the family know.

'However,' he added, 'on the actual day of your sixtieth, you and I, just the two of us, will go up to town and have evening dinner at the Ritz. Would you like that, Polly?'

Polly said he was an utter darling, that she couldn't think of anything she would like better.

Everyone belonging to Chinese Lady's extensive family, except Philip, now in the Middle East with his squadron, turned up for her eightieth, and Polly's sixtieth, birthday carousal. The turnout included family members whom Chinese Lady thought of as living in foreign parts: namely, Alice and Fergus from Bristol, Bess and Jeremy from their farm down in Kent, and David and Kate from their Westerham farm. Together with old friends and some new ones, the guests totalled a most appropriate number. Seventy, which was midway between eighty and sixty. Boots, with the support of Lizzy, Tommy and Sammy, had arranged that very neatly, and no-one of any significance had been left out. Some of Polly's old friends of the '14–'18 war were present, as was Lady Simms, of course, as well as old Eli Greenberg and Mrs Greenberg, and Rachel Goodman.

On arrival, each guest was greeted by Chinese Lady, welcomed by Sir Edwin and presented to Polly, who implored all of them to take absolutely no notice of her, but to concentrate on the marvel of Boots's enduring mother, who looked all of upright. She wore a new dress which, out of family loyalty, she had bought at Sammy's Brixton shop, Lizzy accompanying her and helping her to choose an oyster-coloured creation with a well-fitting bodice that showed her bosom still seemed firm and proud, although not in the least buxom. She had never been that. Her dark brown hair, now tinted with grey, was dressed high in an Edwardian-style upswept crown that suited her perfectly.

Rosie, on arrival with Matt and their children, was greeted with warmth and affection by both Chinese Lady and Sir Edwin, and then by Polly.

And Polly, of course, said, 'Aren't they a darling couple, Rosie? I beg you to take absolutely no notice of myself, even if it is my sixtieth, curse it. I want nothing taken away from Boots's mother, nothing.'

'In that case,' said Rosie, 'why are you wearing such a stunning dress?'

'Darling, this dowdy old thing?' said Polly, shimmering in a Paris-inspired sheathline Tricel creation of turquoise green, mid-calf length.

'In that old thing,' said Rosie, 'you can't fail to be noticed.'

'Rosie darling, I assure you, I merely wanted not to look like something the cat left over for the mice,' said Polly. 'Out of respect for Boots and in honour of – oh, hello, Matt, how well you look on lamb and chicken. As I was just saying to Rosie...'

By six-twenty, all guests had arrived, and from then on they circulated, chatted, gossiped, talked of Grandma and Grandpa Finch and how marvellous they were for their age, and wasn't Polly at sixty simply ravishing, stunning, terrific or whizzo, according to who was paying the compliment. Drink also circulated, keeping pace with general intake, and a team of caterers ran a buffet of unlimited food of first-class quality. Lizzy, Tommy and Sammy were all contributing to the costs, along with Boots.

Young people gradually became a congregated clump of vitality, and Phoebe asked when the jiving would start.

'Oh, I'm afraid we're not having that,' said Gemma, originator of the wild session at her dad's sixtieth.

'No, not this time,' said James.

'No rock 'n' roll?' said Linda, sister of Philip, the one absentee.

'Or jiving?' said Anneliese's stepdaughter Cindy, who frequently regarded James as someone who could make himself useful to her by carrying her shopping bag. She was fond of shopping, mostly for teenage items. Anneliese, her well-off mother, and Harry, her generous dad, kept her purse well stocked.

'Isn't it going to be a proper party, then?' asked Clare, wife of Sammy's younger son, Jimmy.

'Of course it's a proper party,' said James, 'it's in honour first of all of Grandma Finch–'

'And there's no-one more proper than Grandma Finch,' said Gemma.

'–and secondly in honour of our dignified mother,' said James.

'Mrs Polly Adams,' said Gemma.

'Dignified, did James say dignified?' asked Linda, almost spluttering white wine.

'It's a newly won condition,' said James amid the buzz of conversation going on in the lounge, the living room, the dining room and the spacious hall. 'And much to be respected.'

'Gemma, I've got to ask,' said Maureen,

recently Walworth's girl next door, 'is your brother real? I mean really real?'

'Well, no, not really real,' said Gemma. 'Our dad says he's what you call a one-off, but it's not my fault. I'm just lumbered with him.'

'Oh, I sort of like him,' said Cindy, 'even if he's not much good going round shops with me.'

'Nor's Jimmy with me,' said Clare.

'I admit I've got some faults,' said Jimmy, enjoying a second half-pint of old ale. The caterers had mounted a cask of it on a stand, and it had been well tapped already.

The atmosphere was warming up.

'Is it serious there's going to be no rock 'n' roll?' asked Maureen, dying for someone to ask to see her *Weekend* splash. She had a cutting in her handbag.

'Oh, there'll be music,' said James, 'my Aunt Lizzy's going to play the piano sometime during the evening.'

'Play the piano?' said Linda, looking numbed. 'Play the piano?' She had a feeling it would be one of those concertos that went on for ever.

'Oh,' said Maureen, who had a different feeling, a hopeful one, 'does she play boogie-woogie like Louis Armstrong and Fats Waller?'

'Well, no,' said James, 'she's going to play tunes like "Irish Eyes Are Smiling" and "My

Bonnie Lies over the Ocean".'

Collapse of the best part of the young people.

Some of the older generation were on a different level.

'Got to admit it,' said Sammy, 'the old lady's fit to go on for ever. Look at her, giving old Eli Greenberg a bit of a talking-to. Probably telling him it's time he put his horse and cart out to grass.'

'Wouldn't do the cart much good,' said Tommy, 'carts don't eat grass.'

'Now you know what I mean,' said Sammy. 'Vi, you've got an empty glass, let me get you a refill.'

'Later, Sammy, thanks,' said Vi, 'but I wouldn't mind another slice of that lovely salmon.'

'Here, young 'un,' said Sammy, grabbing the arm of a passing lad, who happened to be Giles, son of Rosie and Matt, 'do your Aunt Vi a favour, eh? Bring her a helping of salmon.'

'Give us your plate, Aunt Vi,' said Giles. He took it from her and darted to the buffet set up along the wall of the large dining room.

'Where are all the children?' asked Tim, eye on Felicity, who was talking by the door with Rosie and Lizzy. He could guess this was one more frustrating occasion for her, hearing everything but seeing nothing and nobody. No moments of further hope had happened during the last week or so, no headaches and no vision. She was at the stage of actually wishing for a headache, since she was sure it would lead to a marvellous if brief interval of clarity. 'Yes, where are all the young kids?'

'They're upstairs, in the twins' old playroom, taking turns to ride the rocking horse,' said Susie. She was referring to the four- to nine-year-olds, all of whom considered a rocking horse much more fun than being crowded in among chattering grown-ups. All children under four were at their respective homes being looked after by obliging neighbours or babysitters. 'Boots thought it a good idea for them to ride the rocking horse, he said it would avoid them being trodden on down here. Polly's Flossie and your Maggie are keeping an eye on them, Tim.'

'My old man can still have brainwaves,' said Tim.

Giles returned. He handed Vi's plate back to her. It was piled high with goodies, including two slices of the salmon.

'Goodness,' said Vi, 'I didn't ask for all that, Giles.'

'Do you good, Aunt Vi,' said Giles, and went to join some of his contemporaries.

'I can't eat all this,' said Vi, 'I've already had plenty.'

'No problem, Vi,' said Sammy, and he, Tommy, Freddy and Jeremy raided the plate, leaving Vi with just one slice of salmon.

'Great, this Scotch salmon flavour,' said Jeremy, Bess's American husband. 'Do you guys come here often for your eats?'

'Of course,' said Susie, 'every time Grandma Finch has an eightieth birthday.'

'Bless us,' said Cassie, 'I can't wait for the next one.'

'Lend me your ear, Sammy,' said Jeremy. 'I know you import American denim for the manufacture of jeans. Try importing New England lobsters – they're great too.'

'What for?' asked Sammy. 'Manufacturing shell-armoured bras for shy ladies?'

'No go, Sammy,' said Susie, 'shy ones went out when Hitler's bombs blew skirts off.'

The celebrations went on, Chinese Lady circulating to make sure she had a chat with everyone, while Boots, carrying bottles of red and white wine, saw to it that glasses requiring refills were serviced. Other drinks were being served by the caterers.

Nine o'clock came up all too soon, and he then rang a bell. It caught everyone's attention.

'Friends, family, relatives, time for some music,' he said.

'Oh, hurray!' exclaimed a young feminine voice.

'My talented sister Lizzy will oblige with some piano melodies,' said Boots, looking easy and casual in shirt, tie and trousers. All the men had been invited to shed their jackets, for the September evening was warm. 'So shift to the lounge or as near to it as you can get.'

'What's he mean, the lounge?' asked Chinese Lady of Sir Edwin. 'Doesn't he mean the parlour?'

'Correction,' said Boots, 'I meant the parlour. Where's Lizzy?'

'Here,' called Lizzy, emerging from a ruck and looking splendidly buxom in a dress which, with its long, slightly flared skirt and defining bodice was remindful both of the New Look and the modern look. Lizzy didn't believe in being frumpish, even if she was fifty-eight.

'The piano's waiting,' said Boots.

'Oh, I'd like some nice piano tunes,' said Chinese Lady.

'Go on, Aunt Lizzy, swing it!' called Rosie's daughter Emily, which made Chinese Lady look mystified.

Lizzy reached the lounge piano, seated herself, touched the pedals, struck a few notes and, amid encouraging voices, began a musical repertoire.

She commenced with what she knew was a great favourite of Chinese Lady, 'Soldiers of the Queen'.

Young people looked blank, older people hummed the tune, which Lizzy played with the verve of a natural. She followed that with 'Roses of Picardy'. Young people looked at each other, older people began to sing the refrain.

Then came 'Shine on, Harvest Moon' and 'Drink to Me Only with Thine Eyes'. Young people began to think the party was in a state of disintegration, but older people sang rousingly when the next tune, 'I've Got a Lovely Bunch of Coconuts', arrived from under Lizzy's rhythmic fingers.

Feet began to tap when 'Down at the Old Bull and Bush' came forth from the ivories. Mature voices belted out the lyric. Chinese Lady looked quite misty-eyed. Every song reminded her of her young days, and of the time when she was being courted by the man who became her first husband, Corporal Daniel Adams of the Royal West Kent regiment, the long-gone father of her children.

'There's No Place Like Home' followed, at which stage one or two inwardly groaning young people thought they might as well go home. Old Aunt Victoria, sitting with Ned, said songs like these made a party. Ned said some of the young people probably thought them a bit old-fashioned. Old Aunt Victoria said they didn't have a right to.

Lizzy, quite enjoying herself at the keyboard, was smiling. She'd had two glasses of port and lemon, and there was a twinkle in her eye. Suddenly, she found different chords, and what happened then? A rousing piano rendition of 'Roll out the barrel'.

Young people perked up. Young legs began to jig. And Chinese Lady said, 'Boots, that's a catchy tune, what is it?'

'Oh, something about a beer barrel,' said Boots.

'Well, fancy that,' said Chinese Lady, 'Lizzy's doing my birthday celebrations proud, bless her.'

It was the young people who were singing now, and they were also swinging it. Lizzy, her twinkle brighter, went into another popular number, 'Ragtime Cowboy Joe'. She followed that with her own rendition of 'Singing the Blues'. And then, of all things, 'Rock around the Clock'.

The young people were well away now, and Chinese Lady was thinking what nice catchy new tunes Lizzy was playing. Of course, the rippling notes of a piano were delightful to her ear compared to the sound of Gemma's record player blasting forth at full pitch from the loudspeakers.

'Dig it, Linda.'

'Move, Maureen, move.'

'Crikey. Gemma, your Aunt Lizzy is hep, nearly as good as Fats Waller.'

And so on.

Revelry was the order of the moment.

Chinese Lady only knew the tunes from the piano were really quite catchy, but she had no idea why the young people were doing all that funny dancing. She asked Boots if he could get them to do foxtrotting and waltzing.

'Well, I could, old lady,' he said, 'but I think you'd find them falling over their feet.'

'Don't none of them go to dance classes?'

'Some do,' said Boots, 'but not, I fancy, for waltzing and foxtrotting. Have a little more port.'

'Well, perhaps I will have just another little drop, Boots.'

Chapter Thirty-Three

Lizzy took a rest. Boots thought it a good time for the birthday cake to be made public and for the caterers to uncork the champagne. The cake, wheeled into the hall on a trolley, was hailed with enthusiasm, its white icing top decorated with the pink figures 80 and 60 entwined with green ivy leaves, chosen for ivy's longevity. There were two slim candles, one eight inches high, the other six. The champagne fizzed, glasses were filled, and it was Lizzy who proposed the combined birthday toast.

'Oh, hello, everyone,' she began.

'Hello, Lizzy!' responded a wag.

'It's me that Boots said–'

'Hello, Boots!' responded a host of wags.

'Because I'm her only daughter, Boots said it was me that ought to make this speech to my mum and–'

'Hello, Mum!'

Chinese Lady, having had a couple of neat ports, and a little drop more, nodded graciously.

'To my mum and Polly–'

'Hello, Polly!'

'Stop interrupting,' said Lizzy. 'Look, it's a kind of honour–'

'Hello, Honor!'

'What kind is she?'

'If some of you don't shut up,' said Lizzy, 'I'll get my big brother to–'

'Hello, big brother!'

'I mean the one with the big shoulders.' Lizzy was persevering, and she still had a twinkle, no doubt brought about by a glass of white wine that had been topped up several times. 'Yes, Tommy, I mean–'

'Hello, Tommy!'

The wags included Tommy himself. He'd had two pints of old ale.

'If I might be allowed to finish?' said Lizzy.

'Carry on, Lizzy,' said Boots, his smile permanent.

'Well,' said Lizzy, 'it's my pleasure to ask you all to let our mum and Polly know how much we admire them for being eighty and sixty respective–'

'Hello, respective!'

'And to ask them to step forward and cut their birthday cake together.'

'Hello, birthday cake!'

Shrieks of laughter ran around the hall.

Chinese Lady advanced purposefully on the cake, Polly approached in gliding fashion. Anneliese, watching both of them, saw one as a magnificent matriarch, the other as surely every foreigner's idea of sublime English poise.

Boots struck a match and applied the flame to one candle, then the other.

'Carry on, Lizzy,' he said.

'Come on, Mum, come on, Polly, blow the candles out together,' said Lizzy.

'Hello, blow!' shouted almost everyone.

'Boots,' said Chinese Lady, 'I don't know why you let hooligans in.'

'Blow,' smiled Boots.

Chinese Lady bent forward, Polly dipped, and they looked into each other's eyes.

'Together, then, dear lady?' murmured Polly, and together they blew. Out went both candles.

There was a farrago of rousing cheers.

Boots raised his glass of champagne.

'Friends, family, relatives, here's long health to our birthday girls, and may they always be as close in your affections as they are in mine. I give you Maisie and Polly.'

'Hello, Maisie and Polly, long health and

long luck!' called Ned, getting through the evening without any problems.

The rest of the guests echoed his words, and champagne glasses glittered with light as they were tilted to lips.

After which, Maisie and Polly cut the cake together.

If Lizzy's speech had been short and Boots had said only a few words, that was what Chinese Lady had wanted, while Polly had asked for as little mention as possible. All through her many years, Chinese Lady had discouraged being fussed, while Polly had always preferred good company to windy speeches.

Jeremy, a dab hand himself at inducing a piano to bring forth melody, took over the ivories and jazzed them up. Delight grabbed the young people as they accepted the invitation to swing it. Chinese Lady, now seated in company with Sir Edwin, old Aunt Victoria and Ned, looked on with a feeling it had all happened before, at Boots's sixtieth. Except the sound of the piano was a lot nicer than Gemma's records. But all those girls, well, what had happened to modesty she couldn't think, and said so to her husband. Sir Edwin said he couldn't think, either, and perhaps it was all due to the changes brought about by the war. Chinese Lady said that that was something else to blame Hitler for, that

378

he ought to have been drowned at birth.

'I never knew anyone more horrid,' said old Aunt Victoria.

'I never knew him myself,' said Ned, 'but I'm willing to believe Satan was either his brother or his dad. Well, he's long been a heap of ashes, so don't let him spoil the celebrations.'

Old Aunt Victoria closed her eyes, not because she was tired but to blank out what some of the girls were showing as their skirts or dresses swirled high.

The jiving, the rock 'n' roll and the champagne went on until a few minutes before midnight, when Boots established a little order and asked for quiet.

'What for quiet, Uncle Boots?' asked Phoebe.

'So that we can hear Grandma Finch's mantelpiece clock strike twelve o'clock,' said Boots.

'But we won't hear it from here,' said Lulu, Socialist wife of Paul, younger son of Tommy and Vi.

'Take a look,' said Boots, and took a covering off the old Westminster chimes clock, now reposing on the trolley in the hall, where most guests were gathered.

The wags responded.

'Hello, clock!'

It showed a minute to midnight. Everyone took the cue and waited, while Boots brought Chinese Lady to her feet. She was a little flushed on port and champagne, but not in the least cross-eyed.

The clock struck, and the chimes spelled out the musical passing of time.

Midnight became morning.

A rousing welcome.

'Happy birthday, Grandma, happy birthday!'

'And long may it last,' said Boots, and kissed his mother. Up came Sir Edwin, Lizzy, Ned, Tommy, Vi, Sammy, Susie and Polly, all of whom kissed the birthday lady in turn.

Boots looked at Lizzy, whose twinkle had taken on the sparkle of champagne. She nodded, entered the lounge and sat down at the piano again.

Delighted shouts accompanied the first chords of 'Knees up, Mother Brown'. Action followed immediately, and Anneliese experienced her first viewing of a knees-up, into which she was dragged by Harry and Cindy.

Floors, walls and ceilings vibrated, hitched skirts whisked, and old Aunt Victoria shut her eyes again. Respectability had always meant more to her than even to Chinese Lady.

'Mummy darling, come on, you can do this,' begged Jennifer of her blind mother. Felicity was on her feet. Every light in the house was on, and the light was hurting her eyes. And her eyes were wide open, staring at her precious daughter. This time she moved without effort, she flung her arms around the girl she was seeing for the first time in her life.

'Jennifer!'

'Mummy?' said Jennifer amid the noise of stamping feet, singing voices and general revelry.

'I can see you! Darling, where's Daddy?'

Jennifer, overwhelmed, hugged her mother for long seconds before turning her head. She spotted her father in his white shirt and blue trousers, doing the knees-up with Aunt Susie.

'Daddy! Daddy!'

Tim, hearing her, and seeing her with Felicity's arms around her, knew immediately what had happened. He rushed over. Felicity lifted her head, and as he arrived beside her, the wonderfully clear vision faded. Her daughter and husband blanked out, but what did it matter? It was happening, the process of recovery, she knew it was, and she had seen how lovely Jennifer was.

'Happy birthday, Tim' she said, groping to touch his cheek.

'It's not mine,' said Tim, understanding the touch.

'Yes, it is, old thing, it's yours and mine and Jennifer's.'

The knees-up went on, a rousing,

rumbustious and traditional gesture in this joyous celebration of Grandma Finch's eightieth birthday.

Felicity, Tim and Jennifer danced it together.

Tuesday. Midnight again. Out of the Ritz Hotel came two people, one a tall, long-legged man in a dinner-jacket, the other a slender woman in a gown. Around her head was a colourful bandeau with a long glossy feather tucked into it, and anyone who had known the years of the Wild Twenties would have recognized that the bandeau and feather were the emblems of the flappers.

The night was rainy. The uniformed doorman sheltered them under his umbrella as they walked to their chauffeur-driven hired limousine. He opened the passenger door for them. Polly slipped in, Boots following. He tipped the doorman a pound.

'Well, thank you, m'lord, thank you, and good luck.'

'I've had that all my life,' said Boots, and put himself beside Polly.

The limousine purred away into London by night, the wet streets shining under the street lamps, the windows of clubs glowing, the caped bobbies keeping an eye out for drunks. Polly, head resting on Boots's shoulder, was dreamy with well-being and deep affection.

'Boots?'

'Well, Polly?'

'Lovely.'

'The dinner?'

'Everything. If I could have my years with you all over again, I'd ask for nothing more.'

'I'm touched, and I'd like to ask for something myself.'

'Ask, old darling, and you shall receive.'

'Could you do something about your feather? It's getting up my nose.'